Niobrara Crossing

A NOVEL

G. Gray McVicker

PAINT HORSE BOOKS   WEST DES MOINES, IOWA

A CONVERSATION ABOUT

The Niobrara Crossing
With Author G. Gray McVicker

1. What was your inspiration for the novel *Niobrara Crossing?*

Growing up in Nebraska, I was left with some lingering reflections that have haunted me throughout my adult life. Those thoughts, that were precipitated by actions of certain individuals, manifested into a storyline left hidden and uncovered. Although *Niobrara Crossing* is a fictitious story, it transformed, for me these haunts and allowed them to be brought out in the open.

2. Why the name *Niobrara Crossing?*

The Niobrara River, a physical dividing line, has historical significance to the State of Nebraska. This story, that comes out of the Sand Hills, actually starts as far back as the late 1800's. It begins on one side of the winding river and moves across its waters several times before coming to a conclusion. Because the crossings have a significant impact on the story it only seems right to inform the reader.

3. You were an educator most of your life and your writing, by in large, consisted of technical expose. Was it difficult switching to fiction?

Yes, because in writing a novel you must create heartbreaking emotion yet, not get in the way of all the wounded characters lives and the secrets they carry. It is a story about them, not about you the author. Fiction writers eventually become comfortable in that, but for me the *Niobrara Crossing* was so compelling it was difficult to stay out of.

4. Your book tends to portray the Sand Hills as a violent place. Certainly not a place one would want to visit or live in. Aren't you distorting it a bit?

Life is life no matter where one lives. The violent story line in the book is only a small part of that vast land. In reality, it is a beautiful, serene part of our country. In fact if the reader wants to visit the Sand Hills, I strongly encourage it. And when they do, they will find it a most beautiful land, recognized for its fullness of nature and the treasures that are displayed from all sides of the culture, especially its people. If I had my wishes, I would live and write in a log home situated on the sun swept plains beside the Niobrara Valley with paint horses in the corral to ride daily across this liberating ocean of grass.

5. What is this story about? I don't mean how it's described by the choice of descriptive words, but what is it really about.

Whether true or imagined in a dream, the *Niobrara Crossing* is written out of memory. As novelist Lewis DeSoto states in his book *Blades of Grass*, "It's not the facts of history but the emotions caused by history that are important."

I remember as a young man growing up in Nebraska and learning about the intensity that was played out in many western communities not far detached from my own. But to remove myself and to retain some objectivity in the story, the mythical characters in the novel have been designed to fill a factious look at life in modern day Sand Hills. The saga talks about the lives of Jim and Sandy, Raymond, Dean Gillette and Ed Hardin, Earl and Maria and others whose lives are changed by their actions. Some of the characters accept the change and others live (or die) with it: It is not my story, but their story. One of struggle and sacrifice that had its beginnings over a hundred years ago yet continues to this day.

6. Will there be a sequel to the Niobrara Crossing?

My next book is listed in the back, but now it's time for the reader to experience first hand this riveting land and the story of the *Niobrara Crossing*.

Enjoy your time in the book!

G. Gray McVicker

Niobrara
Crossing

PUBLISHERS NOTE

This is a work of fiction. Names, characters, places, and incidents either are the product of the author's imagination or are used fictitiously. Any resemblance to actual person, living or dead, events, or locales is entirely coincidental.

Published in the United States by Paint Horse Books
www.painthorsebooks.com

Library of Congress Cataloging-in-Publication Data
McVicker, George. Gray 1939-

ISBN-10: 0-9798191-0-5
ISBN-13: 978-0-9798191-0-0

Library of Congress Control Numbers 2001012345

Printed in the United States of America

Design by Emily J. Greazel

10 9 8 7 6 5 4 3 2 1

First paperback Edition February 2008

ACKNOWLEDGMENTS

Special thanks goes to my family for their part in helping me write the *Niobrara Crossing*.

To Scott and Matt for not raising their eyebrows too high when I told them I was writing a novel. Thank you, Nina, for believing in my work, even after hours of pre-editing and to Owen and Lincoln for just being special grandsons. And to Mary Jo who even before I knew I could, was telling everyone that I was writing a novel. She even said it was good. Her support and love was and is always, greatly appreciated.

And to my Nebraska family and friends who I leaned on to get accurate and timely information about the geographical and historical data necessary to keep the story flowing naturally, I thank you. All this help and encouragement enabled me to reach back into my home state and create, in a sense, one of the truest sand hills novels in modern times.

Also I would like to thank the various reading and writing groups who critiqued me and encouraged my writing. Especially Lee Martin and my classmates at the Nebraska Summer Writer's Conference.

But most of all I would like to thank you the people, who bought my book. As authors we tend to forget that our writing will only move, entertain, and inspire people if it is read. You are the soul reason this book will be successful. Thanks a million, or at least $13.95 plus tax.

Niobrara Crossing

PROLOGUE

North Platte Herald: Dateline 1893
"Homesteaders Burned Alive"

After chasing several head of cattle away from a Sand Hills watering hole and driving them down into the Niobrara River Valley, two homesteaders found themselves facing a bevy of angry cattlemen. As the cowboys tried to place them under arrest for stealing stock, a gunfight ensued, and Horace Lincoln, one of the accused, shot and killed a rancher. He and John Caldwell then raced down the river valley on their mustangs and made their escape.

Several days later, both Caldwell and Lincoln were captured by Sheriff Seth Pottoff and taken into custody. Immediately, the sheriff made arrangements to have the two men transferred to the county jail in Cottonwood Springs for trial.

As he and a small posse were en route to the county seat with the prisoners, a group of well-armed masked men overpowered them. With rifles holding the lawmen at bay, one of the kidnappers grabbed the reins of the prisoners' horses, and they took off across the prairie without a single shot being fired, a signal many believe meant collusion between the two groups.

According to court records, the kidnappers carried out their own justice. After stacking dry buffalo grass around the base of an old cottonwood, they tied Lincoln and Caldwell to the dead, dried out trunk and set it on fire. As the black smoke cascaded up, tainting the clear prairie sky, it's said the homesteaders' screams could be heard for miles. Once again the Nebraska Sand Hills were marked with a brand of lawlessness and violence to which the country had become accustomed.

Modern day cowboys know the rest of the story that appeared in that 1893 copy of the North Platte Herald.

But each time an old paper is brought out, or someone tells the story of that caustic vigilante justice carried out almost a hundred years ago, the toughest of the tough still wrench.

At the time it was especially troublesome because violence and murder in the form of torture, such as skinning or burning, had never before been perpetrated upon Anglo-Americans, and the burning alive of the two homesteaders signaled the beginning of a long, fierce struggle between cattlemen and homesteaders in the Sand Hills.

Today the Nebraska Sand Hills are beautiful and quiet. It's a land where cattle graze on sparsely populated ranches among the rolling grass-covered sand dunes that spread over twenty thousand square miles of western Nebraska.

As we learned from the newspaper article, though, the persona of the Hills has not always taken on a quiet, peaceful agenda. The communities scattered throughout Northwest Nebraska have adopted many facets of modern living. Still, it's a land tied to a past that grudgingly lingers. The flavor of the Old West is evident, and the horse and cowboy are still king.

Prior to the mid-1800s, the land was ruled by the Ogallala Sioux, Pawnee, Cheyenne, and other native tribes. They were nomadic, living in tepees and surviving by hunting buffalo. There were skirmishes, but most of the tribes lived in peace and harmony. After the Civil War, westward settlement began. Cattle ranchers began to set up residence in the Sand Hills. Once the cattle ranchers began arriving, the Indians felt more pressure to protect their primordial land, the sacred land of the Lakota. Soon battles broke out among ranchers and Indians.

As the conflicts escalated, troops were sent out by the federal government in large numbers to protect the white ranchers. The fighting between Indians and cavalry soldiers became more frequent, and some of the bloodiest battles in our early history were fought right there on the central plains. The struggles continued through the 1890s and were documented in Plains Indian history as some of the darkest days their people had ever known. As a result of those struggles, most of the Native American population was eradicated or forcefully removed from the area.

Cattle ranchers accumulated great wealth after the federal government controlled the Indians. They could graze their cattle on the open ranges where buffalo once roamed without interference.

Word soon spread about the unspoiled prairie land and into that paradise trickled farmers and homesteaders, wanting to make their lot. Wagonloads of sodbusters with their plowshares and oxen soon arrived. They threatened the cattlemen's fortunes by fencing in areas that otherwise would have been available for grazing. Then they began plowing under the grass.

The cattlemen were backed into a corner. They continued to fight for their right to a free range. The disagreements that had taken the form of violence continued, but much of the conflict now moved into the courts.

Then, what the ranchers couldn't do, drought and hard times did. By the mid-1920s, most of the homesteaders had been driven off their land, not by their greatest adversaries, but by difficult times.

Violent events in history have a way of healing themselves. Now, in 1985, the people of the Sand Hills are allowing the land to do what it does best—nurture cattle. Or is it?

CHAPTER 1

July 20, 1985

Wakinya, the great Thunderbird of the Lakota nation, was angry. He spoke, and a lighting bolt pierced the heavens. Shooting out from this celestial explosion were jagged gold streaks that were quickly absorbed by the dark rain-filled sky and cajoled into loud, sonic-like thunder. Seconds later, the Super Eagle beat its wings and tumultuous waves of boiling air reverberated across the engulfing space with savage, unrestrained report. Havoc was created high above the plains of Nebraska.

The ferocity of this age-old legend violently shook the twin-engine aircraft flying through the black, solid turbulence. Inside the cockpit, a modern day warrior full of conquering energy was struggling to keep the plane on course in the wake of Wakinya's wrath.

Jim Grey Sparrow Grant stared into the churning darkness with heightened concern, because he had let safety and common sense take a backseat to the urgency of the trip. He knew he should have waited out the storm in Denver.

But when that surprise call came a couple of weeks ago from Sandy Williams-Gibbons, a Nebraska Sand Hills rancher, it was too scintillating to turn down. She wanted him to take on an appeal for Raymond Two Bears, her former employee and Jim's boyhood buddy, who had been convicted of second-degree murder. According to her, Raymond was rotting in the state penitentiary for no reason. And you just don't turn down a state senator, even if she is your former girlfriend who departed from your life in a rather abrupt way.

Regardless, was it vital that he visit Raymond today? Perhaps, but more importantly, he didn't want to disappoint Sandy, a woman he still had feelings for after twenty years. Besides, her power and position had wrangled an appointment with the Nebraska Attorney General's office. Jim wanted to ask the attorney general for some assistance in getting an appeal granted in Raymond's case. He wasn't confident of being successful, but he definitely needed their help.

Right now, though, defeating the legendary giant was of utmost importance, and it was crucial Jim land the plane—soon.

Static and weak, garbled radio signals greeted the anxious pilot as he searched the dial for a transmitting frequency out of Lincoln Municipal Airport. Not yet frantic, but nervous about the circumstances, he finally located what he was searching for and clicked on the handset.

"Lincoln, this is Piper Seven Five Four Quincy, requesting clearance for an emergency landing, over."

Jim listened intently for a voice to come back as the Super Eagle continued to rock the small plane back and forth. Had they heard him? Had his SOS been picked up? His nervousness increased.

Then a crackling, nearly inaudible voice came back at him from the speaker, and he strained to hear the words above the drumming thunder.

"Piper, this is Lincoln tower. We have you on radar. You're approximately fifty miles out. Continue on your present course. Our current listing shows heavy cloud cover around a thousand feet with visibility below that of three miles. Do you read?"

"Roger that, Lincoln, but can you guys hurry the emergency clearance along? I don't want to be sacrificed up here."

"Relax, Piper, we'll get to you. There are other aircraft on the runway we have to deal with." The radio went dead.

Jim worried about its ability to come back to life as he sat and waited for further instructions.

Too much time was passing. He feared trouble.

Then, like an angelic declaration penetrating the heavens, a voice finally returned. "Okay, cowboy, this is Lincoln tower. You're now cleared for an emergency landing on runway 2, over and out."

Jim reeled from the disrespectful radio contact but was forced to ignore it in the face of a life-or-death situation.

With a creaking sound the hydraulics let out a metallic groan and began to push the flaps down. The plane slowly descended through the misty blur—3,000 feet, 2,000 feet, 1,000 feet—finally, clear air.

Wakinya had been beaten. Breaking out of its veil, the red-and-white Piper Seminole turned into the headwind and began its final approach toward the airport off in the distance.

"Piper Quincy, this is Lincoln tower," the radio squawked. "Currently, there's a twenty-knot variation between boundary winds and airport winds. Do you read?"

Jim understood and knew it was a bad sign. Low-level wind shear can be devastating. All pilots fear dead air. He remembers seeing the devastating carnage of a twisted wreck left beside the Denver runway after it was literally sucked out of the sky.

"Piper Quincy, do you read?"

The tower sounded concerned, but Jim didn't respond. His fighting initiative as a triumphant warrior was at question in the wake of a disaster that could strike any second.

"Piper, Piper, do you read? Come back."

Momentarily taking his concentration off of flying, Jim called back, "Tower, this is Piper. I gotcha. Now let me bring this bird home, okay?"

Lining up with the runway, Jim started in. If he hit dead air, there would be nothing he could do.

He held his breath.

The wheels of the turbo-charged, twin-engine plane came grinding down. They locked and, moments later, contact was made on the rain-soaked ribbon of concrete.

Only then did Jim let out a deep breath.

The aircraft bounced a couple of times before departing the main runway. It could be seen taxiing toward a Quonset-shaped hangar at the far edge of the airport. Reaching the building's tarmac, the small plane slowly turned and began rolling toward a shiny black town car parked in front of two large hangar doors.

Minutes after the engines shut down, Jim opened the door to the Piper and stepped out onto the wing. A deep languishing sigh could be heard as he expressed relief after his battle with the legendary thunderbird.

He removed his brown leather flight jacket and tucked it under his arm to protect it from the misting rain. Dressed in jeans and well-polished cowboy boots, he rubbed his hands through his coal-black hair, showing gray at the temples, and pushed it aside. His mocha-colored skin and deep-set eyes identify him as a mixed blood—not the kind of person most would expect to be piloting an expensive plane like the twin-engine Piper.

He hesitated briefly, perhaps apprehensive about continuing his mission, but then jumped down onto the tarmac. Opening an umbrella, he walked in a straight, crisp fashion, almost military-like, toward the black town car.

His thoughts were clearly written across his face, reflecting the agonizing flight he had just completed. Then, realizing his state of affairs, he adjusted to the moment, and his look turned into one of intensity, a law warrior ready to do yet another battle.

Reaching the car, he boldly introduced himself to a man standing there in the rain. "Hello, I'm James Grant. Thanks for meeting me."

"Pleased to meet you, Mr. Grant," the man said, shaking his hand. "The attorney general is waiting for you."

Just then the back window of the town car powered down and a voice came from within. "Mr. Grant, I'm Abigail Finnigan. Won't you please join me?"

Jim was surprised to see the attorney general in person. He'd imagined he'd be meeting with an associate, but seeing her there in person spoke volumes. He hoped it didn't mean that a quick turndown was forthcoming before he had a chance to review Raymond's case with her.

"Pleased to meet you," Jim said as he slid into the seat beside her.

As the driver closed the door, Jim noticed the attorney general was at first taken aback by his half-breed status. He had seen that surprised look before. Usually it comes from people who consider themselves an elite breed, a step above. But mostly they are strong candidates for political snobbery.

He is used to raw treatment, though. As a Native American attorney, he has learned to wall off his heritage and assume a white man's attitude when it becomes necessary.

As they exited the airport through a special VIP gate and headed toward the downtown loop, Jim soon recognized that he was wrong. It wasn't going to matter, his being part Native American. He wasn't going to have to reach for his shield after all. In fact, the attorney general began talking about growing up in a small community outside of North Platte and graduating from the University of Nebraska Law School. So much for elitism. She also knew quite a bit about the Sand Hills and the Native American population living there.

Jim started to relax even more as the conversation continued. But could this just be small talk, ignoring the big question? He wondered, will she or won't she help with Raymond's appeal?

"Attorney Finnigan," Jim finally said, "I need your help and the help of the State of Nebraska. I'm working on an appeal for Raymond Two Bears who was convicted of shooting his father to death. Perhaps you heard about the case. There is reason to believe he is innocent.

"The attorney in Houston County has a lock on all the avenues I'm pursuing to get my client's case to an appellant court."

Jim noticed an upbeat look on the attorney general's face.

"I've been dismissed by the county judge in my request for a search warrant. I'm at a standstill getting papers filed for his appeal and generally just being put off."

Jim waited for her reaction, but when none came, he continued. "I don't know how far the county attorney's power spreads, but, off the record, I believe him to be a very controlling, dangerous man. His rule apparently includes the sheriff and others he has in his back pocket. I'd like your help in breaking down that wall."

Jim wasn't quite sure what to expect from his direct approach. Usually prosecuting attorneys, especially ones as high up the ladder as a state attorney general, don't like to get involved in local politics, especially if it has a negative effect on their career. It wasn't long though, before Jim knew he'd hit the jackpot. Still, he was surprised Abigail would tip her hand so quickly.

"Mr. Grant," she said, "I must tell you that your request excites me. I've had a number of complaints about the Houston County attorney. I've been trying for over two years to nail him and the county sheriff but to no avail. Therefore, it will give me great pleasure to personally look into your problem."

That was great news. Jim was feeling better about his trip.

As they neared downtown, the attorney general asked Jim to schedule an appointment so they could talk further. This was good news to Jim's ears. He thanked her for her interest.

With the perfunctory part of his trip a success, he needed to get on with the emotional part. He wanted to get to the penitentiary as quickly as possible.

"It's been a pleasure meeting you, Jim," Finnigan said as she reached for his hand. "Please do contact me later. John will drive you out to see your client." With that, she stepped from the town car and disappeared into a crowd of people entering the capital.

Leaving downtown, the car turned up a side street leading to a small, well-fortified guardhouse. A gray-jacketed guard, hesitant about stepping out into the rain, finally exited the building and stepped toward the car. He checked Jim's papers against a list he was holding in his hand and, after a couple of moments, nodded to an assistant to open the gate.

Jim knew he was back in real time, and he knew what lied ahead, but he was not prepared for the ghastly specter of the thirty-five-foot-high, medieval-looking Nebraska limestone wall that loomed before him. Prisons sit rather mundane on the landscape until you come face to face with their captive reality.

Jim stepped out, looked around, and then began to walk up a razor wire-lined path that led to an old gray door sitting atop some crumbling concrete steps. The rain began to fall harder, so Jim quickened his pace, taking the steps two at a time.

"Please identify yourself," came the echoing voice as Jim backed off from the speaker button located by the visitors' entrance door.

"Hi, I'm Jim Grant, attorney. I called yesterday to schedule a visit with Raymond Two Bears."

There was a long silence. The rain began to come down even harder. As he stood waiting, Jim began to reflect on the last four nightmarish hours. His flight from Denver had begun smoothly enough, but had soon become difficult and surreal.

He knew that his decision to fly here probably hadn't been a good one, but now that he was finally at the prison, he couldn't help but wonder if the emotional meeting with his client would be just as torturous. His lawyerly instincts were chomping at the bit, but his friendship gene was hesitant. Still, he couldn't have known the disaster that lay ahead.

He reached to push the button again. He heared the buzz of an electronic lock and the door unlatched.

"Please enter," the voice barked.

Jim stepped through the doorway.

"Sir, would you place your briefcase on the table, empty your pockets, and remove your shoes?"

Looking to his right, Jim could finally see the person behind the voice that had been directing him over the past few minutes. Emerging was a sweaty, overweight guard with a Marine Corps haircut dressed in a tan, semi-starched uniform. Shuffling some papers on his table, the guard zeroed in on one, and then motioned for Jim to step forward.

"Oh, and welcome to the Nebraska state penitentiary," he said in a voice full of himself, quite pleased with his position of being able to direct people and tell them what to do.

An echoing buzz rang out, and Jim heard steel on steel as the door to a holding room clanged shut behind him. He was again reminded of how terrible and humiliated one can feel when entering a large penitentiary. Strangers inspect your clothes and body, cameras focus in on you from all directions, and disembodied voices direct you to holding cell after holding cell as steel doors slam shut behind you. Jim had never been comfortable entering and leaving prisons because it was such a stark reminder of the terrible places society has created. Prisons are brutal places.

Jim remembered a movie scene where docile inmates were sitting around in blue jeans playing harmonicas—what a false stereotype. Maybe it happens in Hollywood, but in real life, forget it.

Respect for life and property is nonexistence because prisons are places where the strongest set the rules, and you're handled in whatever way the strongest see fit.

Jim was no stranger to life behind steel doors. Twenty years earlier, while a student at the Air Force Academy, he had spent time counseling prison inmates as part of an outreach program. Since then, he had spent time visiting prisons all across the country. From Statesville to San Quentin, from Attica to Leavenworth, he had gone with groups, ministering to prisoners in cellblocks that were large, echoing rooms stacked several stories high as far as the eye could see. Cold, hard steel was everywhere.

He remembered the noise—the deafening noise, twenty-four hours a day—of thick steel doors constantly slamming shut—metal striking metal—producing loud, toneless clanging; stereos blaring loudly with a dozen different beats; and TVs cranked up, echoing the blended sounds of several soap operas playing at the same time. But above all, he remembered the yelling—prisoners marking their territory like rams or bulls with full-voice, top-of-the-lungs screaming—sounds that sent chills down his spine.

Then he'd get smacked across the nose with the smells forced on him—pungent, sweet, medicinal smells from cheap deodorant or no deodorant at all. Harsh, irritating smells of stale tobacco smoke circulating in the cellblock. At certain times of the day, hot plates in cells would be on high, cooking fried potatoes and onions in greasy frying pans, with the strong smell of burnt lard and cooking oil permeating the air. But the worst was the sour, ammonia smell of the open door urinals at each end of the cellblock. It was that blend of smells that got caught in his mucous membranes and remained with him long after he'd left a prison.

"I'll kill you, I'll kill you," came the fitful words from Statesville B during one visit as two guards tried to keep an inmate from getting a choke hold on him. Jim could still see the guards wrestling with that man, struggling to get him in an arm lock and fighting to push him out the door amid his threatening screams.

All those thoughts passed through Jim's mind as he sat waiting, wondering if he'd made a mistake by accepting Senator Gibbons' offer to appeal Raymond's case.

Suddenly, those thoughts were interrupted by a security guard who stepped up to the holding cell. "Mr. Grant, please follow me."

They walked ahead of slamming steel as they edged down the corridor. Along the way, Jim saw young men with cold, lifeless eyes and slumping shoulders sitting on the edges of their bunks. Some glanced up as they walked by. Others decided to confront.

"Hey, Red, check this out," a young inmate shouted as he gestured to his genital area.

Over here, Coconut Man," another yelled, which Jim knew meant brown on the outside and white on the inside.

"Did your fucking daddy sneak onto the reservation one night?" yelled a third inmate.

So it went, all the way down the corridor.

The guard didn't react to the comments. They are a daily occurrence, but he warned Jim to keep his distance from the cell doors to keep the inmates from spitting on him.

Arriving at the visitors' room deep within the prison, the guard asked Jim to wait outside as another guard opened a side door. Looking through a small window in the entrance door, Jim could see Raymond being led into the room from another hallway.

He had handcuffs on his wrists and leg irons around his ankles.

"Isn't that a bit overboard for a general population prisoner?" Jim asked the guard standing next to him.

"You mean for *old crazy?*"

The description took Jim aback because he remembered Raymond as an easygoing, laid-back person.

"Why do you call him that?"

"Demons have him."

"Do you really believe that?"

"Well, ever since he came here about eight years ago, he's been acting crazy. He's up all night yelling, usually naked. When he gets the chance, he mutilates his body, cutting it, scraping it against the concrete walls till it bleeds, or digging his nails into his flesh. He's been in and out of the *hole* several times, but he goes back to his weird ways as soon as he's released. Lately he's been rather quiet and passive, but we never know when he'll explode again. That's the reason for the irons."

Struggling to walk due to the constraints around his ankles, Jim watched as Raymond shuffled in and sat at a table in the middle of the room, his back to the door.

Jim waited for the guard to open the entrance door, and then walked in. The guard followed. Walking to the far side of the table, Jim sat and looked at Raymond. Printed above the pocket of his rumpled blue prison shirt were the numbers 31473. His hair, long and black, rested on his shoulders. Jim could tell that it hasn't been washed for several days because it shone with grease and prison grime. He had the same reddish brown skin as Jim, but it was furrowed and aged well beyond his thirty-nine years.

Then Jim noticed the scarring on his face and neck—self-inflicted, no doubt, based upon what the guard had said.

As their eyes met, Jim looked into a hollow stare that had come from eight years of harsh prison life. They were as close to the eyes of a dead man as Jim had ever seen, yet there was a man inside that Jim had once known well. This man had been Jim's closest friend when they were boys growing up in the heart of the Nebraska Sand Hills. They had been like brothers.

"Raymond, do you remember me?" Jim asked softly.

With eyes fixed straight ahead, staring over Jim's shoulder, Raymond's answer came in a slow head movement from side to side.

"I used to live up the blacktop road from your house. Don't you remember?" Jim asked.

The silence was nerve-wracking. After what seemed like a minute or more, Raymond shrugged his shoulders and looked down at his cupped hands. Either it wasn't registering who Jim was, or Raymond was just pretending it wasn't. Jim wonders if eight years in that place, plus the twelve years before that, have erased Raymond's memory of him. Then again, maybe he was just in a defensive, self-protective mode.

"We used to go bareback riding in the Niobrara River Valley," Jim tried again. "Do you remember that?"

Still no response—still that downward, absent stare.

Jim desperately wanted to help Raymond.

Then, in the midst of this hellhole, a proverb suddenly came to him: "As iron sharpens iron, so one man sharpens another."

Yes, he wanted to help Raymond, but more than that, he now knew he *needed* to help him because times and feelings had changed.

Jim looked directly at Raymond, extended his hand, and, in a strong, forceful voice, said, "Raymond, I'm Jim Grant, your new attorney, and I'm here to get you released from prison."

CHAPTER 2

October, 1986

The words, "Raymond, I'm here to get you released from prison," echo back to Jim as he sits in his vacation home high in the Colorado Rockies. It's been a year and a half since that revolutionary day, a day to excite any synapses. The hair-raising flight across the stormy skies of Nebraska and a draining visit with an old friend at the state penitentiary both created an upshot. Ya! The upshot, that's where the problem is. Jim still wakes in the middle of the night with vivid memories that can only be made translucent with time.

Sitting alone in the quiet solitude of the mountains, all he hears is the crackling of the fire as it licks at the inner walls of the Colorado stone fireplace. He tries to push the prison visit and subsequent happenings from his mind, but even his quiet, lonely home on a majestic mountaintop won't let him take his mind off the visit that so upset his world.

Jim walks over and looks out the high arched windows. The faded gold blush on the aspens tells him winter will be coming early.

Looking across the valley, he can see bare limbs silhouetted against the steel-gray sky, and he knows he'll soon feel the cold, moist air as it rolls down from the high peaks into the Lake Dillon basin. The frostiness and dampness of the mountain air will leave a biting, stinging feeling in his nostrils, telling him that winter is arriving long before it should.

The intermittent waves of heat from the fireplace feel good. He hugs his coffee cup a little tighter to let its warmth seep into his fingers. Jim comes to his mountain hideaway whenever he can to rest and reshape his mind. Fall is his favorite time in the mountains.

It brings a striking peace to this country and is a welcome respite between two fast-paced tourist seasons. Rest is provided from the summer's throng, allowing the mountains to recover and prepare for the onslaught of snow and skiers.

Although fall is welcomed by the mountains, the ending of summer and its luscious beauty brings sadness as it transitions into the most peaceful, tranquil season the mountains know. For many, it is hard to let go.

But for Jim, he is glad this past summer is over. The more distance he can put on the calendar, the better. To put it bluntly, there have been times this past year and a half that have been like hell itself. That wicked reaction has nothing to do with the beauty and gentleness he experienced during that time, nor is it associated with the work he did or his accomplishments. It did heighten his sensitivity to the promises of life and brought about a connection with the land and people of his birth that he had lost, but he remembers it as more than a passionate and engaging time; it was also a stressful, nerve-wracking time. The prison visit had been typical of the intensity and strong emotions that followed.

Sitting there reflecting on that time and mulling over its conclusion, Jim can still feel a churning in his gut. He knows the mountains won't be able to heal everything. His attachment to the people he encountered during that time was deep, and—Jim's mind begins to drift back to how it all began.

————

July 6 was circled on his desk calendar, and Jim was just back from a late lunch at Risone's, a favorite on the Denver scene. As he glanced at the old Roman invention, he thought to himself, "It can't be 1985 already. It seems like I just moved to Colorado yesterday, but that was twenty years ago."

The order of the day was to work in his office. He needed to set aside time to write a closing argument in the Roberto Alveraz case. The stack of paper sitting in the inbox begging for his attention would have to wait. Needless to say, his work as a defense attorney for one of the most prestigious law firms in Denver was overwhelming, and it enjoyed jerking him in several directions at the same time.

Whenever he'd get ahead of the game, he would think about backing off. Then his conscience would bug him. "You haven't reached the pinnacle of your career yet with Duncomb, Morris, Merriweather, and Kline, and that corner office is still out there," it would shout to him. With that, his laid-back attitude would dissolve, and he'd be back on a fast track.

The nameplate on his door reading 'James Grant, Attorney at Law' was temporary at best. He knew that if he worked harder, there would be a partnership just around the corner.

His Native American friends chastised him about that nameplate. They'd asked him why he didn't use his full name. James Grant is his Americanized name, after his father. His mother's maiden name was Grey Sparrow. Thus, the given name of James Grey Sparrow Grant, which he felt was a bit long for legal purposes, caused him to go by James Grant professionally, even though Americanizing his name didn't sit well with the Native American community in Denver. As Jim saw it, why ruin a good thing?

In addition to all the work stacked up on his desk, Jim, his wife Christine, and their daughter Molly were getting ready to leave in three weeks for a vacation to British Columbia. It would be their first real vacation in five years.

Jim remembered the day he met Christine. He'd just finished a high profile murder case, in which his client had been acquitted. As he walked out of the Douglas County courthouse, a microphone was suddenly shoved into his face.

"Jim Grant, in light of the acquittal some think brought about by mismanagement of the Englewood police department, would you consider your win more or less a Hobson's choice?"

His immediate reaction was, "What a dumb question!" But his next thought was, "Who is this beautiful young woman standing in front of me?"

The woman persisted, "Mr. Grant, the KATV viewing audience would like an answer!"

He couldn't remember what response he'd given. He only remembered thinking, "How can I get a date with her?" A year later, they were married. At about that same time, she became the evening news anchor.

Her prestigious position carried with it many public appearances and, in some cases, Jim went along—that was, until management hinted to her that his aspect wasn't in the best interest of the station. He didn't like that, but they were working their way up the ladder, so he put it aside. Besides, Jim had left his Native American heritage long ago in the Nebraska Sand Hills when he'd come to Colorado, and he didn't want to be reminded of it. He remembered it, though, as a fissure in his and Christine's young marriage.

Now, twelve years later, Christine was producing the local news for a national news network and much of Jim and Molly's schedules revolve around Christine's work. Their marriage was surviving, but their work schedules were causing problems. They were no longer able to spend as much time together, and they didn't seem to be as close.

Jim's thoughts were interrupted by the ringing of the interoffice phone. It was Rose Martinez, his secretary.

"Mr. Grant, you have a call on line 1. She says her name is Sandy Williams, and she's from Cottonwood Springs, Nebraska. Shall I put her through?"

"Wow," Jim thought, "that's a name and place I haven't thought about in quite some time."

He hesitated because he was taken aback, hearing those names again. "Mr. Grant? Are you there?" Rose asked.

Still pausing, Jim decided that he needed to get his thoughts together before taking the call.

"Mr. Grant?"

"Uh, yes, Rose. Tell her I'm not available right now, would you? I'll call her back when I'm free."

He was surprised at his hesitation, but Sandy was an old girlfriend from his hometown, a small cattle town in the upper regions of the Nebraska Sand Hills. His parents' ranch had bordered Sandy's family's ranch, and they were both just across the line from South Dakota's Pine Ridge Indian Reservation. He'd read awhile back that she'd been elected to the Nebraska legislature as a senator from her district, but the last time he had talked to Sandy was a year after their high school graduation, twenty years earlier.

They'd gone steady during their last two years of high school and talked about getting married, but he had left during the summer of '64 to enter the Air Force Academy. Upon completion of his first year, he had gone home for a visit, and that was the last time he had talked to Sandy.

Things had changed while Jim was away from that small ranching community for a year. Sandy wanted to break off their relationship. Jim didn't know it then, but she'd been seeing a ranch hand from over by Milford—Mick Gibbons, an RCA World

Champion bull rider—and Jim was out of the picture. He tried to contact her several times, but she wouldn't take any of his calls. She slammed the door hard on their relationship, and Jim later learned that she and Mick had gotten married and were living on her father's 60,000-acre cattle ranch in the Sand Hills.

He had known Sandy most of his life, as a neighbor and schoolmate, then as a lover. Her decision to break off their relationship hit him hard. She didn't say as much, but Jim believed that she had been under a lot of pressure from her family, especially her father, to break up with him. Jim thought being part Native American had a hand in it.

Sitting at his desk, Jim began to wonder why Sandy would be calling him after all these years. Also, he had been startled by the name she'd given. Williams was her maiden name. Why hadn't she used her married name of Gibbons? Perhaps she'd used it to be sure he'd know who she was. But Cottonwood Springs wasn't that big and certainly hadn't changed much in the last twenty years, so such a marking out wasn't really necessary.

The Williams name was well known in that part of Nebraska, as well as throughout the state. Ransom Williams, Sr., Sandy's grandfather, had settled on the land in the early 1900s and immediately began to expand his wealth, power, and influence. It eventually allowed him to control much of the political and business interests in that part of the state.

Even as late as 1920, life in the Sand Hills was rough and rugged. Range wars still raged between homesteaders and cattle ranchers and you had to be tough to make a living in that desolate windswept country.

Sandy's father, Ransom Williams II, continued the family's appetite for cattle and land, forging a Texas-like empire in the hills. Eventually, he built and expanded the ranch into one of the largest in the area. In 1958, he was elected to the United States Senate. His influence, plus his banking and real estate interests, allowed him to control much of the finance in the area. That control included buying Jim's parents' ranch shortly after they filed for bankruptcy.

Jim and Victoria Grant had worked hard on their small spread where Jim grew up, but hard times ensued, and three years after Jim left for the Air Force Academy, Sandy's father, with the aid of the local bank, bought out their ranch for next to nothing. Some even say Ransom Williams stole the land. Jim believed that the failure and subsequent hard times his father went through contributed to his early death, which left his mother, a Lakota and former member of the Pine Ridge Indian Reservation, bitter and angry. That bitterness and anger spilled over into Jim and after helping his mother move to North Platte, where she later died, he ardently put Cottonwood Springs behind him.

Jim should have been thankful for Senator Williams' assistance in getting him an appointment to the academy and for helping him break through the buckskin curtain. He wondered, though, if it wasn't more out of a need to remove him from the scene than personally taking an interest in his education.

After Ransom Williams retired from the United States Senate, Jim read about his death in a small plane crash along the Nebraska/Wyoming border while on a hunting trip. He didn't know exactly how he felt about the senator's death, but he did know that his level of anger seemed to subside after reading about it.

Jim remembered the pain of losing Sandy. Even after all this time, he still felt a bit of the fire they had. It had never completely gone away. However, he also remembered the pain he'd felt when his parents lost their livelihood. It had taken him a long time to get over the guilt of leaving the Sand Hills, which he felt contributed to their losing the ranch.

Even so, he took some comfort in knowing that not many with Native American blood manage to reach the plateau that he had, and he was thankful. He'd worked hard and aggressively over the years, but lately a measure of serenity had come over him. He no longer felt victimized and no longer went about his work with a sense of martyrdom. He had even lost the feeling of being trapped in the dreams of others.

Turning his chair to the west, Jim looked out the large window of his office and saw the beckoning foothills of the Rockies rising up to meet the clear blue sky. Just beyond that, he could see a couple of *fourteeners* with their snowcapped peaks anchoring the scene. With the exception of being buried in work, life in Denver was good. He'd become his own man and lived his life pretty much as he chose.

But Sandy's call, coming from a time and place that had such angst in Jim's life, was upsetting and brought back pain-filled memories. As the afternoon progressed, he spent time working on the upcoming closing argument and reading the pile of legal documents on his desk. In the back of his mind, he kept thinking about Sandy's call. Debate concerning the follow-up raged on in his mind, but late in the afternoon, his professional conscience won and he decided to call her. He buzzed for Rose.

"Yes, Mr. Grant?"

"Rose, would you please get a hold of Sandy—uh, Senator Gibbons—for me?"

A minute or two later, Jim was again standing at the window looking out at the mountains when the phone rang. It rang once, twice, three times. He hesitantly walked over and picked it up.

"Hello, this is Jim Grant. May I help you?"

"Jim, this is Sandy Williams-Gibbons from Cottonwood Springs. Do you have a few minutes to talk?"

Although he hadn't heard Sandy's voice for more than twenty years, he would have recognized it anywhere. It's funny how things stay with you, he thought. Voices can create a picture, and Sandy's low, husky, sometimes mysterious-sounding voice brought to mind a bright face surrounded by short blonde hair, carrying a heart-remembering smile. It was a voice that still triggered vivid memories after all these years.

"Yes, Sandy—uh, Senator Gibbons, I have a couple of minutes," Jim stammered. Then he added, "It's been a long time."

"Jim, please call me Sandy," she said. "I know you're busy so I'll skip the chit-chat and get right to the point. I'd like to hire you and your firm to represent a former neighbor of yours, Raymond Two Bears. Perhaps you've heard that he was convicted of murder eight years ago."

Although Jim hadn't kept in touch with what had been going on in Cottonwood Springs, he was familiar with Raymond's case. Raymond had been charged with murder and convicted of shooting his father, Silas. He was sentenced to forty-five years to life in the Nebraska state penitentiary. Jim had thought at the time that it was a harsh sentence for voluntary manslaughter that had turned into second-degree murder.

Raymond, according to the county prosecutor, had stood by the corral fence outside of their living quarters on the R Bar W Ranch and killed his father with one shot through a window as Silas sat in his lounge chair. He then fled across the state line to the Pine Ridge Indian Reservation but was caught two days later and extradited to Nebraska. It appeared to be an open-and-shut case, and a jury convicted him of second-degree murder after only one week.

When Jim had read the news release, he'd felt sad for Raymond since they had been close friends in Cottonwood Springs. Jim had never followed up with Raymond, however, and soon forgot about his plight.

"Jim, are you still there?" Sandy asked.

"Yes, Sandy. Excuse the pause, but I'm confused as to why you'd want to hire defense counsel for a convicted murderer who's already spent eight years in the penitentiary."

"I don't believe Raymond shot his father," Sandy said firmly. "Some new evidence has come up, and I believe an innocent man was sent to prison. Not even considering the problems of legal maneuvering that led to his unlawful extradition from federal land, there's some limited evidence that the county attorney who prosecuted the case may have withheld evidence and permitted false testimony."

As Jim listened, he was thinking that prosecutorial misconduct is never easy to prove, especially in a murder case—and, in a case that old, it would be doubly hard.

"Sandy, if you have new evidence to discredit the prosecuting attorney, why not take it to defense counsel in that area, someone with more knowledge about the case?"

"I can't get anyone to take the case. They don't believe there was enough violation of the law to take it to an appeals court and get the verdict overturned, but I believe there's more to it than that—and, honestly, I don't trust the legal community out here."

Sandy's response surprised Jim, and he responded with the question that was on his mind.

"But, I still don't see why you called me, I—"

Before he could finish, Sandy interrupted. "Jim, your reputation for helping the down-and-out, as well as being an excellent defense attorney, is well known. I believe you'll see an injustice here and want to make it right. I know you're the best attorney we could hire and, quite frankly, your old friend and community needs you. I'll pay you well for your time and expertise. Won't you at least come and check it out?"

Sandy's statement took Jim by surprise—not her promise of paying him well, but how did she know about his reputation?

"I'll need to think about it; our case load is quite full here," Jim said. "Besides, I'm going on vacation in a couple of weeks, so I don't know if I can."

"It's important to us. We—"

This time, Jim interrupted. "Sandy, I'll consider it, okay? I'll check my schedule and get back to you by the end of the week. Thank you for calling."

He hesitated before hanging up the phone because he wasn't sure he wanted to lose connection with Sandy. The call stirred something in him. But his professional restraint won, and, grudgingly, he hung up the phone. He quickly buzzed Rose again and told her to hold all of his calls. The emotion got to him. He needed to leave early.

The drive to his home in Littleton seemed to go faster that afternoon. Even though the eighteen-mile route was always good for pondering the problems of the day, Sandy's call was on his mind all the way home. Besides debating the business importance of it, there was the haunting remembrance that carried his thoughts back to a painful time that he had tried to wipe from his memory.

That evening, Christine and Jim sat down for a late dinner. Lately, she had been spending more time at the TV station, and their quality time together had become shorter and shorter. Molly was at her best friend's house, so they were dining alone. Jim was lost in thought as they ate in silence.

Christine spoke, breaking the quiet. "Tough day, Jim?"

"Why do you ask?"

"Well, you haven't said a word since we sat down."

"It's just, well, I received a phone call today that has me upset. It was from Cottonwood Springs, and the caller requested my services as counsel for an old friend. I don't quite know what to make of it."

"You mean your old hometown?"

"Yes."

"Who called?"

"Oh, nobody you'd know—Senator Sandy Williams-Gibbons."

"Didn't you once tell me she was your old girlfriend?"

Christine's response surprised Jim. They had never talked much about his old hometown. She'd never seemed interested.

"I'd say more a neighbor and classmate. We did date some," Jim said, glancing away quickly and realizing that he was inadvertently adding to their marriage problems.

His attempt at downplaying the relationship didn't fool Christine, and she stared at him with an intense look. Jim felt foolish for lying to her and tries to smooth over the situation.

"It doesn't matter, anyway," he said, turning to look directly at her. "I'm going to call first thing tomorrow and decline the request."

He could still see the distrustful look in Christine's eyes, and it bothered him through the rest of dinner. After they cleared the table and sat down with coffee, Jim felt the need to explain his comment.

"Look, Christine, you were right, she was an old girlfriend, and at that time in my life she and I had a strong relationship. But she broke it off and married a rancher from a neighboring town after I left for the academy. I'm sorry I didn't tell you the truth. I'm not being secretive. It's just that the pain of what her family did to my parents is still there, and her call stirred up some strong emotions."

"Emotions about your family or emotions about her?" Christine asked.

"Do you care?" Jim replied.

Christine appeared to be surprised by Jim's response, but she didn't say anything.

"Yes, I'm sure the emotions aren't about her," Jim said finally. "First thing tomorrow, I'm going to turn down the senator's offer."

CHAPTER 3

Locality rocks, especially here on the mountainy fringe of civilization. A magnetic intersection, the city of Denver is right outside of the peaks and valleys that meet in a place where time and space are inseparable.

High above downtown on the twenty-seventh floor of the Metro Building were the offices of Jim's law firm. The huge company that occupied the entire floor was Denver's best known. Its show of shock and awe when defending its clients reminded prosecutors of General George A. Patton's crushing defeats in North Africa—no pearl handled pistols, but the same tenacity and bravura.

The firm's strategic planning center sat on the west side of the high office configuration. On this bright, clear morning, it was nearly full as high-priced attorneys gathered around a large, oval-shaped, mahogany table in the middle of the rich-looking room. Strategically placed expensive pieces of art stood out against the light gray walls. Lights directed toward the brushwork shone down from their silver and crystal luminaries on the rotunda-like ceiling, their direct convergence making the exquisite paintings look both exciting and pastoral at the same time.

If you gazed out the wide expanse of glass covering the entire west wall, you could see the towering, lifeless mountains at the edge of the city, waking up to the day. In town, the morning sun, locked behind the fifty-two-story Metro building, was still creating long shadows on the streets far below. Like organized labyrinths, they waited for the inevitable: a time when the sun's rays would inch around the tall steel and concrete pillars to wipe out their tenuous existence.

Some of the people in the room were seated while others stood by the breakfast bar. The atmosphere was relaxed for the time being and most were engaged in causal conversation as they drank their coffee from silver-and-black mugs emblazoned with the DMMK logo.

Then the mahogany door at the far end of the room opened and Tom Duncomb, company president and senior partner, came in. He immediately took his place at the head of the table. Quickly, the tone changed from casual to professional, and those standing around the room promptly took their seats. It was 8:30 on a Tuesday morning, and the weekly briefing was about to begin.

Shuffling the papers in front of him, Tom suddenly stopped, looked up, and glared around the room. Like a well-rehearsed signal, the last of the conversations immediately ceased and everyone focused on the president.

"Good morning, all. Let's get started!"

He returned to his papers, but something was still amiss. Glancing up again, Tom noticed a lone, empty chair at the far end of the table.

"Has anyone seen Jim this morning?"

"Would you like me to check his office?" Rose asked.

"No, I'm sure he'll be here shortly. Let's get started."

Directing his remarks to various attorneys around the table, Tom always began the meeting in an interviewing, probing, and querying way that humbled many of the ego-rich lawyers. There were questions about their weekly dockets as well as their present cases.

In most law firms, the term "defense" is multifaceted, and DMMK was no exception. Each attorney around the table shifted into defense mode after stating his or her position on each case. The attorneys seemed well prepared for a barrage of questions, not only from Tom but also from everyone present.

Sometimes the questions and responses that came from other attorneys in the room could be helpful in the handling of a case. Many times, though, their egos got in the way, and this morning was no different. In fact, it was easy to sense that a power struggle was taking place among those in attendance, because the meeting seemed more contentious than usual.

After listening to the injurious banter, Tom sensed this gathering tension and broke in. "Look, what we need this morning is problem solving. Quit butting heads and put your ambitions to the side. You can save all that stuff for cocktails after work down at Risone's."

Tom, as usual, placed the firm's success above all posturing.

Jim was late getting to the office. He had been visiting with Molly before she headed out the door for summer school. It seemed they hadn't been spending much time together as father and daughter. Tuesdays weren't a good day to be late, however, and he knew he'd catch Tom's wrath.

As Jim walked into the conference room, he said, "Sorry I'm late. I had a bit of a conflict."

Tom stopped giving his fatherly advice to the attorneys and directed his attention toward Jim as he sat down.

"Tell us where we stand on the Alveraz case."

Jim was caught off guard and was not prepared to articulate so quickly. He started to respond.

"About as well as can be expected," he said. "With added testimony from good witnesses and some luck, we'll wrap up the defense argument tomorrow."

As soon as the words came out of his mouth, Jim knew he'd made a mistake.

"Damn it, Jim, this is a law firm. You need to use the tenacity and quick thinking you were hired for and win this case. Luck, as far as I'm concerned, doesn't have anything to do with it. You need to win the argument and get the jury to see it your way."

Tom was starting to get upset, and Jim could tell it wasn't going to be a good morning. Realizing he'd gone about as far as he could with his chastising, Tom asked Jim to meet him later in his office to continue the discussion of the Alveraz case.

Turning back to the group, Tom asked about the acquisition of new cases.

"Where do we stand with new prospects? I'm talking about paying customers, not pro bono ones," he said. "Come on, lay some pleasing words on me—or are you all thinking about your vacations?" The room was quiet.

Taking advantage of the situation, Jim stood up. "I received a call from Senator Sandy Williams-Gibbons of Cottonwood Springs yesterday, requesting defense counsel for Raymond Two Bears. She's requesting that the case be petitioned to the appellate court to have the verdict overturned. According to the senator, new evidence has come up."

Jim paused a moment, then continued. "Without taking a hard look, I'm going to recommend against our office taking the case. If she proceeds, I think it could best be handled by a local defense attorney, somebody more familiar with the original case. Besides, it's been eight years, and much of the evidence presented during the trial could be tainted."

"Jim, think money here, okay? I don't like to see our office turn down clients without at least exploring the possibilities. If what you say is correct, this one may be a reach for our firm, but we'll decide that after details are laid out. Follow up on it, okay?"

But Jim had made up his mind. It wasn't worth dredging up old memories, and he really did believe a local attorney could handle it better. He'd talk to Tom about it later in their private meeting and explain why he wasn't going to take the case.

The meeting ended at 10:00, and the attorneys began to leave. Some had court dates, some were interviewing witnesses, and some would be going over depositions and other paperwork in their offices.

Jim was headed to the Jefferson County courthouse to continue his defense of Victor Alveraz. Before leaving, Jim asked Rose to put a call through to Senator Gibbons.

"I'll be here another fifteen minutes or so," he told her as he stepped into his office.

After about five minutes, Rose came in. "The ranch answered and said that Senator Gibbons is out for most of the day. Shall I try her again later?"

"Please do," said Jim. "If you do get a hold of her, tell her I'll be back around 3:30 to take her call."

Then he left for the Jefferson County courthouse.

————

It was a quarter to four as he drove into the parking ramp below the Metro Building and parked his new Cherokee. The day in court hadn't gone well, and Jim was beginning to worry that he might not win Victor's case.

Taking the elevator to the twenty-seventh floor, he walked in the side door of his office, hung up his jacket, and sat down at his desk. He began to work on the closing argument he was scheduled to give in two days when Rose walked in.

"Are there any messages?" Jim asked.

"Two," she said. "One is from the Latino Law Association, wanting to follow up with you on the Alveraz case, and the other is from your wife, reminding you that she and your daughter will be driving to Colorado Springs tonight to stay with her mother."

Jim had known his wife and daughter were going to the Springs. He just wished he had a portable car phone like other attorneys in the office. It would make it a whole lot easier to get messages on time. He'd call her later. The Latino Law Association, well, they'd have to wait.

"Rose, did Senator Gibbons call?"

"No, she didn't, but you might be surprised about what she *did* do."

"Surprised? What do you mean?"

"She's waiting in the outer office to see you."

"She's here?"

"Yes, she arrived about thirty minutes ago."

After a pause, Jim said, "Give me five minutes, and I'll step out to greet her."

He was surprised to learn that Sandy was there, but in the short time he'd known her, both Sandy and her father had always had an air of urgency and intensity. They both had a strong passion for getting things done. After all, Ransom Williams hadn't become one of the richest cattle barons in the plains states by waiting for things to happen, and Sandy had no doubt inherited that same touch of steel.

Jim put on his coat and opened the door to his office. As he stepped into the outer lobby, he was immediately taken aback by the elegant, handsome woman who rose and walked toward him. Her trim body and confident walk portrayed a sense of charisma and confidence. She looked like a pathfinder, a woman to be reckoned with—not at all like the young lady he'd lost so long ago. He was stunned by her mature beauty and elegance, something you usually see in movie stars.

She extended her hand. "Hi, Jim. It's good to see you again."

"Sandy—uh, Senator Gibbons," he said, his nervousness apparent.

She gripped his hand tighter and says, "I told you earlier, please call me Sandy. 'Senator Gibbons' sounds too formal. After all, we're old friends."

Stepping back from the warm handshake, Jim invited Sandy into his office.

"Please, have a seat. It's good to see you again, too, Sandy."

He couldn't get over how attractive she was, even in her 40s. She had a smooth, seductive face, set off by an infectious smile. Jim could feel himself being drawn in.

The soft, intelligent look that used to burn in her gray-blue eyes when she was a young lady in Cottonwood Springs was missing, though. She looked harder, somehow, and it should have come as a warning to Jim.

"May I get you something to drink?" asked Jim. "I'm afraid all I can offer you is water or coffee."

"No, thanks. It's getting late and I need to wrap up my business. I came because I want to try and convince you to take on Raymond Two Bears' appeal. I know you have reservations about the case, but I'd like you to hear me out, reconsider, and then look into it."

Jim gathered his courage. He needed to speak directly. It was either that or fall by the wayside like a bumbling idiot.

"Sandy, I appreciate your confidence in me and your willingness to help one of my blood brothers, but I've decided not to take the case. My time is limited, and the firm doesn't believe we can add it to our docket right now. I'm sorry you came all this way for nothing."

He prepared himself for further rebuttal but was surprised when it didn't come.

"Well, if you feel that strongly about it, I won't push," she said. "I just feel that you'd be the right person to get his appeal overturned. Since I did come all this way and I'm not going back till tomorrow, would you consider having dinner with me? Just as friends. I promise I won't try to change your mind. I'm staying at the Hyatt Regency, and I'll meet you in the dining room around 7:00. Dinner's on me. What do you say?"

Jim started to decline, but then he remembered that Christine and Molly weren't going to be home that evening. He might as well accept.

"I guess it *would* be nice to catch up on old times," he said as he stood and walked toward the door. "If you promise not to talk business, I'll meet you. May I drive you to your hotel?"

"No, thanks. My pilot's waiting for me in the front lobby. We'll take a cab. I'll see you at 7:00," she said.

She turned and walked out of the office.

Jim sat at his desk, laced his hands together behind his neck, leaned back in the soft leather chair, and stared out the window toward the mountains. His smug look was misleading. He knew that having dinner with Sandy would only mean that he'd have to say no again—but could he? Would his feelings allow him to remain firm, or would they betray him?

CHAPTER 4

Picking up the phone and hitting his wife's speed dial number, Jim heard it ringing at the other end of the line.

"Hello, this is Christine Grant. May I help you?"

"Christine, I wanted to reach you before you and Molly left for Colorado Springs. I won't be home after work. I have a dinner appointment downtown, so you won't be able to reach me till later this evening."

"You didn't mention it this morning."

"No, it just came up this afternoon. I should be home around 10:30."

"A new client?" Christine asked.

"In a way. It's with Senator Gibbons. She showed up at my office this afternoon and, well, Tom asked me to meet with her and hear her story. I'm still not going to take the case, but he wants me to show her the courtesy of listening to her. You guys have a safe trip, and kiss Molly goodnight for me. I'll talk to you later tonight or tomorrow."

He hung up the phone quickly, not wanting to have to explain further. Turning toward the window and staring out, he wasn't sure why he'd told Christine that Tom had asked him to meet with Sandy.

It had just seemed like the best decision at the time so she wouldn't worry about him—though maybe it was out of fear that Christine would have detected some of the feelings that Sandy had aroused in him. He thought briefly about calling her back and telling her it had been his decision to have dinner with Sandy, but his thoughts were interrupted when Rose opened the door.

"Mr. Grant, the affidavits are all finished. Do you need me for anything else?"

"No, not today, thank you," he said. "I'm going over to the club to work out. I'll see you in the morning."

Leaving the Colorado Athletic Club after pushing around some weights, Jim drove to the Hyatt Regency and parked his Cherokee at the front curb. He was somewhat familiar with the hotel and restaurant. It was well known around town how fast your wallet could be cleaned out.

"Maybe when I get the corner office, I can dine in this kind of luxury," he thought as he stepped up to the valet booth to have his Cherokee parked.

While filling out the check card, the parking attendant kept raising and lowering his eyes, checking Jim out. Even though he was dressed to a "T" with a dark suit, cufflinks, stripped tie, and patent leather shoes, being Native American still brought suspicious looks. Jim resented the silent interrogation. He had ignored his heritage since leaving Cottonwood Springs, but the put-down by a parking lot attendant caused him to take offense to the slight.

"Is something wrong?" Jim asked sternly.

"No, sir," the attendant replied, realizing his indiscretion. "Enjoy your evening," he added, handing Jim his claim ticket.

Walking through the hotel lobby, Jim felt for a brief moment the type of mistrust that must have dogged his ancestors over the centuries. In their case, it was grounded in life and death, but for Jim it was a minor annoyance—but it still bothered him.

Was his attitude changing, or was he just becoming more self-protective? Perhaps that was why much of his legal work recently seemed geared toward defending indigenous people and minorities.

He stepped into the restaurant and was greeted by the maitre d'.

"Hello, I'm Jim—"

Before he could finish, the maitre d' interrupted. "Good evening, Mr. Grant. Please follow me. Senator Gibbons is waiting for you."

As he followed the maitre d' through the dining room, Jim caught sight of Sandy sitting at a far corner table, sipping white wine from a tall crystal glass. She saw him and waved.

Her dramatic change from a business look earlier in the day to an elegant, classy evening look was astonishing. Her garnet earrings had been replaced by expensive diamond studs, and a low-cut black dress that revealed her mature figure took the place of her blue business suit. Jim was still focused on the low-cut dress and what it revealed when a stunning diamond necklace around her bare neck flashed in his eye.

His mind was suddenly flooded with a tidal wave of memories—memories long suppressed—and not just about his parents' ranch problems. Taking a deep breath, he took a hold of her extended hand. Before he could release it, she stood and embraced him. It appeared to Jim to be more than a courtesy hug between friends. As they parted, Sandy looked strongly into his eyes.

"Thank you for having dinner with me, Jim," she said. "I really didn't want to fly back to Nebraska without having a chance to visit with you and catch up on everything you've been doing."

They sat down, and Sandy took another sip of wine. Then, looking directly into Jim's eyes, she continued.

"I want to tell you how glad I am that you chose to have dinner with me, but I want to learn more about your life since you left Cottonwood Springs. Please, help yourself to some wine, and tell me about the last twenty years.

Jim had a feeling it wouldn't all be new to Sandy, but he began.

"I'm afraid it's quite boring, like barking at a knot, as they say in the Sand Hills."

Jim didn't know why he'd used that old expression, and, after he'd said it, he felt a little foolish, but Sandy ignored it.

"No, please, I insist," she said. "I want to know about your life. I took the liberty of ordering for you. Sirloin steak, rare, is that right? It should be here in a bit. Please go on, tell me more."

"Well, after graduation from the Air Force Academy, I applied for entrance to Denver University Law School. The air force allowed me to put off my active duty through an educational delay program. That was pretty amazing in itself, since it was during the height of the Vietnam War. That not only allowed me time to attend law school, it also allowed me to meet my active service requirements by serving in military law."

Taking another sip of wine, Jim continued. "After passing the bar, I began a five-year active duty commitment as a JAG officer, starting out in civil law. My real love, though, is criminal law, so I eventually changed, serving as prosecutor for the Air Force in several different court marital cases. My desire to become a defense counselor was even stronger, so after spending a couple of years as a prosecutor, I switched sides and went on the defense. That lasted for eight years before I moved into private practice."

"You were defense council in the Rubin Whitehorse murder trial, weren't you?" Sandy asked.

"Yes. How did you know?"

"Oh, I don't know. I read about it in some congressional review, I think. Wasn't Rubin accused of breaking into the officer's quarters and shooting his lieutenant to death?"

"Yes, he was. But there were no witnesses to the crime and only circumstantial evidence. In addition, the prosecution brought up *supposed* racial conflicts that had erupted between Rubin and his superiors, but I knew that wasn't true. From the start, we knew Rubin wasn't guilty, and our team worked hard to obtain an acquittal."

"Not guilty or justified?" Sandy asked.

The silence that followed was deafening. The warmth Jim had been feeling suddenly turned cold, and he saw the hardness in her look he'd noticed earlier in the day return.

Jim poured another glass of wine, hoping to diffuse the tension heightened by her comment.

Sandy also felt the icicles and, to melt them, changed the subject. "Jim, would you like to dance?"

He accepted and they walked hand-in-hand to the dance floor. Slow dinner music is playing and the small dance floor held only one other couple. As Jim brought Sandy into his arms, he felt her warm body, and it brought back memories of long ago times.

After a few moments, Sandy pushed back to arm's length. "I'm sorry. I don't know why I said what I did. I think I read it in one of the editorials relating to the trial, and it just stuck in my mind. I didn't mean for it to sound like it did," she said.

Jim told her he understood, but the damage had been done. He pulled her close despite his feelings, and they danced until the trio finished.

As dinner proceeded, Jim grew curious about what had happened to Sandy after he'd left their hometown, so he turned the conversation over to her, to fill him in.

"After we broke up, I returned to the university," she said. "Mick and I didn't really start dating till after you and I broke up. I told you that we had dated some—to justify the break-up, I guess. I was being pressured hard by my father to end our relationship."

After twenty years, Sandy had finally verbalized what Jim suspected. Even though it didn't matter anymore, just hearing it stirred something in him.

Sandy continued. "Jim, I didn't want to, but, well, it's hard to explain the influence my father had on me. Until you've lived in the Williams family and felt the pressure on you, day and night, you can't understand. I think that pressure was why my mother committed suicide, or at least I believe she did, even though everyone thought it was an accident when her car rolled several times and ended up in a dry gulch off Highway 61."

Sandy paused, showing a bit of emotion, but then took a sip of wine and continued. "Mother wasn't prone to driving as fast as the accident investigators suggested, and she certainly knew how to handle a vehicle, especially on a straight stretch of clear highway. It was declared an accident, but it was hard for me to believe it was accidental. I think my father knew the truth, too, but he wouldn't discuss it with me. Even as tough an old bird as he was, I think it took him down several notches and played on his conscience, but it did little to change him, at least outwardly.

"My marriage to Mick Gibbons was more or less arranged by both my father and Mick's father, a banker in Red Pine. After our wedding, Mick went to work for my father at the ranch and continued on as a bull rider on the PRCA circuit, winning back-to-back world championships. After my father's death, Mick's rodeo winnings helped pay off some of the ranch debt. Now we each own half of 60,000 acres of grassland, several thousand head of cattle, and some of the finest brood mares in the country."

Sandy paused again, and then said with a sigh, "We're currently separated. Mick lives in Cottonwood Springs and has retired from bull riding. He drives back and forth from his house in town to the ranch. He has set up an office in the bunkhouse and still manages the day-to-day operations as well as the purchasing and sale of our cattle, but our relationship is strictly professional now. I know if a divorce goes through, the Williams ranch will be split in half—but that's something I'm *not* going to let happen."

The conversation continued while they ate and, as Sandy had promised, she never brought up Raymond or his case. But after a while, Jim's curiosity began to get the best of him. He kept wondering why Sandy was so interested in getting Raymond's conviction overturned and what new information she had that was strong enough to take to an appeals court. Somehow, he just couldn't believe that she was doing it simply to right a wrong. Surely she had another motive for wanting to reopen the case.

Finally, not being able to stand it any longer, Jim asked, "Look, I know we promised not to talk about it, but I just need to know why you're pursuing Raymond's case."

He was prepared to disregard any statement she'd make about wanting to help based on the generosity of her heart, but her reply sounded so sincere that he was taken aback.

"Jim, it just seems so unfair that one person, whether he's a neighbor or a friend, should have to spend such a chunk of his life in prison for something he didn't do, and as a public servant for the state of Nebraska, I feel it's my responsibility to do everything possible to get Raymond out of jail. That's why I contacted you. I thought that you'd also feel the need to right a wrong done to one of your blood brothers once you'd heard some of the evidence I've uncovered that's contrary to the facts that were originally put forth during the trial. You're also the best defense attorney in the four-state area—I know because I've been following your work the past several years."

That inadvertent confession seemed to surprise her. She continued with some uncharacteristic nervousness.

"In addition to some physical evidence, other information has surfaced regarding the county attorney and the county sheriff. I believe they were working together and may have been covering up a number of illegal operations in the area. What those operations were, I'm not sure. I believe that Raymond knew about some of them, though, which made him a threat. I also believe that one of them paid somebody to kill Raymond's father, and then they framed Raymond to get him out of the county for good. If Raymond had been murdered, it would have caused too many questions—questions they didn't want to answer."

Sandy paused for a moment, studying Jim's face for a reaction before continuing.

"They gambled that nobody would listen to him. Raymond had been acting strange for a couple of years before Silas' murder. He spent a lot of time walking alone at night, as well as spending long nights in the cemetery. People began to notice signs of self-mutilation. Whether it was caused by demons, as the natives believed, or he was mentally ill, he was a sitting duck, just waiting to be framed—and his running to the Pine Ridge Indian Reservation after the shooting played right into the prosecution's hands. He never stood a chance of being acquitted."

As Sandy spoke, Jim's thoughts drifted back to a day when he and Raymond were boys, horseback riding. Raymond had ridden into a willow thicket along the Niobrara, and a few moments later, had come running out on foot, babbling incoherently. It took some time before he could understand what Raymond was saying.

He claimed that he'd seen a demonic face rising from the ground that had knocked him off his horse. At first, Jim had thought it was a joke, but the terror on Raymond's face said differently, and Raymond would never go near the place again.

"Jim, are you listening to what I'm saying?" Sandy said when she noticed his trance.

"Yes, Sandy," Jim said, snapping back to the moment, "but you said something about new physical evidence on the phone. You know, of course, that new evidence can't be used by an appellate in most cases. Exactly what were you referring to?"

"I don't know if it is so much new evidence or just old evidence that was dismissed in the trial," Sandy said. "Raymond's rifle was brought to trial and evidence was presented to the court that it was his rifle that had killed Silas, due to bullet casings found and the bullet removed from Silas' body. The defense didn't even challenge that supposed evidence. In fact, they didn't challenge the authenticity of *anything* during the case.

"A couple of months ago, Earl Sweet, our ranch foreman, found another rifle wedged in one of the walls of our stable. Although it was rusty and corroded, it resembled the one that was exhibited at Raymond's trial. I went to Sheriff Dean Gillette, who was at the trial, and asked to see the rifle and bullet fragments presented as evidence, but he said they were long gone. I asked to see the testing photos that determined the bullets used, but he said they were gone as well. It just seemed strange that they'd be missing. I believe that evidence is still there.

"Without the exhibits from the evidence room, I don't know for sure whether the found gun can be put into play. I know it's not a strong reason, and I don't know if an appeal would even be heard based on it, but I believe that if an appeal *is* heard, we could get access to the old evidence. I don't believe it's disappeared as the sheriff claims, but it's going to take a court order to be able to get a look at it the way Sheriff Gillette has everything locked down.

"Jim, whether or not it's of any consequence, I'm convinced that the second gun may be the real murder weapon, and whoever shot Silas Two Bears planted Raymond's rifle at the scene and then hid the real murder weapon in our horse barn."

Jim looked at Sandy intently and asked, "Are you insinuating that the murder was committed by someone connected with the R Bar W Ranch?"

"I think the rifle was placed there because it was a quick hiding place close to the house where Silas lived. Whether that someone was connected to the R Bar W, I don't know. But if it was an outsider, chances are they would have been seen driving off the ranch.

"Tell me why you suspect a cover-up by the county attorney and Gillette," Jim said.

"Earl is kind of my eyes and ears around the ranch. He was very loyal to my father, he doesn't trust Mick, and he relays everything directly to me. From time to time we have had ranch hands from the Pine Ridge Indian Reservation on our payroll, and bits and pieces of information would surface about drugs, payoffs, and kickbacks.

"Ten years ago, a government plane from the Denver mint disappeared while flying across the Sand Hills in a heavy rainstorm. Its last radio contact put it northwest of Cottonwood Springs when it disappeared. As you know, Jim, sand ridges in the hills can become quite tall as the wind-blown sand continually builds them up. The downwind side of those slopes can reach forty-five degrees or more. If the plane crashed into one of those slip faces, the impact would cause the ridge to break off and send sand cascading down the slope. Because it was raining heavily at the time, the wet sand would cascade down like an avalanche and bury everything, even a good-sized plane carrying over $3 million in gold eagles."

"Several of those coins turned up in a minor drug bust ten years ago, and eight years ago, some of them turned up in a house on the Pine Ridge Reservation. The ones at Pine Ridge had been purchased at a reduced price, but the man couldn't or wouldn't identify who had sold them to him. Over the years, several others have shown up in a number of the southwestern border states, so somebody has been laundering them, probably through drug purchases. The bulk of them are probably scattered throughout Mexico, but just last year, some of them turned up at a cattle auction in Crawford County. The feds had swarmed all over the area ten years ago and followed up on the sightings in the Southwest, but strangely, the latest incident hardly drew any attention. There still appears to be more than $2 million missing, though."

"It is hard to pin down anything because most people are scared to talk. Some of the information that has leaked out, though, seems to place Raymond in it with the county attorney and Gillette. I believe that Raymond, in one of his nightly escapades, may have found the wrecked plane with its dead or injured pilot and contacted the sheriff. Seizing the opportunity, I believe Gillette raided the site and had Raymond help him hide the gold.

"They probably thought of Raymond as a liability and framed him for murder. Simply murdering him after the stink being raised by the International Indian Movement about a dual standard of justice in the Nebraska Sand Hills would have set off another firestorm."

Jim just shook his head as Sandy continued.

"If local authorities like the sheriff and the county attorney are involved, the last thing they need is an incident that could be exploited by activists. That would have had federal authorities climbing all over the place and maybe dredging up information about the stolen gold or illegal drug operations. It was risky, but much cleaner just to frame Raymond."

The more Sandy talked, the more Jim found himself becoming interested in the case, but he still couldn't understand why she wanted to bring in an outside attorney to help.

"Sandy," he said, "as a Nebraska state senator, why can't you start an investigation that will get to the bottom of what you perceive as an injustice?"

Sandy's pause was longer than Jim had expected. It was as if she didn't want to answer the question.

After a few moments, she finally said, "All right. Since you asked, my direct involvement wouldn't be a good political move. Besides, I'm about to be involved in a potentially bitter divorce settlement, and if Mick is somehow involved—not that he is, mind you—it would create some serious problems."

Jim sat back, drinking in what she'd just told him. Then he asked his next question. "Do you think Mick is involved in Silas' murder?"

"The only answer I can give you right now is that I don't have any concrete information one way or the other," Sandy said.

When they'd finished dinner, they embraced. Before saying goodbye, Jim told Sandy his interest in the case had peaked. But he left it at that.

Thirty minutes later, Jim was on his way down Santa Fe Drive toward home. Sandy had kept her promise and hadn't tried to persuade him to take the case, but the more he thought about their conversation, the more he found himself being persuaded in a seductive, tantalizing way.

Jim remembered the times he had fallen down, physically, after slipping or tripping over something and how the ground came to meet him so fast there was no time to try and break the fall. That's how it felt when Sandy told him the things she did.

There was no time to break the fall. Sandy's dramatics had done their job. A seed had been planted.

As Jim drove through the darkness, a feeling of distrust began to set in, but it was quickly swept away by his passion—the need of a dedicated defense attorney to obtain justice. He wrestled with the dilemma all the way home.

"Hello, Christine? Yes, I just got home. How are you and Molly doing? Christine, we need to talk. I have something important I need to discuss with you."

CHAPTER 5

Stapleton International Airport was busy this morning. On the near east side of Denver, it was one of the smallest hubs for commercial air traffic in the country. Traffic patterns, short runways, altitude—all of those factors played a part in keeping it small. The layout of the airport also made takeoffs and landings tricky, and many experienced pilots had to abort takeoffs when the hot, thin summer air failed to lift the plane.

The air traffic control system was outdated and caused its own problems. Even trained F-15 pilots like Jim Grant worried about Stapleton more than any other airport—but Jim had no choice. He had to leave all his concerns behind, because it had been five days since he'd visited with Sandy. Throughout the Alveraz embezzlement case—at the end of which the jury had found Alveraz guilty of eight of the ten charges—Jim had tossed Sandy's story around in his mind. Once an appeal in the Alveraz case had been filed, Jim could finally leave town to resolve some issues.

He pulled into the private parking lot next to the main hub and walked to the small craft terminal where a Piper Seminole with twin engines and low-swept wings waited for him. It was the company plane, perfect for short-range, quick destination flying.

Jim felt his tension beginning to build as he sat on the tarmac waiting for the tower to give him instructions. Much of the stress he was feeling came from discussions he'd had with Christine and Tom Duncomb prior to leaving for the airport.

Christine had sensed that he was seriously considering taking Raymond Two Bears' case, and she was disturbed at the thought. Jim had tried to downplay the aspects of taking on the case, but when he told her that they might have to postpone their vacation, she had stopped talking to him.

The discussion with Tom hadn't gone well, either. Tom had decided he didn't want Jim to get involved in Raymond's case. Although it promised to be a lucrative case—one the company needed—Tom felt that the firm's docket was already too full and that Jim didn't have time to pursue it—especially when it was a case he stood a good chance of losing. Jim understood Tom's concern.

After a few moments of waiting, the radio came on.

"Piper Seven Five Four Quincy, this is the tower. Please taxi into position and hold. Do you read?"

"Stapleton tower, this is Piper Quincy, roger that."

Clearing his mind of all his troubles, Jim revved the engines to a high-pitched whine and taxied to the end of the runway, waiting his turn to take off. Just as he was wondering why the tower was delaying so long, the radio came on again.

"Piper Quincy, you're now clear for takeoff."

Such delays weren't normal procedure, but Jim's mind was focused on getting airborne, so he let it go. He responded to the tower and slowly pulled back on the throttle. The turbo-charged engines kicked in and the plane sped off down the runway. Suddenly, all hell broke loose.

Jim heard the tower yelling on the radio, "Piper Quincy! Brake! Brake!"

Reflexively, Jim pushed hard on the brake handle as the cries continued, "Brake! Brake!" He pushed harder, wondering what the emergency was.

Then a huge shadow engulfed his plane, followed by a loud whine. Looking up while the radio continued to scream, Jim saw the huge white underbelly of a DC-10, its landing gear only inches away from the top of his cockpit.

Jim continued pushing the brake until finally the huge plane cleared and touched down on the runway just ahead of him— exactly where Jim would have been if he had continued full throttle. But he wasn't completely spared. The DC-10's wake hit him and spun the small plane around, kicking it off the runway. Luckily for Jim, it didn't tip. He looked up just in time to see the plight of the large plane that touched down on the runway in front of him.

With tires smoking and brakes howling, the DC-10 fought to stop before it crashed into the chain link fence at the far end of the runway. Because it didn't have the speed or power to abort the landing and climb out, landing long was its only option.

Jim watched in horrified shock, holding his breath until the huge aircraft finally came to a stop just before the airport fence. He let out a huge sigh of relief. It was over.

Then he noticed his hands, which were pale and clammy. He'd been clutching the brake controls so tightly that all the blood had been squeezed out.

He slumped back in his seat and took a deep breath as he watched the emergency vehicles race toward the DC-10. He felt like throwing up, but his stomach eventually settled down. So did his nerves. There was a lot of turmoil at the end of the runway, but it appeared that everyone was safe.

Jim replayed the incident in his mind, thankful to the tower for aborting his takeoff. They had saved his life—and the lives of everyone on the DC-10. At the same time, he was pissed off that they could have made such a stupid mistake.

Then another terrible thought crossed his mind. Since he'd been so preoccupied when he taxied onto the runway, had he misinterpreted the tower's instructions? No, he was sure he hadn't. They had definitely given him clearance.

For Jim, the worst part now was that it would be several hours before he could get airborne. There would be paperwork to complete, questions to answer, and reports to fill out—accompanied by lots of screaming and yelling. It was also possible that his plane wouldn't even fly. It would have to undergo a thorough mechanical inspection to make sure nothing had been blown apart.

A half hour later, Jim watched as his plane was pulled onto a flatbed by a large winch. He rode along in the truck as they hauled it to a repair hanger. From there, it took him several minutes to get to the FAA office, where he sat down at a small table in the sterile-looking room. Across the table sat the air control tower supervisor and an FAA official. Jim was preparing to defend myself, because he was the low man on the totem pole. He waited quietly for them to try to place the blame on him, but the two men just sat in silence, not saying a word. The tension was nearly unbearable.

Suddenly the door sprang open and the DC-10 pilot ran in. He bolted straight for the control tower supervisor.

"What the hell's going on?" he screamed in his face.

The FAA official quickly jumped between them to prevent any blows.

"Let's all sit down and talk this through," he said as he struggled to keep the two men apart.

The DC-10 pilot, still agitated and emotional, continued to resist for a few seconds. Then he backed off, but it took him several more minutes to calm down before he answered their questions and filed an official report. Eventually, Jim and the rest of them began to discuss the incident, almost calmly.

Thank goodness for tapes.

Jim was right. The mistake had been made by the tower.

Ironically, it had been a second air controller who aborted his flight. The controller who'd given Jim permission to take off wasn't even in the room with them at that time, which made sense. The chances were good that the air control tower didn't want him in the same room with two angry pilots.

Some four hours later, Jim was finally back in his Piper, nervously waiting for permission to taxi onto the runway a second time. His plane had been completely checked out and given a release to continue.

While all that was going on, Jim had thought briefly about postponing the flight, but it was important that he keep his appointment that day.

Permission finally came from the tower, and Jim slowly taxied onto the runway.

"This time, I think I'll look both ways," he thought.

The second takeoff went without incident, and Jim felt a familiar exhilaration as the plane lifted off the runway into the clear Colorado sky. Departing in a left climb, he headed east.

Looking back, he saw the foothills of the Rockies disappear behind him and the brown plains of eastern Colorado begin to flow out in front of him.

Banking left, the plane turned to the northeast, and, after reaching cruising altitude, it leveled off. Jim set the navigation system on course, and settled back for a three-hour flight. Only then did he allow himself to finally take a deep breath and relax.

On the console next to him was a copy of his flight plan—Cottonwood Springs, Nebraska. It was listed on the plan as City Airport, but if his memory was accurate, it was just a level strip of grass at the south end of town with limited facilities. As the plane glided through the clear sky, Jim put the airport incident behind him and began to ponder the events of the previous week.

After flying across Interstate 80 and into Nebraska, he reached under the seat for a flight map. He began looking for landmarks that would assist him in setting the plane on the right course. There was nothing below him at that moment but brown earth interspersed with green irrigated circles as far as the eye could see. The land looked flat, and the only indications of its rolling nature were dark shadows cast by the afternoon sun that left patches of black on the landscape.

After about an hour, he sighted a set of railroad tracks. If he followed them, he knew they'd lead him to his destination, so he lined them up and continued north. Soon, he could see an old silver-gray water tower, its four steel legs holding up a pot-shaped container, rising above the houses and buildings of a small rural town in the distance. It was Cottonwood Springs.

Lowering the flaps, Jim inched the plane down toward a narrow green strip lying off in the distance. It was only distinguishable from the land around it by a darker green color. Actually, it looked more like a cow path from his altitude.

Gliding in at reduced air speed, Jim brought the Piper lower. At about 200 feet, he passed two working windmills alongside the runway. Not wanting to land without getting a complete visual, he made a low-level pass, then throttled up the engine and climbed out. He hoped the townsfolk didn't think he was buzzing their town. The few cattle in the area could be seen scattering as Jim flew overhead.

Everything appeared to be okay, so Jim banked around and took a second shot, this time without the fear of being hit by a DC-10. After a rough landing on the grass runway, Jim rolled up to the end of the landing strip, next to Vauders Mobile Station, located at the end of Main Street. He would have flown directly to the ranch, but their only level strip had been washed out by a torrential rain a couple of weeks earlier, so he had been directed to land at the Cottonwood Springs airport.

He came to a stop next to the only two aircraft on the strip. One was a blue-and-white Cessna 210 with the R Bar W brand on the side, probably used for flying the senator around the country. The other, a small red Piper Cub, was probably used on the ranch to herd cattle and check windmills.

Next to the filling station sat an old Ford Bronco. It belonged to Earl Sweet, the Williams' ranch foreman, and had been left there for Jim to drive out to the ranch.

Jim secured the plane with a couple of tie downs and then walked over to the old Bronco. Throwing his clothes bag in the backseat, he climbed in, turned the key, and gunned the engine. Its dual exhausts, sounding like the husky voice of a seventy-year-old smoker, bellowed as Jim guided it down Main Street toward the outskirts of town. He'd check into the Woods Rooming House later. Now he was anxious to get to the ranch.

Outside the city limits, he turned the Bronco onto the blacktop, shifted into fifth gear, floored the gas pedal, and headed north—toward the R Bar W.

CHAPTER 6

Even though Jim was in a hurry to get to the ranch, he allowed himself to take in the sights as he drove along. It was scenery he had grown to despise.

The land on either side of the oil road that ran like a black ribbon through the landscape was alive with prairie grass. There were blue satin hues of tall grass prairie and strong yellow-copper tinted shades of short grass prairie. But the dominant colors were the greens and browns emanating from buffalo grass, bluestem, and others that rocked with the wind as far as the eye could see. To Jim, it was like a rolling memory that came flooding back as he bounced along in the old Bronco.

He recalled his geography class. More than 10,000 years ago, according to Greek legend, Eolus, better known as the Keeper of the Wind, took eroded sediment washed from the Rocky Mountains by glaciers and blew it into western Nebraska. Grain by grain, the sand piled up, forming dunes, brinks, valleys, and troughs. Soon the sand was covered with emerald green vegetation and the lowlands filled with brilliant blue lakes.

As a kid, though, Jim thought the land was discordant and ugly. He struggled to appreciate the harsh beauty of the wind-scoured dunes and the prairie land that rolled out like the ocean floor.

Driving on, he soon began to feel the same awesome sense of loneliness that many people experience when driving through that land.

The locals tolerate the loneliness. They see the land as a place where they make their living. They've also come to appreciate the infinite beauty and magnetism of the hills. For Jim, however, the allure had died long ago, with the prejudicial treatment of his parents.

In spite of that, he still felt the energy and spirituality that his early ancestors had known—people who had lived on this self-sustaining land 'long before the white ranchers or homesteaders. Their nomadic ways forced them to turn to the land for spiritual comfort as well as for physical existence.

Looking down the road, his thoughts were interrupted by the transparent waves of heat wafting up from the black oil surface. Nothing unusual, except today the mirages took on a desperate look as they leaped with urgency out of the blackness. "I suppose it is the degree of heat that speeds up their motion," Jim thought. He couldn't help but wonder, though, if there was another reason. Could it be they were trying to escape the clutches of Satan himself? Jim hoped it was not a sign of things to come.

After a couple more miles of rolling hills, he finally saw the Williams ranch sign at the side of the blacktop. Weatherworn and faded, it still beckoned travelers westward down an old double-rutted dirt road.

First time visitors are always nervous about leaving the blacktop and navigating that dusty road that looms ahead because of its winding nature into undefined, desolate, abandoned space looking distinctly untamed. The feeling of being alone is instantly magnified, and most people find it daunting. In just a matter of minutes, however, it straightens out and has destiny written on it. Soon the once foreboding road becomes friendly territory.

Cresting a large hill with the road dust billowing skyward from the Bronco's tires as it caught the wind, Jim spotted a cluster of old, tattered, whitewashed outbuildings. Now ramshackle and in disarray, they sat at the entrance to the Williams ranch just as they had done for over half a century.

The tone they set was anything but one of wealth or power. Instead, they suggested poverty and neglect and seemed out of place to anyone who was familiar with the fortune the Williams family had amassed.

Beyond the cluster of run-down buildings was the first indication that the R Bar W Ranch was actually a prosperous business. On the flat land, down from the outbuildings, sat a large octagonal-shaped Tuscan-style stallion barn with more than 10,000 square feet of covered stalls. To say it was impressive was to do it injustice.

Adding to its grandeur were horse corrals fanning out on three sides. It was home to a large number of horses, mostly paint and quarter. The mares and foals were out on the summer range and wouldn't be gathered up until early fall. Clearly the large barn was built to house the breeding as well as riding stock.

About one hundred feet west of the stables stood a huge hay and cattle barn, forty feet across with a high gabled roof, twin cupolas, and red clapboard siding. It was magnificent under the hot July sun. Having worked inside that building as a young man, Jim could still visualize the sawed softwood timbers caressing the huge roof of the haymow. The inside wasn't all that pretty. It had been built lean and solid for holding massive amounts of hay.

Driving past the barn and around a stand of cottonwoods, he finally saw it. There on a hillside, standing like a monument to fine living amid the rugged grass-swept slopes of the Nebraska Sand Hills, was the large, eloquent, ranch house.

It had been built in the late '20s by Sandy's grandfather and was crafted from giant ponderosa pines trucked in from the Grand Tetons of northwest Wyoming. There was no other house in the hills like it.

Parking the Bronco, Jim got out and walked up the natural stone steps to the entry portico. Stepping beneath its graceful arch he reached for the tarnished brass doorknocker and rapped on the nine-foot high rustic brown door. During the short wait, his mind flashed back to the first time he had stood there as a nervous young man of sixteen—the first time he called on Sandy.

Then the door swung open, and Sandy's housekeeper greeted him.

"Maria, is that you?"

"Hello, Mr. Grant. Please come in."

Although Jim didn't remember much about her, Maria had been a good friend of his mother's on the Pine Ridge Indian Reservation. She had worked for Jim's mother and father on their ranch when he was a very small boy. In fact, he vaguely remembered the day long ago when she left and moved back to the reservation. Shortly after Jim's parents lost their ranch, she came back to the area and started working for the Williams family.

"Senator Gibbons will be down shortly," Marie said as she walked him from the entrance hall into the great room. "She's been out riding with her husband. Please make yourself at home. By the way, Mr. Grant, it's exciting to know you are going to get Raymond released." With that, Maria disappeared through the side door into the kitchen.

Jim thought about her last statement. She certainly had confidence in him—maybe too much confidence.

The vaulted great room, with its timber-framed ceiling, looked the same as it had twenty years before.

Jim remembered entering the house on his first visit and being greeted by Senator Ransom Williams. The senator was the personification of power and wealth, which had made Jim uncomfortable at the time, and, in spite of himself, some of those same feelings came flooding back as he looked around. The room still reflected the elegance and strength that had so long been a part of the Williams family heritage.

Like the first time, he became captivated by the high-gabled ceiling that soared twenty-five feet upward to the elaborate roof above. Dressed with collar pins and a large queen truss, its flowing lines were mesmerizing. Then there were the hand–peeled posts and beams at the edges of the room that contributed to its rustic feel. In fact, the entire room was a whimsical homage to the American West, especially the American cowboy. Many of the lamps and wall decorations were the same and still created drama and inviting warmth as he remembered it.

Hanging from the center of the room was the original hammered brass chandelier, suspended by a long chain from the ceiling. Its twelve oil lamp sockets had been replaced by softened white bulbs topped with brass half-globes, adding a bucolic patina to the warmth.

He walked over to a grouping of reddish-brown distressed leather furniture and sat down on one of the club chairs. The furniture sat on a large southwestern–style rug in the middle of the wide plank dark pine floor. Sitting there, his vision was funneled toward a large Colorado stone fireplace at the far end of the room.

Jim could imagine many bygone evenings spent by men in front of the fireplace with whisky and cigars, making cattle deals, talking politics, and extolling life in the Sand Hills. He couldn't imagine Sandy doing that now. But on second thought, he could.

He leaned back onto a colorful Pendleton blanket draped across the leather chair.

It still felt like a powerful room.

Looking around, his eyes landed on a familiar sight that made his heart skip. Above the mantel on the wide hearth fireplace hung a larger-than-life oil painting. A William Cormish original, crafted in the style of Remington or Russell, the forty-eight-by-sixty-inch painting leapt out at Jim as he sat there staring at it.

Good paintings have a way of telling a story. This painting burned its story into your mind.

Colored in bold yellows, blues, and browns, the painting brought to life dozens of anxious cavalry soldiers astride shoe leather-brown mustangs, racing through the icy waters of the Niobrara River. With long manes lifted in the wind, the horses were in full gallop as they charged crossed the river toward the barren snow-covered bluffs in the distance.

On a bronze plate at the bottom of the frame were the words "The Niobrara Crossing."

Most people who saw the painting believed that Cormish was depicting a charge by the Ninth Cavalry in the winter of 1890 as they raced in a bloodthirsty manner toward the Pine Ridge Indian Reservation to quell a sudden Lakota uprising. That so-called uprising was thought to have been fueled by the ghost dances, a religious movement that was growing in popularity among the Plains Indians at the time.

These dances promised the revival of traditional Native American culture for those who participated, but they were perceived as a threat to white settlers.

That charge across the Niobrara ended in an encampment and eventually a battle—or, more accurately, a massacre.

As Jim sat there, he imagined the sights and sounds coming from that moment in time. His mind focused out of the painting, ahead to his ancestors' village . . .

On that bone-chilling December morning, chaos reigned on the snowy banks of Wounded Knee Creek. The early morning silence was broken by the deadly sound of military carbines ringing out, slaughtering men, women, and children. Soon other guns could be heard echoing along the bluffs, killing many who attempted to flee.

Jim could see the 250 Lakota lying dead after the massacre. A day later, their frozen bodies were buried in several mass graves.

Some people who viewed the Cormish painting saw only a historical scene, but as Jim sat there, he could see only impending tragedy, heartbreak, injustice, and abject poverty. It was the same feeling he'd experienced the first time he'd seen that painting twenty years earlier. To Jim, the painting was a symbol of the callous manner in which a land and an entire way of life had been stripped away from an innocent people by a never-ending stream of lies and deceit. Jim saw the painting as symbolic of the tragedy that was about to befall his ancestors on that dark and horrible winter day—a day that marked the eventual dismemberment of the Lakota tribe.

He felt beads of sweat beginning to well up on his forehead. He could have blamed it on the hot July day, but he knew better. It was the zeal he'd lost for reconnecting with his people since leaving the Sand Hills. It was coming back to play upon his mind. Just as he was thinking about leaving the room, his torment was relieved by a familiar voice.

"Jim, thanks for coming," Sandy said as she appeared on the balcony above a large pine staircase. "I'll have Earl bring your things in."

"That's okay," said Jim. "I've made arrangements to stay in Cottonwood Springs."

Walking to the bottom of the steps, Sandy responded, "Oh, no. I won't have that. You're here as my guest, and here at the Williams ranch we treat our visitors special. Besides, I want to fill you in on some more information I've learned about Raymond's trial and conviction. Then, early in the morning, I want you to ride with Earl and me out to a spot where there are some curious signs of recent airplane landings."

Moving over to the couch, Sandy motioned to Jim. "Please sit. Dinner will be in an hour."

Then, calling to her housekeeper who was standing in the doorway to the kitchen, she said, "Maria, will you please bring us a bottle of our best wine?"

CHAPTER 7

Jim had forgotten that at 4:30 in the morning it would still be dark outside. An early morning ride hadn't seemed such a big problem for him last night. He and Sandy finished off two bottles of Sacramento Valley sauvignon and talked until midnight, forgetting that morning in that part of the country started at four. Breakfast was over and the ranch hands were heading out for the day's work. Sandy looked over and smiled at Jim as they walked out of the house toward the horse barn.

Last night he'd seen Sandy as an elegant, demure hostess in a long skirt, white puffy blouse, and what looked like expensive turquoise jewelry, but as she walked along beside him this morning, she looked every bit the tough, hard-driving ranch owner she was. She was sporting tight fitting, well-worn blue jeans beneath her rough-cut leather chinks. A large silver belt buckle accentuated her tiny waist and paired well with her blue-checked shirt. A Dakota straw cowboy hat sat atop her short blonde hair. With a pair of honed leather gloves tucked into her belt, she looked more like a rugged cowhand than a cowgirl.

Earl was in charge of the cowboys, but it was easy to see who was in charge of the ranch. Jim soon learned that Sandy had the respect of all the men who worked for her. She'd inherited her position as co-owner of the oldest family-owned ranch in Nebraska, but the deference she was given by her ranch hands had been earned, and her passion for ranching was clearly evident.

Jim sheepishly suggested that they take the Bronco instead of riding, explaining that his sudden exposure to a saddle after so many years might be hard on his body, but Sandy wanted Earl and a handful of the men to move a large herd of cattle closer to a particular watering hole before the midmorning heat affected them. Not wanting to appear too citified, Jim backed down and agreed to ride.

The stable was bustling as the cowboys worked on getting their mounts ready. Even though much of the range work was done by plane or four-wheel vehicle, a lot of it still had to be done on horseback. A few of the mounts were registered quarter horses, but most were American paints—in flesh, blood, and spirit. On the Great Plains, paint horses represented sheer athleticism and were proudly called the "athlete of athletes." Dutiful yet feisty, they were well suited for ranch work.

Long before cattlemen controlled the land, paints could be seen carrying Sioux hunters across the Sand Hills after fleeing buffalo. Groomed for survival and spiritual well being, they were the lifeblood of the Plains Indians. In fact, the Lakotas measured wealth by the number of paint ponies a man owned. The horse the ranch hands had selected for Jim was a sorrel gelding with tobiano markings.

The Tuscan style of stable fit well. Sandy's father had picked up a passion for the vaquero style of horsemanship, which still continued at the ranch. A 300-year-old tradition, the gentle training style took advantage of a horse's natural instincts. The subtle commands from a rider's hands to a horse's mouth allowed the horse to cut and break gently in a short time. Keeping the horse's mouth soft and its neck flexible was also important. Ransom Williams had insisted that all his riders learn the vaquero style and had hired Earl Sweet to train them.

Even though it had been many years since he'd ridden, Jim remembered what his father had taught him. A good rider needed to use his body to direct the horse. The key was to lean back when stopping and to use the legs to get the horse moving and driving from the rear.

Jim had just finished saddling his paint and was walking him toward the door when a short, stocky cowboy in a large black hat walked over to him. He knew who the cowboy was by the large silver belt buckle he was wearing, emblazoned with the words "World Champion."

Waggling a finger in Jim's face, the cowboy spoke. "I'm Mick Gibbons, and I don't want you to put stock in my wife's cockamamie ideas about Raymond Two Bears. He shot his father and deserves to be in prison. I don't see why she has to bring an attorney out here to rehash an eight-year-old crime. It's a waste of your time and my money, I'll tell you that right now." Then he turned and walked out of the barn.

It wasn't the friendliest greeting Jim had ever received, but he hadn't expected much more because he knew about their impending breakup. Even so, he was somewhat surprised by Mick's comments.

When Jim emerged from the barn, Sandy rode over. "I see you met Mick. Don't let him scare you off," she said.

Before Jim could respond, Earl gave a crack on his bullwhip and signaled for everyone to mount up. Some of the cowboys rode south toward the hill country, but Earl, Sandy, Jim, and four other cowboys rode around the corral fences and headed northwest toward the grasslands along the Niobrara.

Although Mick's words lingered with him and were worrisome, Jim soon forgot about the encounter and a magical sense of anticipation began to come over him. He remembered that dawn and dusk were the two most spectacular times in the Sand Hills. Even while riding in the dim morning light, Jim knew that a glorious Sand Hills sunrise would appear like magic over his shoulder in less than thirty minutes, and when that happened, the world would come alive and draw him away from the rigors of the everyday life he had come to know.

At breaking light with the sun's rays still hidden by the far-off horizon, Jim could feel a cool breeze blowing from the north across the Niobrara bluffs and down onto the grassland. He was just shifting in his saddle to adjust to the cool wind when, without warning, his paint horse began to rear, pawing at the sky with his hooves. Instinctively, Jim rocked forward, grabbed the saddle horn, and rode the paint back down to all fours.

Even with their easygoing manner, paint horses still have an inbred need to control the situation around them, and Jim's lack of firmness in the saddle had signaled his mount to make an attempt to take control.

The paint wasn't finished, though. He dropped his head. If Jim hadn't grown up around horses, the horse's next move would have thrown him off. Reflexively, he sat back in the saddle, pulled hard on the reins, and dug his heels into the paint's sides.

It was all over in a moment, and Jim was once again in charge. To let the paint know further who was in control, Jim pulled the horse's head back until his nostrils were tucked tightly against his chest.

After holding him there for a few moments, Jim relaxed the reins and gave the paint his head. The horse instantly bolted forward and carried Jim across the grass-covered plains toward the group, now several rods ahead.

Sandy was smiling when Jim finally caught up. Nothing was said, but everyone's body language told it all. That particular paint had been given to Jim by Earl—either to test his toughness or simply as a trick. Whichever, Sandy's smile was her way of telling Jim that he had passed the test.

The sun's rays were beginning to pop up behind them, creating long shadows across the prairie grass as they rode toward the northwest quadrant of the ranch in search of cattle—and the area where Earl had seen signs of possible aircraft landings.

Jim thought his tussle with the paint would be the excitement of the day, but the peace and quiet of the early morning was soon shattered by what happened next. It all happened quickly, but it left little doubt in Jim's mind that Sandy was as savvy as anyone on the ranch when it came to handling a rifle.

A raw-boned, undernourished coyote suddenly appeared one hundred yards to the north. He hadn't yet picked up the group's scent, so he was loping along in search of small rodents or whatever he could find for his morning meal.

Stopping her horse before the coyote could react, Sandy reached into her rifle scabbard and pulled out her Winchester carbine. Raising the gun and splitting the lever at the same time, she fired. A perfect shot! The coyote flew back about five feet and died on the spot.

Jim suddenly remembered how accurate the shot was that killed Silas, but he dismissed it quickly.

"They've been known to take down some of our new calves," Sandy said, putting her rifle back into the scabbard. "It's important that we keep them thinned out."

With shooting like that, nobody in the group even thought about questioning Sandy's motive. Jim was impressed that she needed only one shot to accomplish the kill.

Thirty minutes later, they found part of the herd they were looking for.

Cattle on the R Bar W Ranch were mostly Charolais, a deep reddish-brown animal, almost auburn in color. Hundreds of them were milling around in the early morning sun with the grass-covered dunes framed in the background. It was a sight Jim had seen many times before, but he'd forgotten what a spectacular picture they made.

With the rifle carrying cowboys and the deep red animals looking like a herd of buffalo, it was easy to imagine riding through this land 150 years ago.

Earl signaled for the cowhands to start moving the cattle. He wanted to begin walking them southeast toward a large watering hole. If enough of the cattle started moving in that direction, most of the rest would follow. They couldn't possibly drive all the cattle in that quadrant toward the watering hole, which was about a mile and a half away, so they were just playing the odds.

"Over this way," Earl said as he broke out from the rest of the men. "The landing area is just north and west of here."

As they rode along, Sandy filled Jim in. "The reason we're curious about the site is that it appears to be heavily used. There's an unwritten law out here that any aircraft landing on private property should notify the owners, even if it's eight or ten miles out from the ranch base. This site appears to have had heavy traffic, not just one or two emergency landings. No one seems to know who's been doing it."

"And you think it has something to do with the county attorney and Sheriff Gillette?" Jim asked.

"One of our ranch hands out on an all-nighter tending some of our newborn calves heard what he thought was a plane taking off," Sandy said.

"What do you mean, he thought it was a plane? Isn't a sound like that pretty easily distinguishable out here?"

"Jim, have you ever heard of singing dunes? Sometimes they're described by the Lakota as evil prairie spirits."

"No, I can't say that I have."

"Well, some crescent shaped-dunes, barren of grass, have singing sand. Grains of sand on the crescent roll and collide in a synchronized motion that can create a roaring sound up to one hundred decibels. The low pitch of the moving sand can resemble a low-flying propeller aircraft.

"Anyway," continued Sandy, "after he heard the sound, a four-wheeler much like what the sheriff drives was seen racing across the grass toward the blacktop several miles away. That, combined with signs of heavy air traffic in such a remote place without anyone knowing about it, raises some questions."

As they continued to ride toward the site, Jim mulled over the information, trying to fill in the blanks. How could any of that be connected to an eight-year-old murder case, and would any of that information really be helpful in making a case for the appeals court?

At the top of a large grass-covered dune, Earl stopped and pointed to the valley below. With the sun at his back, Jim could make out what looked like worn paths in the grass approximately the width of an airplane's landing gear.

They rode down the dune for a closer look. The tracks weren't as distinguishable, but they had definitely been made by some type of vehicle, even though it was difficult to tell how old the tracks were. Only repeated landings over an extended period of time could have left such distinctive marks on the ever-changing surface. Jim assumed the landings had been made at night. Otherwise, someone would have seen them.

He turned to Earl, "How often do you or your ranch hands come out to this area?"

"Not often. Usually we come out here during calving season in the spring or fall."

"Always in the daylight?" Jim asked.

"Usually, but we draw some overnighters during early spring calving season."

Sandy added, "Most of the time, unless they're flying extremely low, an aircraft could be seen and heard three or four miles away, and we often have cowboys in that area."

"Any others who might come into the area," Jim asked.

"Only antelope or grouse hunters, and maybe some of the young men from Pine Ridge, showing off their entrepreneurial spirit by growing pot," Earl said.

It seemed unlikely that the planes had landed in the daytime, Jim thought, but he wondered how planes landing at night would have been able to see the landing area, since it was flanked by large rolling sand dunes.

Earl turned his horse around and told Sandy he was going back to the men.

"Go ahead," she said. "I'll stay here and ride back with Jim."

As Earl rode away, Jim surveyed the area, still puzzled. How could any pilot find that narrow strip in the dark?

"Sandy," he said, "let's follow the landing marks and see where they play out."

Dismounting, they began to walk along the landing area. To keep the sun out of his eyes, Jim tilted his hat down. Suddenly, he caught a glimpse of something shiny on a large grass-covered sand dune about a quarter mile away. They climbed back up on their horses and began riding toward the reflection off in the distance.

To their surprise, the reflection disappeared as they drew nearer. The object was apparently only detectable from a certain position and a certain angle of the sun. Reaching the dune at the end of the trough, they found nothing that seemed out of the ordinary.

Sandy waited with the horses as Jim searched for the object of the reflection. Near the top, he noticed that a particular clump of buffalo grass was taller than the rest. He walked up, bent down, and pushed back some of the grass.

Then he saw it. A large circular light was hidden in the tall grass.

Taking a closer look, he saw that the light was mounted on a steel frame buried halfway down in the sand. Attached to it was an empty metal container that appeared to be a battery box of some kind.

"It looks like we've found out how the night landings are carried out," Jim called down to Sandy. "This light is turned on at a certain time so an incoming plane can line up with it and make a safe landing."

"But who turns it on?" asked Sandy. "It would have to be somebody who knows the area and can drive or ride out to the spot at a designated time. And why are the batteries missing?"

"Sandy, let's get back," said Jim. "I want to go into Cottonwood Springs and talk to Sheriff Gillette. Will you please keep this a secret?"

"Absolutely, but first I want to show you something. It isn't far out of our way."

Jim was curious about the statement, wondering if there could be something else important to Raymond's case.

They rode northeast for about thirty minutes until they came upon a set of conical hills four miles from the ranch house. Dismounting and leaving the reins of the bridles trailing the ground, they climbed one of the hills to get a better look. From the top, they could see the buttes rising out of the Niobrara Valley across the way and the river winding below.

"Remember when we used to come up here and sit?" Sandy said. "Do you remember how we'd stay here until the night sky lit up with a million stars? Then we'd ride double back to the ranch. Afterwards, you'd ride on home." The memory of those times came flooding back, and Jim suddenly felt as if he'd never left.

As they stood there side-by-side taking in the scene, Sandy—in a surprise moment—put her hand on Jim's shoulder, reached up, and kissed him.

Before Jim could react, she turned and quickly walked back down the hill, where she picked up the reins of her horse and mounted.

"For old time's sake?" Jim asked as he started down the dune.

"Jim Grant, I still love you!" she shouted as she dug her heals into her horse's side and sped toward the ranch house.

Jim stood there, shocked at what had just happened.

He finally caught up with Sandy about two miles from the ranch, and they slowed down, riding side-by-side in silence.

Back at the stable, Jim turned Sandy's horse and the paint over to a stable hand and walked toward the house. The hot July sun was directly overhead.

"Would you like to come in for lunch and a cold beer?" Sandy asked in a nonchalant manner, as if nothing had happened.

It sounded intriguing as well as refreshing, but Jim declined, telling Sandy that he wanted to snoop around town a little that afternoon. In the back of his mind, however, he was also thinking about the kiss and Sandy's confession. If nothing else, it seemed like a good way to avoid having to confront her about her sudden emotional outburst. He grabbed his clothes bag, walked down the brick path, and tossed the bag into the Bronco as Sandy walked along behind him.

"I'll be back tomorrow," he said, "I want to talk to some of your ranch hands."

Looking around and seeing that no one was watching, Sandy reached up and kissed Jim again—and Jim returned her kiss. Then she turned, walked back up the steps, and disappeared into the house.

Jim cranked up the Bronco and started down the lane and onto the double rutted dirt road, his mind focused on Sandy. Coming to a stop at the blacktop, his thoughts changed. He remembered the old house where he'd lived as a boy. It was only two miles up the road from the Williams sign. But did he want to see it again? Could he control his emotions? After all, it was part of a very poignant time in his life. He decided he did want to see it again.

Turning left, he headed north. In a couple minutes, he saw the rundown, weather-beaten farm buildings still standing about one hundred yards off the road. He drove up to the buildings and parked the Bronco next to the old clapboard house. Walking along the path he'd walked hundreds of times, he could feel tears welling up in his eyes.

He opened the broken back door and stepped into what had been the kitchen. It looked like it had been home to every raccoon and coyote in the sand hills.

Then he walked into the back hallway that led to a set of stairs. They were still climbable, so he carefully made his way up to the second floor. Soon he found himself standing in the doorway of his old bedroom. His furniture and bed were gone, but the faded red-flowered wallpaper remained. Loose at the seams and peeling around the heat duct in the corner of one wall, it didn't look as fancy as he remembered. The sheer curtains, which had been purchased from the Sears Roebuck catalog, were still hanging in the windows. They were brown and stained from the rainwater that had seeped in around the windowsill, and they were still attached to the same bent curtain rod where Jim had tried to chin himself when he was about five.

Leaning against the sagging doorframe, Jim closed his eyes and let his thoughts drift back to a time when his home was the energetic hub of activity in the area. A tide of memories washed over him as he stood in the doorway.

He remembered lying in bed night after night waiting. Suddenly a light would appear on the south wall of his room as it shone through the dusty north-facing window, with its cracks and glazed-over corners. The light would show up quickly, like a spaceship swooping down from the night sky. Fixated between the bedsteads, it would remain stationary for several seconds before starting to move. After a few scary moments, during which time Jim's imagination ran wild, the light would move around the wall only to disappear behind the curtains as the car that created the light roared by the house on its way to Cottonwood Springs.

Standing in the doorway, Jim's thoughts then turned to Cooney, who had been his best friend when Jim was ten. Cooney was a good cattle dog even though his fur was mangy-looking and matted from sleeping in the barn or the old feed shed.

He remembered playing with Cooney in the cottonwood groves, chasing rabbits and ground squirrels, or trekking down to the Niobrara to go wading. However, his strongest memory was of the day he had to take an old shovel from the machine shop, walk out to the east pasture, pick up Cooney, and place him in his wagon.

Earlier that day, Jim's dad had come in from mowing and, as he climbed down from the tractor, called out, "Jim, come here a minute, will you?"

Jim remembered how his dad's voice shook as he tried to explain, "Son, it's Cooney. He ran out in front of the mower—and I couldn't stop in time. I'm sorry, but—"

His father's voice trailed off at that point, but Jim couldn't hear him, anyway; he ran toward the barn as fast as he could. The barn was one of the few places where a ten-year-old boy could go to cry without the whole world knowing.

Later that afternoon, Jim and Raymond buried Cooney with all the pomp and ceremony a young boy burying his best friend could muster. Even after Jim had stopped making regular visits to Cooney's gravesite, thoughts of his friend would continue to sadden him for a long time.

Moving out of the doorway, Jim smiled as he retraced memories of the ranch. Like the light on his bedroom wall that appeared and then moved on, time also had a way of moving on. However, unlike the light that had disappeared behind his curtains, the memories that had brightened the room of his life would forever leave traces on the walls of his mind.

It was a melancholy ride to town where the Woods rooming house was expecting him. He pulled up to the square two-story house late in the afternoon. Perhaps a hot shower, dinner, and a cold beer at the local bar would settle him down after the emotional roller coaster ride this day had been.

He'd renew his quest for information tomorrow—but *not* at 4 a.m.

CHAPTER 8

The smell of bacon and sausage frying on the grill permeated Malarkey's Bar as Jim sat down for breakfast. The greasy smell mixed with the odor of stale smoke, spilled beer, and dirty oil-soaked floors couldn't be avoided.

The rooming house had stopped serving after 8:00, and Malarkey's was the only place in Cottonwood Springs that served breakfast. Ironically, it was the same place Jim had helped close down the night before. Cottonwood Springs had more than one beer joint, of course. In fact, there were more taverns in town than churches. You might say there was a definite imbalance between rowdiness and righteousness.

He'd had a definite plan for his visit to Malarkey's the night before. Besides downing a long neck or two, he wanted to ask a few questions about the mysterious plane landings at the R Bar W. He wanted to see if any of the local cowboys had any information, and he was hoping to run into someone he'd known as a young man. He thought an old-timer or two might be around from the days of his youth, but he didn't see any familiar faces, which didn't surprise him very much. After all, a cowboy's life was transient, and many of his old friends had probably never started a family or settled down very long in one place.

Most of the cowboys he talked to looked as if they'd just climbed off their horses after a long day of chasing cattle. After an hour of cold shoulders and brick walls, Jim quit buying them beers. Trying to get any answers was hopeless. Then a cowboy sitting in the far back corner of the room got up and walked over to where Jim was sitting at the bar.

It was Mick.

"Those plane landings you're asking everybody about—they're just in somebody's imagination," he said.

Then he turned and walked out.

Jim hadn't recognized Mick with his hat pulled down, sitting in a dark corner, and he'd been surprised when Mick walked up. It was the second time he'd run into him in as many days, and he still hadn't gotten in a single word. He was starting to dislike the guy.

As the evening went on, Jim saw various descriptions of men coming and going through a door in the back of the tavern. The bartender was reluctant to share any information when Jim asked what was going on back there, but after some prodding and a twenty-dollar bill, he learned that it was a local poker game.

"Do they let out-of-towners in?" Jim asked.

"Go see for yourself," the bartender said.

Jim thought, "Maybe I can get some information if I join them."

As he walked through the door, the room suddenly got quiet and the five men gathered around the well-used poker table slowly looked up.

"Have an empty chair?" Jim asked.

At first there was no response, but then a cowboy holding the deck of cards said, "Ante is a buck, and a Hamilton is the limit." It took Jim a second or two, but then he remembered that a Hamilton was a ten spot. The dealer continued. We only play two games—five card stud and five card draw. Nothing wild and jacks or better to open. Are you in?"

"Sounds good to me," Jim said.

He sat down, slid four one hundred-dollar bills across the table, and asked for chips. They weren't exactly a noisy bunch, but the sight of four C-notes brought complete silence.

Then an old cowboy sitting next to the dealer responded, "We usually don't see bills that size here in Cottonwood. I can tell you ain't no ranch hand, tossing around money like that. New to the area?"

"I'm Jim Grant, from Denver, and I'm visiting my old home town as a guest of Senator Gibbons. She hired me to look into an old case—Raymond Two Bears. We're trying to land an appeal for him."

Jim was disappointed that his statement drew only a shrug or two in response.

Then the cowboy who had reacted to the C-note spoke. "This here is Red," directing a thumb in Red's direction. "Over there are Lyle, Wolverine, and Curt," pointing as he went around the table.

Each nodded at the mention of his name.

"And my name's Lloyd."

"Pleased to meet you for now," Jim said. "Maybe after our card game I won't feel so pleased," he added.

"Are you Jim and Victoria's son?" Wolverine asked.

Jim was surprised by the mention of his parents' names. It had been a long time since he'd heard their names spoken out loud. He didn't recognize Wolverine but evidently he had known Jim's parents.

"Yes," Jim said.

"Fine people," Wolverine said. "I hated to see what happened to them."

Jim thanked Wolverine for the comment, fighting back a small tear of remembrance.

The chips Lloyd slid toward Jim had definitely been around some. Those that weren't broken had so much dirt and grime embedded in them that it was hard to distinguish their color. He could only guess that it was four hundred dollars' worth, but soon found he was wrong.

Lloyd said, "Don't have enough chips for four bills, but you can claim the difference when the game's over."

The way Lloyd said it, Jim could tell that he didn't expect Jim to have much left at the end of the night.

"Fair enough," Jim said.

He stacked his chips as best he could, and the game resumed. About a half hour into the game, Jim started asking questions, but no one seemed to want to talk about the plane landings, so he changed the subject to Raymond. This time it stirred some interest.

"I used to work out at the R Bar W until one night about ten years ago," Lloyd said. "I'd just finished my chores. It was 10:00, which wasn't unusual in the summertime. Cowboys ain't a nine-to-five group."

Everyone chuckled and nodded as Lloyd continued.

"I was driving down the lane toward the blacktop when I noticed something lying curled up on the road. I damn near ran over it, but was able to stop in time. I stepped out to see what it was—and the damn thing uncoiled and jumped up. It was the most god-awful sight I'd ever seen."

No one interrupted, so Lloyd continued. "It was a manlike creature, but its face was contorted, and its eyeballs were huge and glowing white. I stepped back, but it came at me. As the thing raised its arms, I could see claws on both hands. They looked like eagle talons."

Jim looked around the table, but no one seemed surprised by Lloyd's story.

"Then that thing started to speak, and his voice echoed across the prairie, but I couldn't make out what he was saying. God, I was scared. Then, as fast as he'd appeared, he shriveled back to his whimpering, mumbling self. It was Raymond, I'm tellin' you, but before I could say anything, he disappeared into the darkness."

"Yeah, Lloyd, we know," said Wolverine with a chuckle. "It couldn't have been whiskey playing tricks on your vision, now could it?"

Lloyd answered emphatically. "I saw him, I tell you, and it scared me so bad that I never went back. I took a job over at Merimen ranch, and I'm glad I did."

The game continued, but Jim kept thinking back to what Lloyd had said. Had Raymond been possessed by demons like people thought, or was he slowly losing his mind? Either way, it was possible that he really did shoot his father.

Around midnight, the game broke up and everybody left. Jim's winnings wouldn't get him to Vegas, but he'd won enough to pay for his room for three more nights.

As Jim left the tavern and started back toward the rooming house, he noticed there were no sidewalks once he left the main area of downtown, so he walked along the edge of Elm Street under several broken streetlights. The street was quite dark.

About two blocks from the rooming house, he saw an old pickup sitting on the corner of Elm and 5th, its engine running and its lights off. His first thought was that it was somebody from the tavern sleeping it off before going home, but suddenly, with its lights still off, it roared around the corner and headed right for him.

Reacting to the danger, he dove headfirst into the ditch. The pickup just missed him as it raced by, throwing dirt and gravel everywhere before disappearing down the street. Jim hadn't gotten a good look at it, but he'd recognize it if he saw it again.

Standing up, he dusted himself off. Then he noticed the blood oozing from his forehead. He must have hit a rock while diving into the ditch. His first thought was that one or more of the cowboys in the back room hadn't appreciated his winning during their poker game, but the more he thought about it, the more he realized that wasn't the reason.

Maybe someone at the tavern had taken his questions seriously. Could it have been Mick?

Whichever, it was a rather rude welcome to the small cow town.

The next morning, Jim's thoughts were swirling as he cut into his pancake and took a bite of toast. No matter who had tried to run him down the night before, he had work to do. He had to keep digging if he was going to take on Raymond's case and win an appeal. To get an appeal heard would take proof of prosecutorial misconduct, and that would take some doing. If the roadblocks became substantial, and it looked like they might, the next step would be to move to an extraordinary motion and try for a new trial.

Jim wanted to schedule an appointment with Sheriff Gillette before making a rush decision. The court documents from Raymond's trial needed to be combed to see if anything popped out that could be used as the basis for an appeal. No doubt a subpoena would probably be necessary to look at the evidence. That could take some time, providing a judge could be found that would go along with him.

Taking the last bite of pancake, Jim reached for the rest of the black coffee getting cold in its mug. As he did, he looked into the large mirror above the bar. He wasn't going to have to wait long to talk to Gillette, because at that moment, the door opened, and Jim saw the sheriff walk in. He was a tall, barrel-chested man with a definite walk of authority. His generous gut was carried well on his large frame, and, although graying, he looked rather physical for a man of his age—which Jim guessed to be around sixty. In blue jeans and a tan shirt, the sheriff looked like most of the locals, but the silver star on his shirt and his clean white hat distinguished him as the sheriff of Houston County.

He walked straight to Jim, took off his narrow-brimmed Stetson, laid it on the bar, and sat down on the stool next to him.

"Mr. Grant, I'm Sheriff Dean Gillette," he said, reaching over and extending his hand, with his shoulders square to the back bar.

The two men shook hands as Gillette called to the woman behind the bar. "Marge, would you get me a cup of coffee and give Mr. Grant here a refill?" Then he turned his attention to Jim.

"So, Mr. Grant, how's your breakfast? I apologize for not having a fine restaurant like you're used to, but this is the way things are here in Cottonwood."

Marge filled their coffee cups and the sheriff continued. "I heard you were in town, and I wanted to stop by and welcome you to Cottonwood Springs. It's unusual for a high-priced Denver attorney to be in our town, but I know you used to live around here, isn't that right?"

The sheriff didn't wait for an answer.

"By the way, it looks like you had a small accident last evening, judging by your forehead. Anything you want to tell me?"

Jim didn't know how to interpret Gillette's comments, but decided to play the game to see where it led. Evidently, some of the questions Jim had asked the night before had echoed outside the bar. Why else would Gillette be paying him a personal visit? He hadn't come in for breakfast. But something puzzled Jim. How did the sheriff know about his close call on the way back to the rooming house last night?

"Yes, my parents used to live north of town, on land Senator Williams now owns," Jim said after putting the puzzling thought aside.

"Are you planning to be here long?" Gillette asked.

"Well," said Jim, "it's a bit more than a visit. I'm following up on some new evidence in the eight-year-old Raymond Two Bears case, and, if it pans out, we'll approach the appellate court to have the case appealed."

Gillette's tone grew darker.

"The *we* you're talking about—does that include Senator Gibbons?"

Jim knew Sandy didn't want her name involved, but it appeared that it was already out there. "Yes," he said, "she's the one petitioning for an appeal."

The sheriff sniffed derisively. "Yeah, that figures. She was happy about the verdict at first, but lately I've been hearing rumors that she's trying to get the case reopened, and since you're here and not on vacation, I can assume the rumors are true. After eight years, I figured she'd just let it go."

The sheriff's answer surprised Jim, because Sandy hadn't indicated happiness or unhappiness with the outcome of Raymond's case. She'd only talked about a need to clear his name. That brought up another question that needed answering.

"I understand that Senator Gibbons requested a look at the evidence from the trial, but you told her it was gone. Is that true?"

"Son," said Gillette, "that evidence isn't available to just anyone in the county. Not even to a pseudo power like Senator Gibbons.

Jim wasn't quite sure what the sheriff meant by his comment, but it was obvious he thought he held the real power in the county.

"Sheriff Gillette, I'd like to review the court records and take a look at the evidence from Raymond's trial. I realize that sitting at a bar eating breakfast isn't the most professional way to make such a request, but it would certainly save both of us some time. Can I stop by your office and look at the evidence before I go to the courthouse and begin combing through the court records?"

"What makes you think you are any different from Senator Gibbons?" Gillette asked.

"So I need to get a subpoena—?"

Sheriff Gillette interrupted, "Damn right, you do! Who do you think you are, anyway? I'm the law in this county."

The sheriff's manner had suddenly changed from that of a welcoming committee to more of a bouncer.

Setting his coffee cup down hard on the counter and reaching for his hat, he firmly said, "I'm telling you, those records are unavailable, and I can guarantee that you won't get any assistance from Judge Madrid at the courthouse."

The sheriff stood and stared directly at Jim. "Don't get too comfortable here, Mr. Grant. This isn't your town." Then he placed his Stetson on his head and walked out of the bar.

Jim's mind flashed back to the stories he'd heard as a boy and read about as a law student recounting the dual standard of justice and abuse of power against Native Americans in the Sand Hills. It appeared that it was still going on.

The roadblocks he'd feared now were out there. To get anything accomplished, his next step would be to bypass local jurisdiction and take his request for a search warrant to a district judge in North Platte, but first he wanted to visit the county courthouse.

He finished his coffee and walked back to the rooming house to pick up the Bronco. A chill came over him as he walked by the corner where he'd nearly been run down. It could've been a drunken cowboy making his way home, but the timing left many questions in his mind. If it had been intentional, should he be on the lookout for more trouble?

The walk and drive from the rooming house to the courthouse was refreshing, considering the staleness of Malarkey's Bar and Grill. The county seat of government was located a block off Main Street, just past the downtown area. He pulled into a parking space in front of the courthouse and stepped out of the Bronco. The courthouse looked the same as he remembered, but Jim saw its architecture with new eyes. It was a two-story red brick Romanesque revival-style building, and its center tower and tall, narrow arched windows reflected a strong counterpoint to the smaller buildings that surrounded it.

Then Jim noticed something above the main entrance that had escaped him as a boy. Carved in the limestone facade over the doors were the words "Equal Justice for All."

"We'll see about that," Jim thought as he opened the large wooden door and walked into the courthouse lobby.

A young, petite receptionist sitting at a table along one of the side walls looked up, no doubt hearing the thumping sound of Jim's boots as his heels struck the floor and echoed throughout the marble-lined lobby.

Stepping to the table, he greeted her.

"Hello, I'm Jim Grant, and I'd like to see the county attorney."

Her eyes went to the cut on Jim's forehead and she stared at it for a few seconds.

Jim wasn't sure if she was taken aback by the cut or by the color of his skin. Suspecting the latter, he flushed with some anger before clearing his throat to get her attention.

Realizing her improprieties, she quickly looked down and responded.

"Yes, Mr. Grant, the county attorney is expecting you. Take the staircase to the second floor and go to room 221."

Jim backed off his anger, realizing she was just a young naïve county employee, but her reaction continued to heighten the divide he felt between the area cultures even in contemporary times.

After the cold reception from Sheriff Gillette, Jim was surprised that he was going to meet with the county attorney so easily. After all, he and Gillette were the two people Sandy suspected of collusion in sending Raymond to prison. But he wasn't in the door yet, and the young lady was only a receptionist. He'd still have to request to see the trial records—and that probably wouldn't be easy.

Reaching the top of the marble steps, Jim turned to walk down the hall. Immediately he saw a man in a blue serge three-piece suit coming toward him. The man was bald, with the exception of two small tufts of hair above each ear that stuck out beneath the stems of his wire-rimmed glasses. His black wingtips lacked polish, which matched the rest of his rumpled look.

"Good morning, attorney," the man said as he removed his glasses and shoved them into his breast pocket. The crooked smile on his face grew wider, showing his large yellow teeth stained with tobacco juice. "I'm Ed Hardin, county attorney. Welcome to Cottonwoods Springs."

Jim saw no need to introduce himself because the county attorney already knew who he was. They shook hands and started toward Hardin's office.

"I understand that you'd like to review the trial records of Raymond Two Bears. My associate is pulling together the files right now, and you can use our side office," Hardin said. "I have a client coming in shortly, but please make yourself at home and take your time."

"Wow!" Jim thought. "That was easy—too easy. He's bending over backwards to accommodate me. This was certainly different from Sheriff Gillette's approach. Does he want me to assume that laying out the records for me means they have nothing to hide?"

Jim followed Hardin into the side office, his thoughts racing. Attorneys who assume too much are attorneys who get burned. There was no way to tell if all the records were there. If some of them had been destroyed or altered, it would be a criminal offense, but from what Jim had heard, it wouldn't have surprised him.

Hardin laid out the court papers and then excused himself.

Proceeding through the records, Jim was struck by three things. Raymond's testimony wasn't there. His name appeared on an early witness list, but it had been stricken from a subsequent list. In fact, the defense had called very few witnesses. Jim himself had kept defendants off the stand, but in a murder trial with such strong evidence, he questioned that tactic. Why hadn't Raymond been called or allowed to testify?

Then Jim remembered what Lloyd had told him about Raymond's strange behavior. It might have hurt his case. Surely, though, there must have been people who could have testified on his behalf—but none were called.

What about Raymond's state of mind? Any smart defense lawyer would have brought forth witnesses on the defendant's behalf to push for mental incompetence. But Jim found nothing—although two medical doctors had testified for the prosecution; it wasn't clear if they were psychiatrists. The first had blamed Raymond's actions on factitious disorder (FD), whereby symptoms are either self-induced or falsified by the patient, and the second had blamed his actions on dissociative identity disorder, something about having two distinct personalities. Both doctors looked like ringers to Jim.

The third thing that caught Jim's attention was that a man named Harold Eagles had been struck from the witness list. Despite the lack of defense witnesses, however, nothing appeared to suggest prosecutorial misconduct. The evidence of Raymond's guilt was there, though it was never challenged. Would that evidence have been looked at differently if the defense attorney hadn't signed off prematurely?

Jim couldn't escape the feeling that the evidence had been presented inaccurately. That was where he needed to prove misconduct. Was Raymond a man who'd been tried for a crime but punished for who he was? It was beginning to look like it, but could Jim convince an appellate judge of that? He needed to find the evidence that had misled the jury, which meant he'd need to get into the evidence room at the sheriff's office.

A young associate stepped into the room a short time later and asked if Jim had any questions.

"Yes," Jim said, "I have two. Where's the defense attorney for the case now, and how can I locate Harold Eagles?"

"The defense attorney left office soon after an appeal had been made in the case," the young man said. "And shortly afterward, he moved to North Carolina, I think."

As for Harold Eagles, the young attorney had no idea where to locate him, since he was new to the county.

Jim emerged from the side door three hours later, thanked the associate, and then walked down the stairs and out to the Bronco. Before he obtained a search warrant to see the evidence from the trial, he needed to ask some questions of the old-timers working at the ranch.

He also hadn't totally dismissed Sandy's kiss and confession. In fact, the incident had been on his mind ever since it had occurred. It certainly hadn't been expected, although he'd seen signs of her feelings during her first visit to his office in Denver. An emotional involvement would make his work here and his life in general more difficult, however, so he decided to let it ride for the moment.

Before getting into the Bronco, Jim took time to look around. It seemed peaceful, but, then again, it had seemed peaceful the night before, too.

As he drove toward the ranch, Jim thought about what he was going to say and how he'd act. He had to admit that Sandy's feelings weren't totally one-sided. The chemistry between them and the riskiness of the situation brought a thrill that he hadn't felt in a long time.

As he thought about the warmth of her kiss, he was undercut by a curious pain—the pain of what had happened in the past. It had put him on the defensive since his arrival, but Jim was determined to tell Sandy how he felt about her before he left.

Earl was tethering his roan-colored paint to a corral fence as Jim pulled up and parked next to the stables.

"Thanks for the use of your Bronco," said Jim.

Earl put a foot up on the lower rung of the fence and rested his arms across his knees.

"Sure enough. Glad you could use it. I don't get around much outside the ranch. Maybe a couple of nights playing cards at Malarkey's, but that's about it. Otherwise, it just sits."

Jim noticed that Earl still had the west Texas drawl and cowboy gait that he'd brought to the Williams ranch years ago. Jim had known him since he was a young boy, and Earl was impressive in his younger days. He was the first real cowboy Jim had ever met, and, according to Jim's dad, Earl was the best bronc buster in the country. But as Jim looked at Earl standing there in the daylight, the bright rays of the sun shadowing his face, he suddenly looked like an old man. Sun and exposure to the outdoors had rutted his broad, deeply tanned face, but he was still the picture of a real cowboy.

Jim joined him along the fence.

"How long have you been working at the ranch?" Jim asked.

"I came up in '54," Earl said. "Things were getting rough in Texas and cowboy wages weren't keeping up, so I took an opportunity offered by Mr. Williams and started here at the R Bar W. He was interested in my vaquero style of training and had a lot of horses that needed attention, so I signed on. I've been here ever since."

"I imagine you've seen quite a few changes."

"You're darn tootin'," Earl said. "Cattle ranching has changed a lot, but three things that have really been a disaster for an old-time cowboy like me—when they quit making Bull Durham cigarettes, when they changed the style of Levis, and when they started putting coffee in plastic containers instead of tin cans."

Then he chuckled, but it was an honest answer from a man who went to bed looking forward to the next day's work, and it let Jim know that humor was still a big part of the cowboy life.

Jim pressed on.

"How well did you know Raymond Two Bears?"

"He hung around the stables, but when hard work was scheduled, he'd disappear like a thistle in the wind. He was always out ridin' that horse of his, and he knew every square foot of this ranch like the back of his hand because he spent so much time ridin' around it. Silas would be lookin' for him in the mornin', and Raymond would come riding in after spending all night on the prairie. Sometimes he'd be gone for two or three days, and lots of times he looked like he'd been in a fight with a wildcat when he got back."

"Did he and his father get along?" Jim asked.

"They got along like any other father and son makin' a livin' as ranch hands. Silas would cuss him out from time to time and call him a lazy bum, but Raymond just seemed to let it roll off. He never got very excited about anything."

"Where was Raymond's mother?"

"I can't answer that one. There are some suspicions, but I don't think anyone knows for sure."

"Do you think Raymond shot his father?"

Earl laughed in disgust and said, "Are you loco? Of course he didn't! He was just a handy target."

"How much do you know about his connection to the sheriff?"

"Rumors, I imagine, although the sheriff did come out to the ranch to see him a few times.

"Would you testify to that?"

"That depends."

"On what?"

"On when and where."

"Okay. How well do you know Sheriff Gillette?"

"Dean? Well enough to know that if I had any trouble, I wouldn't go to *him*."

"Why's that?"

Suddenly, Earl stepped off the fence and turned toward his horse. "I'll let you figure that one out," he said. "Now I've got to get back to work."

Evidently he was tired of answering questions, so he just mounted up and rode off. Earl didn't appear to be a man who shied away from tough questions, but he was definitely ducking Jim's last one. It appeared that Jim would have to get that information from the other hands.

At that moment, Sandy drove up in her pickup and parked by the stables. Seeing her pushed Jim's heart into his throat. As she opened the door, Jim was struck by the realization that he might still be in love with her, and it suddenly made him afraid to talk to her.

"Jim," she said, giving him a hug, "what happened to your forehead?"

Jim lightly replied, "I tried to whip an old pickup truck at the corner of Elm and 5th last night after I left Malarkey's."

"Come on up to the house. I'll get you a cold compress and something to drink."

Log homes have a unique way of staying cool in the middle of the summer without air conditioning, and the air was very pleasant as Jim stepped into the great room.

"What did you find out today?" Sandy asked, handing Jim a cold bottle of beer.

"I found out I'm going to need more evidence if I'm going to take an appeal to the appellate court. If there was any prosecutorial misconduct, it doesn't show up in the records."

"What do you plan to do next?"

"I think it's time to go visit Raymond," Jim said. "I'm also going to talk to the state attorney general. We're going to need help on this one. There's just too much inside control in this county to get straight answers. I also need to get back to Denver and take care of some business. If the weather holds, I'll fly from there to Lincoln first thing Wednesday morning."

"Would you like to stay for dinner?" Sandy asked.

"Sure," Jim said.

CHAPTER 9

Sitting in the visitor's room, Jim looked across the table at Raymond. His presence brought back memories Jim had long suppressed. The rough turbulent flight from Denver to Lincoln hadn't allowed him much time to think about it, but as Jim looked at his old friend, he remembered how close they had been. Perhaps he'd been too young to understand the bond that had developed between them at the time—a union of blood brothers.

Jim continued trying to get Raymond to talk, but his body language told Jim that he didn't trust him—but then, why should he? Everybody Raymond had ever known had abandoned him, and he'd been left here in prison to rot.

"Raymond, talk to me," Jim said. "I want to help you get a new trial. I want to free you and let you go back to the Sand Hills. I want you to ride again through the Niobrara Valley with the wind blowing through your hair."

Raymond looked up and stared at Jim for a few seconds before looking back down at his folded hands. It was a start, but Jim could tell Raymond still didn't trust him. Even though they'd been good friends, Jim represented the establishment, and Raymond wasn't ready to open up and give Jim the information he needed. In fact, Jim wasn't sure Raymond even wanted his conviction appealed.

"Senator Gibbons—uh, Sandy Williams—has retained me on your behalf to try to get an appeal granted to overturn your conviction. Raymond, I've been reviewing the evidence, and I don't think you killed your father."

Raymond looked up again, and Jim saw a bit of life glimmering in his eyes. He straightened up in his chair, threw his head back to flick the hair out of his eyes, but looked straight ahead, right past Jim.

"Raymond, did you shoot your father?"

Raymond shifted his stare toward Jim and looked into his eyes.

"Yes! Why do you care?" came his answer in a low guttural voice.

Jim was surprised by the sound of Raymond's voice and by his answer. He'd hit a nerve.

"Why did you shoot your father?"

"I just did, no reason," he said.

If Jim had believed him, it would have put an end to the whole thing, but he wasn't ready to jump on that wagon yet. Why had he said yes? Had this place conditioned him to accept his fate?

"Raymond, I'm on your side. I'm sorry I wasn't able to help you during your trial, but I remember our friendship, and I remember the good times we had," said Jim, watching as a slight smile tugged at the corners of Raymond's mouth.

"We're blood brothers, and I want to help get you released. I don't believe you shot your father."

Suddenly, Raymond's smile was replaced by an angry look as he said, "Blood brothers? You're a half-breed who left the Lakota nation and the Sand Hills, the spiritual land of our ancestors. We're not blood brothers. We live in different worlds. Why are you *really* here?"

Raymond's words stung. In his mind, Jim had always defended his choice, but he knew Raymond was right. Jim was half Lakota, and he had left the land of his ancestors, but how could he convince Raymond that he hadn't given up his heritage when he left? Somehow, he needed to let Raymond know that he really was there to help a man he considered a brother.

"Raymond, you *have* to trust me. Remember on the prairie when you put trust and faith in your paint pony to always be at your side and to help you? You can rely on *me* now, just like you trusted your paint."

Raymond's look didn't change, but Jim could see his body relaxing a bit. Jim felt that, deep down inside, Raymond was still uncomfortable with his questioning and might shut him out again, but he had to get some answers.

"There are several people at the ranch, including Sandy, who don't believe you shot your father. They think you were framed. There's both circumstantial and actual evidence that strongly suggests reopening the case and getting you a new trial."

Again, Jim was surprised by Raymond's response. "How will a new trial affect the people at the ranch? How will Sandy be affected?" he asked.

At first Jim didn't understand the questions, but he was glad that Raymond was opening up.

"Why do you care whether the people at the R Bar W will be affected, and why are you reluctant for people to find out the truth? Are you protecting someone?" Jim asked.

Before Raymond could answer, it hit Jim that the reason why Raymond hadn't testified at the trial and the reason a second witness had been stricken was because Raymond *was* protecting someone. Did he know who the shooter was? Was it somebody from the ranch? Earl? Mick? Another one of the ranch hands? A friend from Pine Ridge? If Gillette and Hardin were involved, as Sandy thought, why protect them?

Then Jim sensed that Raymond was reverting back to his non-trusting, non-talking frame of mind, so he hurriedly continued. "Sandy wouldn't have hired me to get you a new trial if she or anyone on the ranch would be drastically affected. She's on your side and wants to see you get a new trial. Raymond, you have to give me a lead so I can go to the appellate court. I need some strong evidence of your innocence for the court to receive this petition."

Jim waited in silence for about a minute, watching Raymond weigh his decision. Should he say something that might drastically affect the person he was protecting, or did he want his freedom from this hellhole?

Then, like a clap of thunder, Raymond said, "I wasn't at the ranch the night my father was shot. I was in Pine Ridge, visiting Harold Eagles."

"So you didn't shoot your father?"

"No!"

"Did you have your defense counsel strike Harold Eagles as a material witness because you wanted to take the fall for the murder?"

"It was the right thing to do," Raymond said softly.

"If I can find Harold Eagles and get him to speak on your behalf, we might have a chance at a new trial. Raymond, I think you just gave me the evidence to petition for a reversal."

Jim wanted to continue questioning Raymond, but the allotted time for his visit had expired, and the guard, who'd been standing in the room the whole time, told them they had five minutes to wrap up the visit.

Jim asked Raymond if he could come back and talk to him about his relationship with Gillette and Hardin.

"Is there anything else you want to tell me now?" Jim asked.

Raymond hesitated, looked at the guard, and said, "Yes, I'd like to talk about the crash of the Denver Mint plane.

"Time is up," the guard said as he stepped between them.

"Raymond, I'll be back to finish our talk!" Jim said as he shook Raymond's hand. The guard, appearing nervous, quickly intervened.

"Time to take him back to his cell," he said.

Jim watched silently as the guard escorted Raymond toward the door. Raymond turned, swiped his hair to the side with his hand, and looked into Jim's eyes. Then he turned and left. Having known Raymond from boyhood, Jim interpreted Raymond's last look to be one of trust.

Abigail Finnigan's driver John was waiting outside the prison. The weather had settled down, and they drove to the airport. The flight to Denver would be much calmer than the morning one. Pulling back on the throttle, Jim felt the twin engines kick in and lift the aircraft skyward toward the western horizon.

It had been four long days since he'd left Denver to fly to Cottonwood Springs, and it felt good to be home. Opening the front door, he stepped into the house. The familiar smells and sights were pleasing to his senses after what he'd experienced the past few days.

"Hi, Daddy!" Molly exclaimed as she came running down the stairs.

She was talking a mile a minute as she gave Jim a big hug. Her chatter centered on a class dance, her friends, and many other things while Christine stood watching from the kitchen doorway.

With much less enthusiasm, Christine said, "I'm glad you're home, too."

She walked over and gave Jim a hug.

"Dinner will be ready in about thirty minutes," she said, turning back to the kitchen.

Setting his clothes bag by the stairs, Jim followed Christine into the kitchen. His mind had been on the happenings of the past few days, so he hadn't recognized the cool reception he'd received from her. He started telling her about his trip, but she didn't want to get into that conversation.

"Why don't you go upstairs, unpack, and visit with your daughter? She's happy to have you back."

It wasn't like Christine to shoo him away. "What's going on? I've been away several days, and you don't have time for me?" Jim asked.

"Go, go. Get reacquainted with Molly," she said, flicking her hand toward the door. "Dinner will be ready shortly, and I'll call you down."

Molly dominated the conversation at dinner, as usual. It gave Jim and Christine an excuse not to say much. They did talk after dinner, but the coolness could still be felt. Jim wanted to tell her about Sandy's reaction, but decided to pick a better time.

In spite of everything, it was good to be home. He'd take some time over the next few days and get straight with his wife, starting with the next morning by spending some time at home and going into the office late.

———

As Jim stepped out of the elevator the next day at about 1:00, Tom was waiting for him in the hall.

"Jim, stop by my office, would you?"

"Sure, let me check in with Rose and take care of my messages."

"No, right away," Tom said.

Jim was surprised by Tom's insistence. Tom was known for being direct, but not unreasonable, so it seemed out of character. Jim followed him into his office, and Tom shut the door.

"Jim, I just received a phone call from the warden at the Nebraska state penitentiary."

"Does he have a warrant for my arrest?" Jim said in a joking manner to lighten the mood. "I guess I shouldn't have kept their magazines after all."

Tom spoke softly, "Raymond Two Bears was murdered today coming out of the dining hall after lunch."

Jim sat there in silence, stunned, not believing what he'd just heard.

"Did you say he was murdered?"

"Yes, around 11:00 this morning."

Jim uttered a string of profanities as he jumped up and slammed the heels of his hands on the table, knocking over Tom's expensive bronze cast. He thought that what he was feeling must be what it feels like to live on the outside while dying on the inside.

"How? Why?"

Suddenly, Raymond's last look over his shoulder as he left the visitor's room came to Jim's mind, and he shuttered at the thought. He'd been wrong. It hadn't been a look of trust. It had been a look of *fear*. Jim suddenly realized what Raymond had known. His visit had put Raymond's life in jeopardy. The pain kept coming harder and deeper until Jim felt as if he would explode.

"The warden is expecting your call, Jim. If no arrangements are made, Raymond will be buried in the prison cemetery."

Jim picked up Tom's phone and buzzed for Rose.

"Yes, Mr. Grant?"

"Rose, would you please get the warden at the Nebraska state penitentiary? I'll take it in my office."

Jim needed more details. With Raymond on the verge of telling him about the sheriff and county attorney's misdeeds, he needed to wrench out as much information as he could. Besides, he had to take Raymond home. There was no way he would leave him to be buried by the state that had taken away his freedom unnecessarily.

Tom interrupted Jim's thoughts.

"I hate to say I told you so, Jim, but we should have stayed out of this case. Your friend would still be alive if you'd taken my advice."

Tom's words hit Jim like an F-16 flying into a brick building.

"Damn it, Tom!" he exploded. "As far as I'm concerned, you and this firm can go to hell."

Jim didn't wait for a response. He rose and walked quickly to his office. He needed to get some distance between himself and Tom.

As Jim sat in his office looking out toward the mountains, Rose stepped in and said softly, "Mr. Grant, I have Warden Pulaski on the phone."

"Thanks. Put me through, would you?"

It was hard for Jim to hold back the tears as he picked up the phone.

"Mr. Pulaski, this is Jim Grant. Tell me more about how Raymond Two Bears died."

There was a pause and then the warden spoke. "He was killed with a knife-like object as he walked to his cell from the dining hall. It appears that whoever killed him wanted to send a message."

"What do you mean, a message?" Jim asked.

"I hate to tell you this, but Raymond was slit open from his bellybutton to his chin and draped over the third floor railing. Although I suspect many inmates saw him hanging there, they didn't respond. He was found several minutes later by a guard who noticed blood dripping onto the concrete below. Quite frankly, since becoming warden, I've never seen such a gruesome ight."

Jim's tears suddenly dried up as he felt an intense wave of anger come over him.

"Who killed him, warden?"

"We don't know yet, but an investigation is underway. We're currently in lock-down, and each cell in the block is being searched."

"You mean someone can be cut wide open in broad daylight among all those inmates and nobody knows who did it?"

"The code among inmates doesn't—"

"The hell with a code!" Jim screamed, "I want to know who killed Raymond!"

Before the warden could speak and before Jim embarrassed himself further, he regained his composure and changed the line of conversation.

"I'll make arrangements to take Raymond's body back to Pine Ridge for burial. Please let my office know when the body will be available. I'll personally come and take care of it. Thank you, warden."

Jim hung up the phone, knowing the time had come. Putting his elbows on his desk, he held his head in his hands, and he cried.

Several minutes later, Rose stepped in.

"I'm sorry to hear about your client, Mr. Grant."

"He was more than a client," Jim blurted out. Rose just stood there in silence, a hurt look on her face.

Jim quickly apologized, "Look, Rose, I'm sorry. I know you meant well. I'm just struggling, that's all."

"Can I get you anything?" she asked.

"No, just cancel me out for the rest of today."

Jim knew then that he had to go to back to Lincoln and take care of things, even though leaving so soon would only make matters worse with Christine.

"Perhaps someone else in the office could go," he thought, but then quickly dismissed it.

He needed to go to Lincoln. His wife would just have to understand, and he'd talk to Tom later.

When Jim got home, Christine was anything but understanding. She couldn't see why Jim needed to leave again so soon, and when Jim left the house early the next day, she didn't even say goodbye. She just rolled over in bed and turned away.

John was waiting at the airport when Jim landed the company plane in Lincoln. Jim's clearance had already been approved, so it was much easier getting into the prison this time. Warden Pulaski was waiting as Jim stepped into his office.

"Mr. Grant, thank you for coming. I'm sorry it isn't under better circumstances."

Pulaski told Jim that Raymond hadn't always been a model prisoner. He had sometimes gone a bit crazy, although he never really caused any serious trouble with other prisoners. Jim wasn't interested, however, especially when Pulaski started defending the prison. All Jim wanted to hear from the warden was who had killed his friend.

"Did Raymond leave anything that might indicate who his killer was?" Jim asked.

"We went through his cell and found nothing unusual. With the exception of several old newspaper stories and pictures of Senator Williams-Gibbons, it was the usual stuff," said Pulaski.

Jim took the notebook with the neatly folded newspaper clippings from the warden and leafed through them. Some of Raymond's motive was becoming clearer. Had he been in love with Sandy? Was he protecting her? It was possible, but Jim dismissed the notion.

"What about on his person?" Jim asked. "Was there anything on him to give you a clue?"

The warden reached into the side drawer of his desk, pulled out a crumpled piece of paper, and handed it to Jim.

"Only this in his pocket," he said.

The half sheet of paper looked as if it had been torn out of a notebook. Blood that had soaked through Raymond's pants stained the most of it, but in the middle of the paper, in smudged black lead was a single word, clearly legible.

"Shaman."

"We had it fingerprinted but found only Raymond's prints on the paper," the warden said. "At first, we thought someone might have stuck it in his pocket after slicing him open."

Realizing his casual description of the murder had hit a raw nerve, the warden apologized.

"Sorry about my choice of words," he said. "We believe that Raymond had the paper in his pocket when he was killed."

Jim was struck again by the fact that Raymond knew he was going to be killed.

"Who did Raymond have conflicts with?" Jim asked.

"We try and keep tabs on things like that, but, frankly, it's impossible to pinpoint each and every conflict among inmates. I'm afraid that avenue won't help us in solving Raymond's murder, but we'll eventually hear through the grapevine who was responsible, and justice will be done. Unfortunately, Raymond was a loner. His actions could be described as being like a man who was demon possessed. Most of the prisoners stayed away from him. Many times, inmates who gang together take justice in their own hands, but Raymond wasn't part of a gang."

"You mean the law of the jungle," said Jim.

"Yes, I guess that's what some call it," the warden said.

"Prisons haven't changed much," Jim added.

Before the warden could defend himself further, Jim said, "Well, if Raymond was such a loner and never bothered anyone, why was he killed in such a barbaric way?"

Suddenly, Jim realized that he'd just answered his own question. Raymond hadn't been killed because of his prison contacts. He'd been killed because he was a threat to someone—perhaps someone on the outside.

"Warden, I'd like to take a look at Raymond's visitor list and all the prison phone records over the past two weeks."

"I'm sorry, Mr. Grant, but I can't release them. Privacy issues, you know."

"I can have a subpoena here by this afternoon if you want to go that route. This murder is high profile, and it's already created a stir in the newspapers. I'm sure you don't want any more negative criticism."

The warden backed off, and, after they'd talked about the arrangements for Raymond, Jim spend the rest of the afternoon combing phone records. During his examination, Jim's eyes kept going back to the sheet of paper found in Raymond's pocket.

Raymond knew he was going to die. But what was it he was trying to say? Why that single word for a Native American spiritual leader? How could that note lead Jim to Raymond's murderer?

None of the prison phone records from the last two weeks yielded any leads. It seemed to be a dead end. What next? Whatever it was, it would have to wait.

It was time to take care of Raymond's body!

CHAPTER 10

To days later, a hearse made its way up the dusty red road to St. Stephen's Cemetery on the Pine Ridge Indian Reservation. Four mourners were standing beside a freshly dug grave: Father Simon Running Horse from St. Stephen's parish, Maria, Sandy, and Jim.

Maria had insisted on coming. In fact, when Jim told her of Raymond's death, she took it quite hard. She had come to know Raymond in a special way when they lived and worked together on the ranch.

As they waited, Jim noticed another person—and elderly man in Native American dress—standing next to the rusty wire fence at the south edge of the cemetery. He wore mourning attire, with leather leggings, a full chest plate of colorful beads, and a single eagle feather in his headband. He looked like he'd just stepped off a movie set.

Alongside the man was a paint horse with a single eagle feather tied to its mane. Jim remembered and understood the symbolism. According to Indian ritual, as the body is lowered into the ground, a warrior's pony is released to run free across the prairie, releasing the native soul and carrying his spirit home one last time. Jim motioned for the man to come closer, but he remained where he was, his arms folded, not moving.

Raymond's grave was next to his father's on the barren wind-blown hillside. Although he tried, Jim couldn't remember Raymond ever talking about his mother. Ever since they were young boys, it had just been Raymond and his father in the small house on the Williams ranch. Jim found himself wondering who she was. Where was she? Was she dead or alive? Had she walked out on them?

As the hearse crawled slowly toward the cemetery, Jim leaned over and asked Maria, "Do you know anything about Raymond's mother?"

Maria's reaction came as a surprise. Although she'd been quiet and solemn until that moment, she suddenly placed her hands over her face and began to sob. Sandy put her arm around her and comforted her. Not wanting to push, Jim turned and looked out across the prairie.

Despite everything, he was glad to see Raymond buried next to his father. In a strange way, he was actually happy for his old friend. At last Raymond was free from torment and the demons that had haunted him for so long. Regardless of what had happened in the past, Raymond had finally come home.

Father Simon sensed Jim's troubled spirit, so he walked over and began to offer a history of the area, trying to ease Jim's mind.

"There are three Native American cemeteries scattered about the Pine Ridge Reservation. This one dates back to 1885," he said. "It was started as a mission burial ground, but prior to that, most of the bodies of the dead were placed on a frame aboveground, in the traditional Indian manner."

As Father Simon continued, Jim's thoughts began to drift. He looked around at the unkempt condition of St. Stephen's. There were weeds growing along the fence lines and tall prairie grass covering many of the headstones. It was obvious that nobody took care of the place. Like so many things on the reservation, it had seen better times, and the loneliness and disrepair only seemed to heighten the sadness as they stood waiting for the hearse to arrive.

Most of the gravesites were marked with simple headstones—weather-etched, crumbling, and sagging in disarray. Some had toppled over, and many stones were nameless. Jim wondered how many people were actually buried there. There was no way to know. Had any of them been his relatives? Did any of them die in defense of their native land? How many of them died of a broken heart after having been imprisoned by the white man in this desolate land?

Jim's thoughts turned to his daughter. Would she ever know about her Native American heritage, the good and the bad? He made a pledge to himself at that moment to make sure she understood.

Of course, sadness is normal at the funeral of a friend or loved one, but the sadness that was welling up in Jim's heart threatened to overwhelm him, tugging at his soul in a way that told him his life would have to change.

The hearse arrived at the cemetery gate and slowly wound its way toward the gravesite. Red-brown dust enveloped the long black car as it came to a stop next to Raymond's open grave. Four men dressed in black suits from Albright Mortuary in North Platte stepped from the hearse, lifted out the coffin, and carried it to the gravesite.

The words spoken by Father Simon were over in a short time, and Raymond's body, in a simple wooden casket, was lowered into the ground.

At that moment, Jim looked up to see the warrior's pony set free, its shiny coat glistening like silver as it raced across the prairie, the sound of its hoof beats growing fainter as it galloped toward the horizon.

Jim tossed the first shovel of dirt into the grave. Just as the soil hit the coffin, he heard a drumming sound in the distance. A few moments later, the rumble grew louder. Then, as if it had been planned, Jim saw huge storm clouds rolling in from the southwest—but what he saw next came as a complete surprise. The towering thunderheads began to transform into human shapes. In the darkening sky, Jim saw the figures of Red Cloud, Black Elk, and others he couldn't identify. They appeared to be riding across the tempestuous sky, as if coming to take Raymond's spirit home.

Then, as mysteriously as they had appeared, the figures disappeared, and so did the storm. Jim turned to look for the old man by the fence, but he had vanished also. Jim regretted not having had a chance to talk to him. He asked Father Simon if he knew the man, but the pastor just shook his head.

Father Simon offered to take Maria home as he felt a need to comfort her, so Sandy and Jim drove back to the ranch by themselves. They hardly spoke until they drew close to the ranch. Jim's thoughts were light-years away. He knew he had to get back to Denver and try to get his life back into some semblance of order, but he was fighting a strong, continuous tugging. Part of him recognized it was over now that Raymond was dead, but another part of him insisted that it was only just beginning.

Sandy didn't help his torment when she asked Jim if he wanted to stay with her that night.

In spite of himself, Jim longed to be with her, but could he bring any closure to that part of his life if he let his feelings for Sandy take control? Was he just too weak to deny what was happening? Where was his sense of wisdom and courage when he needed it most? After all, virtues such as humility, sacrifice, and bravery were expected of every Lakota man. The Lakota believed that men were measured by the virtue they displayed during their life's journey. Had Jim's denial of his heritage been the cause of his ineptness? He was beginning to feel as if he'd been on the wrong path.

In the midst of all his turmoil, Jim impulsively told Sandy that he wanted to be with her.

As they pulled off the blacktop and onto the dirt road that led to the ranch, Jim suddenly felt a strange wind on his face, unlike anything he'd ever experienced in the Sand Hills. It seemed to be coming from all directions at once, and although he couldn't explain how he knew, it seemed to be beckoning him. The wind kept wrapping itself around him even as they walked toward the house.

Jim had heard stories about a demon wind that singled out a Lakota warrior and called him out. Was it a demon wind he was feeling? He tried to ignore it and deny its presence. Sandy didn't seem to feel it, so Jim assumed it had to be his imagination, but it kept encircling him.

Then he heard something unnerving.

"Jim, come here and sit by my chair," he heard a familiar voice say.

It was his mother's voice. It was unmistakable, and he would have known it anywhere. He was instantly carried back to the time when he was a young boy of ten.

"You're becoming a young man now," his mother said, "and it's time I told you about *wanagi tacaku*," she said.

"The spiritual path beckons to warriors and hunters who've lost their way, and when they feel a spiritual tugging, it's the keeper of the wind trying to bring them back to their intended path. One day, the keeper of the wind will come to you, my son, and to everyone who has lost their way, and if you choose to listen and follow the spirit wind, you'll be rewarded.

"It will lead you to an isolated, sacred part of the land where you can meditate, pray, and receive a spiritual message, but you must be careful. You must determine whether the demon wind is leading you down a false path or to a true spiritual awakening."

"Jim, are you okay?" asked Sandy. "You seemed to be in a trance."

"What?" Jim said, snapping back to reality. "I'm sorry, I guess I was lost in thought."

How could he tell Sandy that he seemed to be receiving spiritual messages from his ancestors? But there was no denying what was happening. Jim realized that a spiritual wind was calling him back— through his native soul. It was calling him back to the land of his ancestors, and he knew exactly what he had to do. He had to let the wind strip away the pretense of the life he'd piled up around him, like a fortification of sandbags in the white man's world. He had to let the wind disassemble him, force him to take a clearer look at himself, and then put him back together again. He had to pay honor to the spirit in the wind. It had a message for him, and he had to find out what that message was.

Denver would have to wait.

Before they had reached the steps to the house, Jim confessed to Sandy, "I have something I have to do."

"What's that?"

"I need to go for a ride out on the prairie."

"Oh," Sandy said, a little confused. "Do you want me to come with you?"

"Not this time," said Jim. "I have to do this alone. I have to let the wind lead me."

Again, Sandy looked confused, but she said nothing, so Jim continued. "Sandy, you'll never know much how I long to be with you, but that will have to wait for a little while. Right now, something is telling me I have to follow the wind."

"Are you sure you don't want me to go along?" she said. "We'd be alone out there on the prairie."

"No!" Jim said. "I can't explain it, but I have to do this by myself."

He couldn't expect her to understand, but it was clear in Jim's mind that the spirit wind was calling him for a specific reason, calling to show him the way, and he could only confront his true self in complete solitude.

He reached out and held Sandy in his arms for a few moments. They kissed, and then Jim turned and headed for the stable. It was difficult to turn away from her, but the call of the spirit wind was stronger than his physical desires.

Changing into jeans and moccasins, Jim walked to the stable. He called out the paint horse he had ridden earlier. After putting a halter on, Jim grabbed the horse's mane and swung up onto its back. He didn't bother to use a saddle. He would ride the paint the same way his ancestors used to ride in the days before the white man. Instantly, he could feel a bond between himself and the paint horse.

The sun was low in the afternoon sky and the wind now seemed to be blowing from just one direction—the Niobrara Valley. Jim turned the paint into the wind and they galloped at full stride toward the river bluffs. He could feel the warmth of the magnificent animal in his loins and the snorting sound from the horse's nostrils echoed like a steady drum beat as they raced across the prairie, the wind blowing in their faces. Jim hadn't felt a sense of freedom so pure since he'd left that land so long ago. He could feel the big city shackles beginning to fall away. It brought back memories of riding across the prairie with Raymond when they were young—like brothers.

Jim remembered Raymond's exquisite horsemanship. When Earl couldn't break a horse, he'd turn it over to Raymond, and that's when Raymond would truly come alive. There was nothing he liked better than helping train a horse. Through his unconventional methods, usually by lavishing kindness on the horse, Raymond would have it ready in a couple of days. Raymond always rode bareback, controlling the horse using only a neck halter and his legs.

As Jim neared the Niobrara, he could feel the wind blowing even stronger than before. Reaching the bank, he guided the paint into the shallow water and crossed over toward a sandbar beneath a small grove of cottonwoods on the other side. To the Lakota, cottonwoods, or *talking trees*, were sacred, and Jim saw the grove as a sign that he would be on sacred ground. He was even more convinced when, as soon as they emerged from the water on the far side of the river, the wind died. It had to be the spot that *hanhepi wi* had been directing him to.

Jim knew that this was the place set aside for him to pray and receive the gifts being offered to him by the spiritual wind. He would also need to petition the Great Spirit to protect him from any demons that might try to invade his space.

The sun was close to the horizon, so Jim gathered some dead cottonwood branches and started a fire on the sandbar. He hadn't brought any food with him, because fasting was going to be an important part of the ritual. A warrior had to remove all indulgences during prayer and meditation.

Jim sat on the sand by the fire while the paint grazed quietly in the distance. Placing both hands on his knees, he focused on the ground in front of him, closed his eyes, and began to pray, lifting his hands toward the heavens so the Great Spirit would receive him.

His prayers were for change, harmony, and understanding. From time to time, the silence was interrupted by the distinctive sounds of the land around him. He heard the gentle slaps of the river as the current broke and splashed down onto the water. In the distance came the cry of a red-tailed hawk, echoing along the bluffs as the raptor hunted for its evening meal. The wind picked up again, and Jim heard the tops of the cottonwoods begin to whisper as the branches swayed rhythmically.

He didn't know how long his eyes had been closed in prayer, but when he opened them, the sun had gone down, its lingering rays still casting a dim light in the clear Nebraska sky.

Then he noticed something he hadn't seen. A short distance from the sandbar, in the midst of a willow thicket on the riverbank, was a round, skin-covered hut. It blended perfectly with its surroundings and was hardly noticeable. A stream of white, wispy smoke was coming out of a hole at the top. Jim wondered how he could have missed it, and although he tried to continue his meditation, his thoughts were interrupted by curiosity.

Finally, he could stand it no longer. He stood and walked toward the hut. About twenty feet from it, he stopped when the deerskin drape that covered the front opening suddenly parted. To Jim's surprise, out stepped the most beautiful Indian woman he'd ever seen. She was dressed in a tan, soft leather buckskin dress and wore a shimmering silver band around her neck. As she walked toward Jim, her long black hair bounced on her shoulders.

"Hello, Jim. I've been waiting for you. Come sit with me, and eat the food I've prepared," she said seductively as she pulled back the deerskin drape and beckoned to him.

Jim hesitated, partly because he couldn't believe what he was seeing. Why was such a lovely woman living on the prairie by herself? Was her seduction part of a larger plan? Would he be attacked by an unseen partner if he ventured inside the hut? He stood motionless, his mind reeling.

"I'm alone," she said, as if she was reading Jim's mind. "Please, my home awaits you."

Although he was apprehensive, Jim stepped inside the cool, inviting hut, where she asked him to sit on the soft furs strewn on the floor. From a table in the center of the hut, she took a small bowl of fruit and a cup of syrup and handed them to him.

"It's made from buttercups that grow on the prairie," she said sweetly. "I made it especially for you."

Jim raised the cup to his lips and tasted. He'd never heard of such nectar before, but it had a sweet, sensuous taste.

Then the woman walked over and knelt by Jim's side. She put her arms around his neck, and he felt the seductive warmth of her body against his. As he gazed into her dark, piercing eyes, he suddenly remembered something he'd heard while sitting at his grandmother's knee as she talked about their ancestors. That day, she'd been telling him stories about the Deer Woman.

"Long ago," she said, "hunters would go out by themselves in search of food for their families. Sometimes they'd be gone for several days. One year, at the time when the cottonwood leaves were turning gold, my father, your great-grandfather, collected his equipment for an antelope hunt and started out on a three-day journey. Most men who ventured out alone never encountered the Deer Woman, but on that hunt, your great-grandfather did."

Jim remembered listening closely to his grandmother as she continued. "Cursed by a spell centuries ago, the Deer Woman lives most of the time as a deer, feeding on the prairie and drinking from the rivers, but whenever she sees a lone hunter, the demon inside her transforms her into the most beautiful woman any man has ever laid eyes on.

"She seeks the comfort of a man lying beside her so she can steal his spirit—a quest she must pursue in order to keep her own spirit alive.

"Some men have slept with her, but when they woke up, she was gone. Once a man has lain with the Deer Woman, he'll never be the same again. He forgets his family and spends the rest of his life looking for her, no matter how far away he must go or how long it takes. He becomes relentless, desperately trying to find her and regain his spirit."

His grandmother finished her story with an admonition.

"Though it's difficult to resist her, my son, the hunter must turn away, and, luckily for us, when my father found himself face to face with the Deer Woman, he knew what to do, because his grandmother had warned him. Now I am warning *you*."

In spite of his grandmother's prophecy and warning, Jim dismissed his concerns and gently laid down the beautiful woman onto the pile of furs.

Then he knelt beside her.

As he was looking at her beautiful face, he suddenly shrank back, shouting, "*Ahawi winyan!*"

He could see a look of pure evil shining in her dark eyes.

"You're the Deer Woman! No! You can't have my spirit!"

Jim clawed and fought against her grip as he struggled to get to his feet. Finally, he broke free and bolted from the hut. She started to follow him but stopped at the doorway. Jim looked back for an instant—just long enough to see her eyes begin to turn a bright white that shone through the darkness. Then they began to sink back into her head and her feet started to change into hooves.

Jim didn't stop running until he reached his campfire. He turned back toward the willow thicket one more time. The hut was gone. The entire scene was just as it had been when he'd first arrived. Sitting on a cottonwood log, he stared into the empty thicket for a long time. Finally, he sank down onto the sand and fell asleep by the warmth of the fire.

When he awoke, the warm rays of the sun were beating down on him. He looked around, confused, but then remembered why he had come to this spot. He worried that he had failed in his quest to learn the spiritual lesson he'd been brought there to receive.

He looked down the sandbar toward the willow thicket. Nothing was there, but how could that be? Had he simply dreamed about the Deer Woman? He couldn't be sure. It had all seemed so real.

He walked over to where the paint was waiting patiently beside a tall cottonwood. He picked up the halter rope, and together they walked down the sandbar toward the willow thicket. Jim was stunned by what he found!

In the middle of the thicket were the burned out remains of a campfire, and leading away from the thicket were the small imprints of a woman's moccasins in the sand. Was that the message he was supposed to receive, or had she been a demon, sent to interrupt his prayers?

As he turned to leave, Jim heard a soft rustling sound coming from a rain-eroded gully that led down to the river's edge. Looking up, he saw a doe making her way to the edge of the river, where she began to drink. Suddenly, she raised her head and saw him, and for several long seconds, their eyes locked. They were eyes that Jim had seen before. A few moments later, the doe turned and slowly walked back up the draw until she disappeared.

At that moment, Jim understood the wisdom that had been revealed to him. When he was growing up on his parents' ranch in the Sand Hills, he doubted many of the stories he'd heard about his ancestors, sloughing them off as myths and exaggerations. They were interesting and sometimes exciting, but he'd never really thought of them as being true.

But, as of last night, all that had changed. He had encountered a living myth, and he'd seen for himself the reality of one of the stories from his distant past. Whether she'd appeared to him in his dreams or in the flesh, the Deer Woman had brought him a powerful message. He now understood that myths were really roundabout ways of telling the truth, and, myth or not, he suddenly understood the wisdom of his ancestors. A hunter who recognizes the Deer Woman for who she is and acts appropriately in life can save himself from a lifetime of pain and sorrow.

Jim knew without a doubt that he had encountered the Deer Woman. Now it was up to him to heed the message he'd been given. He wondered if he could.

He grabbed the reins, jumped onto the paint's back, and raced through the Niobrara and across the prairie toward the ranch house. The wind in his face now felt free and light—the pull was gone.

CHAPTER 11

Arriving back at the ranch, Jim brushed down the paint and led him out to the corral. As he turned and walked back toward to the stable, he sensed the paint trotting after him. A moment of affection was what the horse was after. Reaching Jim, the horse gently butted him in the lower back—a touch that signified a bond had been created between them.

At that moment, Jim understood how a Lakota brave could put absolute trust in his horse. He'd heard about it all his life, but now he'd experienced it firsthand. He rubbed the paint's forehead and face as if to say, "Nice job, old friend." Then he closed the stable door behind him. A hot shower would feel good, so he headed toward the ranch house. Besides, he was anxious to see Sandy.

As he walked through the door, expecting to see her, he was greeted by Maria with only a note from Sandy.

> Jim,
> I've been called to an emergency meeting with the governor. Mick is flying me to Lincoln, and I'll be back tomorrow evening. I hope you're still here."
> I love you.
>
> Sandy

Following a long shower, Jim sat down to think things through. He realized that his attitude had changed since Raymond's murder. In fact, the whole arena of law was changing for him. It was going from shiny to dull, from brilliant to lackluster. It had been exciting, and he used to find worth in what he was doing, but he was beginning to feel out of place in that world and didn't feel as connected to the rule of law as he had before Raymond's murder.

Many people around him had been trying to discourage his involvement in Raymond's case. Tom told him to let it go, and Christine, through her body language, expressed the same. Maybe he should have gone with their advic—after all, it was his first leaning.

Why had he allowed Sandy to draw him into the case? The choices he'd made were out of a desire to help a friend, and, at the time, they'd seemed right. Then, after deciding to take the case, he'd felt a positive change come over him, like a light that had been switched on. His path had become clearer, and his outlook was more focused, but with Raymond's shocking murder, things had grown a bit murky.

Jim went into the great room and stood before the Cormish painting. He felt different about it now. He could still feel remorseful for his Indian brothers and sisters, but, at that moment, he lived in a different world, and he needed to think like a white man. There was too much at stake. His career was on the line, not to mention his relationship with Christine. The law firm wasn't going to stand for any more time or money being spent on the appeal process, nor would Tom allow him to stay in Cottonwood Springs to investigate Raymond's murder.

As Jim stood staring at the picture, he convinced himself that it wasn't as though he was abandoning his friend. He could turn the case over to state authorities, and they could solve the murder.

Jim pondered the situation, then slowly and reluctantly came to a decision. What did it matter whether Raymond was guilty or innocent of Silas' murder? Who would care if he abandoned his attempts to obtain an appeal now that Raymond was dead? No matter what happened, though, Jim knew he'd have to live with the possibility—no, the fact—that his initial involvement had fueled Raymond's murder.

He stepped away from the painting. Looking out the picture window toward the Niobrara, he began to realize that his rekindled love for Sandy wasn't good for him. Besides, he was beginning to feel pressured. It would be tough to put her out of his mind, but he needed to get on with his life and be there for his family again.

Standing by the window, he thought about one more thing he needed to do before he left the Sand Hills for good. A call to the Lancaster County attorney in Lincoln could help him finalize his decision. It could either provide evidence he could turn over to the state, or it would strengthen his resolve about dropping Raymond's murder case. Jim thought all along that Raymond's murder was connected to someone in the Sand Hills . . . like Sheriff Gillette. Maybe it was a stretch to think that way, but he was convinced after being around Cottonwood Springs for the past two weeks.

He picked up the phone, dialed the number, and waited.

"Good morning. This is Max Lewis."

"Mr. Lewis, this is Jim Grant, Attorney at Law, calling from Cottonwood Springs, Nebraska."

"Good morning, Mr. Grant. What can I do for you?"

"I'm looking for some information on the prison murder of Raymond Two Bears. I was his attorney, petitioning for an appeal when he was murdered. I assume you've heard about it?"

"Of course," he said in a suspicious tone.

"I'd like to subpoena the home phone records of Darrell Goodall. He works as a guard at the Nebraska state penitentiary."

"And the reason, Mr. Grant?"

"I want to see if the records show any connection to Raymond's murder."

"Do you suspect Mr. Goodall?" the attorney asked, sounding even more suspicious.

"No, not necessarily. I think it was an inmate who did the actual murder. Some convict who was recruited to keep an eye on Raymond."

"Then, why Mr. Goodall?"

"He was the guard in the visitors room on the day I met with Raymond, when Raymond told me that he had more information about his father's murder and other illegal activities in his hometown of Cottonwood Springs. We arranged to meet later in the week, and Mr. Goodall was the only witness to that conversation, so I believe that he's the only person who could have leaked that information. I think Raymond's murder was ordered from the outside, and I want to see if any of Mr. Goodall's phone calls support that conclusion."

"Well," Lewis replied, "it'll take some doing, but if I can convince Judge Newsome to draw up a subpoena, I'll fax the records to you as soon as I can, probably later this afternoon."

Jim thanked Lewis for his cooperation, gave him the R Bar W's fax number, and hung up the phone. Would he really be getting information that afternoon? He had his doubts, knowing how fast judges work. Besides, Max Lewis didn't know him from Adam. How could the Lancaster county attorney know that this wasn't a hoax? Jim felt the only thing in his favor was a feeling of pressure by the Lincoln attorney over solving the murder; plus, it wasn't Friday.

Settling into one of the club chairs, he began thinking the process through again. It was probably a dead end, and if it didn't provide any evidence, he could leave for Denver that night and never see Sandy again.

That thought caused him to waver, but he remembered his encounter with the Deer Woman. It was a powerful and life-changing experience, and suddenly he knew he was doing the right thing.

He looked up at the painting again. He couldn't decide whether he had a guilty conscience or simply disliked the painting. Regardless, he turned his chair away from the fireplace.

Sinking back, he began to relax, thinking how simple things would be once again after he'd left the Sand Hills behind. He thought about Christine and how he was going to get things back on track with her. He missed Molly and couldn't wait to hear about her latest adventures.

"I'll give the phone records a quick glance and then be on my way," he thought.

Then he closed his eyes.

"Mr. Grant, there's a fax coming in for you," he heard Maria's voice say.

He must have drifted off. The grandfather clock in the corner told him it was 4:00 p.m.

Jolted and groggy, he jumped to his feet, gathered his wits, and stepped into Sandy's office. The fax machine had finished printing, and he could see two sheets of paper filled with phone numbers, ready for his examination.

He was surprised the records had gotten there so soon. He had been expecting to spend the night, waiting for them to come the next day, if they came at all. It was unusual for the court system to get anything done late in the afternoon. Apparently, the Lancaster County attorney had some influence—or Raymond's case was sending shock waves, and the local law community was putting pressure on. Whichever was the case, Jim was grateful for the quick response.

Scanning the list, he didn't notice any numbers that stood out, although he wasn't sure what he was looking for. Then, at the top of the second page, two calls caught his attention. The first call was to area code 308 on July 13 at 6:02 p.m. Jim knew that 308 was the area code for Cottonwood Springs. At 7:06 p.m., another call was made to Goodall's residence in Lincoln *from* that same area code.

The first number struck Jim as familiar, so he opened the phone book, turned to the blue pages, and there, under the county listings, was the number: It was the sheriff's office!

The call lasted only about twenty seconds, so someone in the sheriff's office had either cut Goodall off or had taken an abbreviated message—perhaps a phone number. The call to Goodall's residence about an hour later was from a different number, but even after a thorough search of the phone book, Jim failed to find the number.

Then he remembered the pay phone located outside Malarkey's on the corner of Main Street. He didn't recall any other phones around. He wondered if that phone might have been the source of the call—but if it was, then what? If someone had used that phone, they probably did it so they couldn't be identified, and he'd still be a long way from having a real lead in the case.

"Good," he thought, "a dead end. I gave it the old college try, and now I'm going home."

He sat down and wrote Sandy a note.

Dear Sandy,
   Raymond Two Bears is dead, so overturning his guilty verdict is no longer necessary, and neither are my services to you. I've decided to return to Denver immediately. I regret that I couldn't stay long enough to say good-bye. Thank you for your hospitality.
                                                                    Jim

He carefully composed the note to sound as professional as possible, doing his best to leave his conflicted feelings for Sandy out of it. He figured that a clean break was best.

He put the note in an envelope and laid it on Sandy's desk.

Borrowing Earl's Bronco one last time, he drove into town to get his plane ready, but as he drove by the phone booth outside Malarkey's, his curiosity got the better of him. Could that be the phone where the call to Goodall's home had come from? He couldn't resist the temptation to find out.

Getting out of the Bronco, he opened the booth door and looked inside. The phone number was printed above the receiver—but it didn't match the number on the phone records.

Jim was actually relived, but now what? He decided that a few minutes over a cup of coffee would help, so he walked into the bar and sat down.

As Marge brought him a black coffee, he was still wrought with curiosity.

"Marge, are there any other pay phones in town besides the one outside?"

"There's one in the lobby of the courthouse and another one at Vauder's Mobil station," she said.

Jim finished his coffee in silence. He knew he should let it go and head home, but somehow he couldn't. Those other two phones weren't that far away, and it wouldn't take long just to have a look.

He checked the one at Vauder's first. No match.

It was 5:10 when he got to the courthouse. Stepping to the front door, he tried the latch, but it was locked. Just his luck. Closing time was 5:00 and there was no one around. He banged on the door and finally drew the attention of a custodian.

"Can you please let me in?" Jim yelled through the locked door.

"Who are you?" the man asked.

"I'm Jim Grant. I'm an attorney, and I need to use the pay phone in the lobby."

Jim could tell that the custodian wasn't happy about his request.

"I'm not supposed to do that," he said, but after more pleading from Jim, the custodian reluctantly opened the door.

"Thank you. I promise this won't take long," Jim said. Then he immediately headed toward the phone.

This time, the number matched! It was the phone that had been used to call Darrell Goodall's house at 7:06 p.m. on July 13th! Jim breathed a sigh of relief—but that information didn't necessarily connect the sheriff to the call. The phone was in the vicinity of the sheriff's office, but anybody could have used it. Lots of people go in and out of the courthouse every day.

As the custodian let Jim out, he glanced at the 5:00 closing time printed on the window—and something clicked inside his mind. Closing time was at 5:00, but the call had been made at 7:06! That meant the call could have been made only by someone who had a key to the courthouse!

Jim knew how hard it had been to get the custodian to open the door for him, so he knew that he wouldn't open it for just anybody. Had Goodall called the sheriff with information about his visit with Raymond, and had the sheriff called him back to order Raymond's murder?

Could the sheriff really have that much power? It was hard to believe, but the location of the calls and the order in which they'd been made couldn't have been sheer coincidence. He knew he needed to talk to Gillette, but as he walked out ahead of the custodian's scowl, he figured the sheriff would be gone for the day. If he was, that would give Jim another reason to sack it all and go home. However, as he walked around to the side of the courthouse, he saw the sheriff's car parked nearby.

Jim tried the latch to the office door. It was locked. Then he knocked.

After a few seconds, the sheriff opened the door.

Standing with his arms folded, he said, "Mr. Grant, I see you've extended your stay here in Cottonwood Springs."

Although the words themselves were innocuous, there was a tone of challenge in the way Gillette said them.

"What brings you to my office so late in the afternoon?" he added.

"As you know," Jim said, "Raymond Two Bears was murdered in prison three days ago. I'm wrapping up some details about his murder before I go back to Denver, so I wonder if you'd mind answering some questions."

"Shoot," said the sheriff, turning his back and walking toward his desk. "I only know what I read in the papers, but if I can be of some help, I'll certainly try."

"Tell me, Sheriff, can anybody gain access to the courthouse through your office?"

"Well, only if you're a resident of the rooms behind those doors," he said, pointing in the direction of the jail proper. "From those rooms, you could be personally escorted into the courthouse through my office."

He was being flippant, but Jim let it pass.

"Seriously, can anybody get into the courthouse from here after closing hours?" Jim asked again.

"Mr. Grant, no one is allowed to use my office to gain access to the courthouse at any time. No one!" Gillette said emphatically.

The sheriff didn't know he'd just narrowed the list of possible callers down to someone who had a key to the front door, someone on his staff, or himself.

Jim pressed on. "Sheriff, do you know Darrell Goodall, a guard at the Nebraska state penitentiary?"

He hadn't expected to get a straight answer, but Jim was surprised by what happened next. The sheriff's expression turned sour, and the tan in his face was quickly replaced by an ashen gray color. He started to declare his separation from the name, but realizing Jim must have some pertinent information, Gillette decided to play it cool. Once he'd collected himself, his response was calm and controlled.

"I come in contact with law enforcement people all the time, so I probably have met Mr. Goodall at some time, but don't remember it."

"Do you remember taking a phone call from him, here at your office, on July 13?"

Gillette exploded. Playing it cool was no longer an option. He'd been cornered.

Slamming his fist down hard on the desk, he thundered, "Since this is an unofficial visit, and you came in here unannounced, your stay is over, Mr. Grant! Now get out!"

Gillette motioned violently toward the door.

"You either leave through that door, or I'll put you behind these!" Gillette yelled, pointing to the steel doors that led to the jail.

"Sheriff, you can threaten me all you like, but you'll eventually have to answer that question, and not to the county attorney, but to a state attorney or the United States attorney," Jim said firmly.

"Like hell, I will!" Gillette growled, placing his hand on the top of his revolver.

Jim knew it was a power play but a caged animal can become violent when challenge, so he decided it was time to move toward the door. As he did, Gillette immediately removed his hand from atop his gun.

"Get out of here now," Gillette warned as Jim opened the door and walked out.

Jim knew he was getting close to something, but now he was *really* in turmoil!

CHAPTER 12

Leaving Cottonwood Springs first meant a preflight check of the plane. It was ready to go—but was he?

The longer he lingered over the gauges and controls, the more he was tempted to bag the flight in favor of staying and finishing what he'd started. Maybe he should go back to the ranch, destroy the note he'd left for Sandy, and continue with the investigation of Raymond's murder.

No! His mind was made up. He had finished his work in Cottonwood Springs. He taxied the plane to the end of the runway, took one last look around, and then lifted off for Denver.

Although it seemed like an eternity, it wasn't long before he finally entered Colorado air space, leaving Sandy and the plains of Nebraska behind. The sunset was spectacular as he cruised along at 6,000 feet. Locked between the horizon and a layer of cumulus clouds, the sun reflected an assortment of colors, its rays painting electrifying patterns on the gray clouds drifting above it. It was a calming scene.

If only Jim's mind was that calm. An empty feeling gnawed at the pit of his stomach. He knew he was doing the right thing, but the pain associated with leaving was always there in his rearview mirror, making it difficult.

When he arrives home, he'll have to decide what to do with the information he'd dug up. He'll probably file an accusatory instrument and turn it over to Abigail Finnigan's office.

As he approached Stapleton, the last bit of sun was descending behind the mountains. He dropped lower and lower as he made his approach to the airport, his eyes glued on the runway lights. The sky was now fully engulfed in darkness as he set down the plane and taxied toward the terminal.

Back home in the city, Jim's mind continued doing flip-flops. He felt light-years away from the freedom he'd experienced earlier that day while riding across the grasslands on the paint. Simply put, he had forgotten the type of peace and serenity that can still be experienced on the prairie.

Sliding into the seat of his Cherokee, Jim recalled something he'd once heard: "Country can keep the heart from getting wrinkled."

He thought to himself, "How true." It would be a struggle to hold onto that feeling, and, as he drove out of the airport and into the city traffic, he could feel it waning already.

His home in Littleton wasn't really that secluded. Normally, he could see their house lights as he got close. Tonight, he only saw a dark house as he drove down his street. It was only 9:00 p.m. Why weren't there any lights on?

Driving into the garage, Jim saw that Christine's car was gone. It was strange that she and Molly would be out so late on a school night. Summer school isn't the same as regular school, but it was still late. Maybe Molly had gone to bed early, and Christine had gone to the store for a few minutes.

Jim walked into the kitchen, turned on the light, and saw a carefully folded note on the counter. Picking it up, he read: "If you get home tonight, you'll find that Molly and I have gone to Mother's in Colorado Springs."

That was all it said.

Jim sat down, picked up the phone, and dialed Christine's mother's number. After a couple of rings, Christine answered.

"Hello?"

It almost sounded as if she'd known it would be him, and she wasn't happy about it.

"Hi, honey," Jim offered in what he hoped was a soothing tone. "I just got home and found your note. Why are you and Molly gone on a school night?"

Christine let out an exasperated sigh and said, "Jim, I didn't know when you were coming home. We just needed some company. The house is lonely without you."

"I'm sorry I've been gone so long. I miss you. Are you coming home tonight?" he asked.

"No, I'll drop Molly off at school in the morning. Then I'll come by the house by 8:30. Jim, we need to sit down and have a serious talk."

Before Jim could say anything, Christine had hung up. No *I love you*, no *good-bye*, nothing.

After a fitful night, Jim awoke to a dismal morning. The sky was gray, and it had been raining. Seven o'clock was early, considering he wasn't planning to go to the office that day, but he was too nervous about the talk Christine had said they needed to have to stay in bed any longer, so he got up, showered, and headed downstairs.

Nothing in the pantry appealed to his knotted stomach.

What was Christine going to say when she got there? Judging from her tone, he guessed that she would say one of two things. Either she'd give him an ultimatum to shape up or she'd simply announce that she was leaving. He hoped it would be the former, but he also knew how his last visit to the Sand Hills must have looked to her. He'd come home from a trip she hadn't been thrilled about, gotten one phone call, and then promptly left again. He hadn't even called home since he'd been gone.

Christine had never been the jealous type, but Jim knew he'd crossed the line, and he felt terrible. The more he thought about his behavior of the past several weeks, the more he realized that he deserved whatever he was going to get.

Then, unexplainably, his mind drifted back to the kiss that he and Sandy had shared and the feelings that he'd allowed to come back. It made him even more afraid, but he realized that sitting there, at home in his own kitchen, was the only place he wanted to be. The Sand Hills had brought back memories, but that's all they were—memories. Denver was his home now. It was where he belonged—at home with Christine and Molly, not running around trying to solve some old mystery that didn't concern him.

The question that was twisting inside him now was, "Will Christine take me back?"

It was raining again and the sky was even more overcast when Jim heard the garage door open and Christine's car drive in. A few seconds later, she came into the kitchen and put her keys on the counter. She didn't look happy. The perfect walk and stance that she'd learned from being a TV personality weren't there. In fact, she looked a bit rumpled. She'd always been upbeat and prepared for any occasion, but that morning she appeared to be ready for a fight.

He got up, walked over to Christine, and attempted to kiss her, but she turned away.

"Jim," she said matter-of-factly, "why are you so willing to give up this home, your family, and all you've worked for over all these years?"

"Christine, I'm not giving it up. My involvement with Raymond Two Bears the past couple of weeks was part of my work," Jim said. "I'm sorry we missed our vacation, and I regret being away from you and Molly, but it was something I had to do. If it was a mistake, I want you to know that I'm sorry, but won't you give me a chance to make it up to you?"

Christine began to cry. Jim tried to console her but she wouldn't have it.

"You expect me to believe that everything's going to be great from now on? You were gone for over a week, and now you're back, and I'm supposed to act like nothing's happened?" Christine said sharply. "What about your ex-girlfriend? I know she was part of the reason you went to Cottonwood Springs. If she needs your help again, are you going to leave us like you did the last time?"

Jim tried to assure Christine that it wouldn't happen and that what he wanted most in the world was for their marriage to be solid again. He knew the dangers of being unfaithful—the Deer Woman had driven that point home forcefully. He'd get over Sandy, and, as for Raymond's murder case, he planned to turn the whole thing over to Abigail Finnigan in the Nebraska attorney general's office.

After a few moments, Christine regained her composure and started wiping away her tears. "Jim, I can't bridle you like a horse, but I *will* tell you that if you give in again to the tug from the Sand Hills, I'll leave you—and I'll take Molly with me."

Her threat certainly had more punch with that last statement.

From the look in Christine's eyes, Jim knew she meant every word she had said.

Then she made a tentative move toward him and let him put his arms around her, and when she finally began to return his embrace, Jim knew that she was going to give him a second chance.

Jim realized Christine had not been completely won over, as she still felt distant to him, but he knew it would take time to heal the split in their relationship. Jim resolved to work at it as best he could from that moment on.

CHAPTER 13

A week had passed since Jim had galloped across the plains in total freedom. His work at the law firm was back on track, and he and Christine were getting along much better. Jim continued to organize the information from Houston County about Raymond's murder, planning to turn it over to the attorney general's office eventually.

He often found himself sitting and staring out the window toward the mountains, thinking about his blood brother, and from time to time he debated his decision to stop working on Raymond's absolution. Every time he put it aside, he was haunted by the reality that someone was getting away with murdering Silas Two Bears—and Raymond.

The chances were less than 50-50 that an appeal would have freed Raymond from prison anyway, Jim kept telling himself, but the hardest reality—one that punched Jim in the gut with guilt—was not being involved in solving Raymond's murder, especially when he remembered how his friend had died. No matter what he did, Jim knew those feeling would be around for quite a while.

For his family's sake, he'd been struggling hard to put Sandy behind him. He truly wanted his marriage to last. It was important to him, as was his life in Denver, but it had been difficult to put his old hometown on the back burner, let alone trying to take it completely off the stove. He kept feeling a tug to return to that lifestyle, but he knew that what he used to have in Cottonwood Springs, including his short stay there, had to be subtracted from his total being if he was going to survive.

Swinging his chair around toward his desk, Jim looked up just in time to see Tom Duncomb and Dick Morris walk into his office. If something important was coming down, he could always count on being called by Tom, but a simultaneous visit from two of the partners told Jim that something radical was up.

As Tom walked over and sat down, Dick closed the door.

"Have you filed a complaint to the Nebraska attorney general's office yet?" Tom asked.

"No, but it's about ready to go in," Jim said.

"Don't file it."

"What do you mean?"

"We're of the mind that it shouldn't be filed," said Dick.

"That's nonsense," said Jim. "I'm going to file it as soon as I get it ready."

"Jim, if you follow through on it, you'll no longer be working for this firm," Dick said firmly. "We'll terminate your contract for insubordination."

"What do you mean? What's this all about? Is it about the time I've been spending on this case? Tom, are you still upset because of the tiff we had when Raymond was murdered? If so, that's a bunch of crap. I've already severed myself from Raymond's appeal case, and once I submit the accusatory information to the attorney general, I'm dropping out of the cases altogether."

Tom interrupted. "Look, Jim, we received a call from the Houston County attorney. He wants you to pull back on your filing with the attorney general's office."

"You mean Ed Hardin," Jim said in a disgusted voice.

"Yes."

"And you are going along with that?"

"Well, normally we wouldn't, but this time we are. Mr. Hardin brought up something to help us in our decision."

"I don't understand."

"Okay, Jim, I'm going to lay it on the line for you. The county attorney said that you went in to look at some court records a couple of weeks ago. Is that right?"

"Yes. I wanted to find out who had testified on Raymond's behalf, as well as get a handle on the evidence that was presented."

"Did anything happen?"

"Nothing to get him so upset," Jim said.

"Well, Mr. Hardin said that after you left, he found some of the records missing. He isn't too concerned yet, but he made a point that if you file your information with the attorney general, he'll change his mind. If you file the papers, he'll start proceedings against you—and this office."

"Tom, that's blackmail," Jim said. "You know I wouldn't steal any of those records. Besides, I can't withhold evidence that's a crime in itself."

Dick interceded. "I don't care if it's dark-black blackmail. I'm not going to have some tinhorn lawyer from some cow town taking money from me, let alone threatening to close down our office. I don't think you understand the gravity of what he's saying or what you could be charged with, so I'm telling you now—you won't file as long as you're employed by this firm! My god, Jim, let the prison officials take care of it."

Jim stood and turned toward the window, trying to hide his anger as best he could. The audacity of Ed Hardin! How evil must that man be to abuse the law like that?

Jim's thoughts were interrupted when he heard the office door shut behind him. Tom and Dick had left him hanging. He was all alone, not just physically, but also to face the terrible injustice. If he bailed out and left it up to the local officials, it would never happen.

All he could think about was the dual standard of justice that Raymond had suffered while alive, and now the same abuse was happening after his death. For the people of the Sand Hills, the healing was far from over.

Jim opened his desk drawer and took out the torn piece of paper that had been found in Raymond's pocket, staring at the single word in smudged pencil script.

Shaman.

What could it mean?

Then he noticed the dark blood stains along the edge of the paper, and he lost it.

Rose must have heard his screams of anguish, because she came running into the office, asking, "Mr. Grant, are you okay?"

Without a word, Jim bolted past her, ran down the stairs to the garage, and climbed into his Jeep.

He must have driven around for hours, because before he knew it, his watch said 4:30. It was time to go home.

As he pulled into the garage, Christine came running out of the house. "Jim, where have you been? We've been trying to reach you all day. No one knew what had happened to you or where you were. Are you all right?"

"Yes and no," Jim said weakly. "I'm not physically hurt or in trouble, but I'm not okay."

They sat on a swing on their back deck, facing the foothills, and Jim told Christine what had happened at the office.

"Ed Hardin has threatened to have me arrested if I don't go along with the selective enforcement of the law in Cottonwood Springs. If convicted, Christine, I could face possible jail time, and my decision will affect my job, not in quality, but whether or not I have one."

But most importantly, and with a great deal more zest, he told her that he was afraid of losing his sanity if he let Ed Hardin take control of him.

Then he took a deep breath and said the words she'd feared.

"Christine, I've made a decision."

He could tell from her eyes that she knew what he was about to say.

"The only way I'll ever have peace in my soul is if I impale myself onto the spikes of this injustice."

She knew he would be leaving again, but she said nothing. They just sat on the swing and stared at the mountains in silence.

In the morning, as they sat at the breakfast table eating without a word, Jim finally broke the silence.

"Please understand, Christine. I have to do this. When it's over, we can go on with our life here in Denver, but right now, I need resolution for Raymond more than anything else in life." He was surprised that he'd used those words. Deep down, it might have been a symbol of where their marriage really was, but he added, "If I win this case, I promise that I'll walk away."

"Jim, you're fooling yourself. It will never be resolved. There will always be something else. Like an eagle, once you get your talons into the prey, you'll feel the need to feed everyone, and it'll go on and on."

"No," Jim said emphatically.

Christine interrupted. "I understand your need, Jim, I really do, but I have to think of our sanity, too—Molly's and mine. I told you that if you left again you wouldn't have a home to come back to, and I meant it. Now you're going to have to make the decision."

They said nothing more until Christine left for work, but Jim's soul was in torment. Why wouldn't it work? Once the case was resolved, he could come back, and they could once again be a family. He was sure that Molly would understand about the short time they'd be apart. Why wouldn't Christine?

It was clear that if Jim went, he'd no longer have a home and family when he returned.

———

The office was quiet when Jim walked in. He stood next to the fax machine but hesitated before dialing the number, knowing that sending that one fax was going to change his life dramatically. He might as well send it, though, since he'd already turned in his resignation. After a few moments, a beeping sound let him know that the information had been sent to Abigail's office in Lincoln.

Before he cleaned out his desk, Jim needed to call Sandy to see if she still wanted him on the payroll. It would be a difficult call to make. Was a continuance for Raymond's case still on the table? Did she still want to clear Raymond's name and solve his murder?

As the phone rang on the ranch, Jim nervously drummed his fingers on the desk until Maria answered.

"Is Senator Gibbons available? Jim asked.

"Yes," Maria said. "I'll tell her you're on the phone."

Jim waited.

"Hello, Jim." Then silence.

"Sandy, I just wanted to let you know that I'm going ahead with an appeal on Raymond's behalf."

"Jim, I've changed my mind. I don't want to continue pursuing a reversal. At this point, it no longer seems important."

"Look, Sandy," said Jim. "I'll do it pro bono. That way you won't have to pay out of your pocket."

"No, Jim, I want to drop the whole thing. I don't even want you to pursue Raymond's murder," said Sandy.

Jim was confused. It made no sense. Had she been that upset about his not wanting to renew their relationship? Was she angry, hurt, or was there another reason?

Although Jim had suspected that Gillette was responsible for having Raymond murdered, he still hadn't dismissed the idea that Mick might have been involved. He didn't know why. It was just a gut feeling. However, having Sandy change her mind so quickly took him by surprise. If she was afraid she'd lose control of the R Bar W, why had she pursued Raymond's case in the first place?

Jim asked the next obvious question.

"Do you want to see me?"

Sandy said softly, "Jim, I don't know."

The tone of her voice didn't sound promising.

"Sandy, it'll be difficult proceeding without you, but I want you to know that I *am* going to continue the case. Now that Raymond's dead, I feel a need to clear his name—and I have to find out who killed him. I'm going to drive out there at the end of the week and do some looking into both cases."

"I wish you wouldn't, Jim," said Sandy.

What next?

He knew he couldn't work from home, and he no longer had an office to work out of, so his first priority was to get busy and scrounge up a place to settle into. Maybe he could call some of his law school buddies who had offices in the area—if he hadn't beaten them up too badly over the years.

CHAPTER 14

It had been a long, hot drive from Denver to the Sand Hills. For most of his seven-hour trip, the view from Jim's windshield was stark and austere as the arid countryside rolled out before him. Now, in the midst of the hills, there were stretches of the highway so long and monotonous that it became difficult to keep his eyelids open. But, as if planned—and just at the right moment—his tired eyes would get a break from the miles and miles of buffalo grass. The landscape would magically turn into lush cattail-lined marshes surrounded by brilliant wildflowers and dotted with smatterings of indigo buntings, yellow-shafted flickers, Baltimore orioles, and, of course, redwing blackbirds. The contrast of these small breaks from the endless grass landscape was a welcome sight, even lifesaving.

The bright colors and surreal marshes were topped only by a sign Jim saw along the road that welcomed him to Houston County. In another twenty-five miles, he'd be in Cottonwood Springs and the long tedious drive would be behind him.

Cresting a long hill several miles into the county, he met a car. As it passed, Jim recognized the county sheriff's emblem and immediately looked down at his speedometer. He was only traveling five miles over the speed limit. Nothing to be concerned about, so he continued on.

Just as he reached the bottom of the hill, Jim glanced in the mirror. The flashing lights reflected there were quickly approaching his car. Pulling over to the side of the road to let it pass, he was surprised when the car pulled in behind him. He couldn't believe that he was going to get a ticket for going five miles over the limit.

Looking again in the mirror, Jim saw the officer get out of the squad car and cautiously walk toward the Jeep, stopping just long enough to glance at the Colorado license plates.

"Look, officer," Jim said as the deputy stepped up to the car door. "I was just barely over the speed limit."

The officer looked at him and then, in a rushed move, stepped back from the door.

"Sir, would you please exit the vehicle."

That seemed unusual for a routine speeding ticket. "Don't you usually just ask for a driver's license?" Jim responded.

Before he had finished his question, the officer stepped back, unbuckled his holster, and took a defensive stance.

"Sir, I want you to exit the car—now!"

Not wanting to be shot on a lonely stretch of Nebraska blacktop, Jim slowly opened the door and stepped out of the Jeep.

"Place your hands on top of the car," the officer demanded.

"But officer, I—"

The officer drew his pistol and pointed it directly at Jim, shouting, "Hands on top of the car!"

He had definitely gotten Jim's full attention.

Using his free hand, the officer pushed Jim toward the car. Again, the thought of being shot crossed Jim mind, and he had a vision of seeing himself lying beside the road in a pool of blood. He was beginning to get a feel for the abusive treatment his people had received for hundreds of years at the point of a gun.

Dutifully, Jim placed his hands on top the Jeep as the officer patted him down. Then the officer grabbed Jim's right arm and yanked it behind him. Jim felt the cold lock of steel around his wrist. Almost as quickly, the officer secured his left arm in the adjacent cuff. With both of his hands locked behind his back, Jim was helpless.

The officer reached into Jim's back pocket, removed his wallet, and took out his driver's license.

"Mr. James Grant, I have a warrant for your arrest."

He read Jim his Miranda rights, and then pushed him toward the squad car. Opening the back door, he shoved him inside. Jim could understand why anger could spill over among his people when they were treated in such a manner.

He wondered about his Jeep, sitting there unlocked by the side of the road. Would it still be in one piece when he got out of jail, which is where he assumed he was being taken?

It still made no sense that all of this was happening because he had driven a few miles over the speed limit. The deputy had seemed dead set on arresting him from the start.

Then it hit Jim.

Of course! Ed Hardin was making good on his threat to have him arrested if he filed his new evidence with the attorney general's office. He hadn't forgotten, he just thought it was a bluff. Maybe he should have taken Hardin's threat more seriously. Jim wondered how long the deputy had been cruising that area waiting for him to return to Cottonwood Springs.

Arriving at the sheriff's office, the deputy escorted Jim though the side door and removed the handcuffs. Jim heard the cell door clang shut behind him. He shuttered from the terrorizing sound he had learned to despise.

Two hours later, Sheriff Gillette walked into the jail. Stopping in front of Jim's cell, grinning profusely, he unlocked the door and said, "Mr. Grant, I see you've found a way to gain access to the courthouse after closing hours."

Jim just glared at Gillette, but he continued, unperturbed. "Seriously, I have a warrant for your arrest. County Attorney Ed Hardin is filing theft charges against you for the disappearance of court records from the Raymond Two Bears trial. Your arraignment will take place immediately in front of Judge Madrid. Your county appointed attorney will meet you in the courtroom. Let's go."

Jim knew there wasn't any reason to get riled, because he was on the short end of the stick at the moment. He'd go through with the arraignment, post bail, and then get on with clearing Raymond's name. He was sure *his* arrest would be cleared up as soon as he absolved Raymond's name.

The sheriff escorted him out of the cell.

"Can you tell me where my Jeep is?" Jim asked as they walked toward the courtroom.

"We had it towed in and impounded," said Gillette. "By the way, you might be interested to know that we searched the vehicle and found some of the missing court papers."

That was the last straw. Losing control, Jim started to struggle against the sheriff's grip, until he came to his senses and realized what he was doing.

"Cool down, Jim," he thought. "Violence isn't going to help at all."

But that didn't mean he couldn't take on the sheriff verbally.

"I've had about enough of this nonsense, and I'm not going to settle for this kind of treatment. You've been harassing the citizens in this county for too long. You know those papers were planted," Jim yelled. "If Ed Hardin said I took those records, he was lying. I'm going to take both of you on, and I'll see to it that your next job will be cleaning out latrines in the state penitentiary!"

At that, Gillette shoved Jim across the hall and into a brick wall. Reeling, Jim slid to the floor. Gillette then reached down and pulled him up by the collar.

The sheriff bellowed, "You can't threaten me. Many men have tried before, and they've all failed. You don't have a big enough dog to take on mine. Now, we either go to the courtroom, or I'll take you back to your cell. Which will it be?"

Jim's first thought was to exact abuse charges against the sheriff, but it would have done no good. There'd been no witnesses. Gillette knew he was in control, and Jim was powerless at that moment, so he calmed down and prepared for his arraignment.

The hearing didn't go as smoothly as Jim thought it would. But what could he expect from a county that was powerless against the likes of Gillette and Hardin. At first, Judge Madrid was going to deny bail. This was just a set-up to jack up the cost of the bond. Even after extensive argument from his defense attorney—who was probably in on the game—Jim's bail was set at $50,000. Ridiculous for a step above a misdemeanor, but what could he do? After the hearing, Jim asked to make a call to Sandy. He wasn't sure she would help him, but she was his only chance to avoid jail until bond money could be wired from Denver. Ironically, it was from the same pay phone that Gillette had used to call Goodall.

"Sandy," Jim said when she answered the phone, "I need somebody to come and post bail for me."

He could tell by her reaction that she was surprised, but he continued. "I'm in the Houston County jail. I'll tell you all about it when you get here."

As they walked back to the jail cell, Gillette made an unusual proposal.

"After Senator Gibbons posts bail for you, I'm sure I can convince Hardin to drop the charges—if you pick up your Jeep, head back to Denver, and never set foot in this county again."

It was the kind of deal Jim would have expected and showed just how the sheriff had been able to run Houston County for as long as he had.

Part of Jim's mind wanted to take the deal and get out of town, but would it be worth it? Since taking on Raymond's case, he'd lost his wife and his job, he'd nearly gotten smashed by a DC-10, he'd barely survived a flight through a fierce thunderstorm, he'd been held at gunpoint, and he'd been thrown in jail for a crime he didn't commit. It had definitely not been an average month.

He found himself thinking, "These *are* things that can put wrinkles on your heart."

His life would be simpler if he just picked up his Jeep and headed back to Denver, but simple wasn't always best. If he left, things would continue to be the way they'd always been, with Gillette on top, untouchable, and the rest of the townsfolk— especially the Native Americans—continuing to suffer. No, Jim decided. He was in it for the duration. He owed it to Raymond and to his mother's people.

He told the sheriff, "Thanks, but I'll take my chances."

Gillette didn't seem surprised.

As he was being led back to jail, Jim pondered his next course of action. In order to get the appellate court to render a decision *de novo* in Raymond's case and to challenge the lower court's findings of fact, he needed to get a look into the evidence room. But being out on bail was going to make that more difficult. Maybe he should call Abigail Finnigan and have her office start proceedings immediately.

Trying to locate Harold Eagles, the witness struck from testifying on Raymond's behalf in the first trial, would be a waste of time, even if he was still alive. And the rifle that Earl had found in the stable wall at the R Bar W would come under the prevue of new evidence. Jim decided that before he called to ask Abigail for her assistance, he would follow up on Raymond's single-word note.

Why had he put the Native American word for *spiritual leader* on that piece of paper? Had he put it there especially for Jim? Had he hoped that his note would lead Jim to his killer?

Before Jim could make use of it, he needed a crash course on Native American spirituality. Even though his ancestors came from that perspective, he had avoided it. Now, he wondered, who could teach him? Then he realized that there was no better person to do that than Maria Red Eagle, Sandy's housekeeper and his mother's dear friend.

While waiting for Sandy to post bail, Jim was allowed another phone call. He called the ranch house, and Maria answered.

When she heard Jim's voice she said, "Mr. Grant, Senator Gibbons is on her way into Cottonwood Springs."

"Thanks, Maria, but I would like to talk to *you*. I want to stop by the ranch later this afternoon for a visit, okay?" Maria was silent, so Jim added, "Growing up, I missed knowing a lot about my mother, and I'd like to know more about her and my father. I know you'll be able to tell me many things I don't know."

Jim heard Maria gasp, but he continued. "It's important to me to find out more about her struggles, especially the struggle she had linking her Native spirituality with her God, the God of the cross. I want to learn more about the friendship you and she had. Can I stop by later?"

Maria said softly, as though choking back tears, "Yes, Mr. Grant, that will be fine."

"Thank you, Maria. I'll see you later this afternoon."

Then Jim hung up the phone and was escorted back to his cell.

Much of what Jim's mother had stood for had been lost on him when he was younger. Before Jim left home, they hadn't spent much time together just sitting and talking, and Jim was only now beginning to realize how much he'd missed.

Twenty minutes later, Sandy came in and posted Jim's bail. As they drove to Vauder's Mobile to pick up his Jeep, Jim told her about Christine's leaving. He also restated his determination to clear Raymond's name and to solve his murder.

Sandy looked troubled.

"Jim," she said, "I'm happy you're here, but I'm uncomfortable with your continuing with Raymond's case. I know that's what brought you back, and for that I am thankful, but I still want you to drop it."

"But don't you see, Sandy? I can't," Jim protested. "It's become part of who I am, even if it means losing you again. I never lost my desire for you, even though I made a life away from you for twenty years, but I can't just walk away from Raymond's memory."

"Jim," Sandy said firmly, "if you really want me, you'll have to decide. If you solve Raymond's murder, you will lose me."

It didn't make sense that Sandy's attitude had changed so dramatically. Why was she so adamant that he drop Raymond's case, and what did she mean when she said he'd lose her if he solved the case? All he knew for certain was that the only thing he wanted to do, at that moment, was hold her in his arms.

"You know that spot out by the Niobrara we used to go when we were younger?" Jim asked. "As soon as you drop me off, will you follow me out there?"

Sandy didn't say anything. She just stopped in front of Vauder's, let Jim out, then turned her pickup around and drove away.

On a knoll overlooking the Niobrara bluffs, Jim waited for an hour, but Sandy never came. Apparently, she wasn't ready to forgive his sudden departure back to Denver.

Jim decided to leave, but just as he was opening the door of the Jeep, he saw Sandy's pickup coming toward him.

Like old times, they played in the cold, clear water of the Niobrara. When Jim saw her come up out of the water with water droplets on her tan body, glistening like diamond in the sun, he'd forgotten just how beautiful she was.

They made love that afternoon next to the Niobrara. Jim could feel their hearts link, and it was if the last twenty years had never existed.

Walking back to their vehicles, Jim told Sandy he wanted to stop by the ranch and visit with Maria. Then he wanted to spend more time with her where they could be alone.

"Jim, I have to go to Rapid City tonight," Sandy replied. "Mick, Earl, and I are going to buy some cattle. I'll be back in a couple of days."

Sandy didn't want them to arrive at the ranch together, so she left first, leaving Jim to sit looking at the river for quite a while before he followed.

CHAPTER 15

Back at the ranch, Maria met Jim at the front door and escorted him into the kitchen. As he sat in a rustic pine chair next to the kitchen table, she handed him a cup of coffee. Jim remembered Maria as a shy, quiet person, but he also recalled a time when she had run him down with a switch in her hand. He couldn't remember why, but he did remember the final results.

"Maria, do you remember chasing me across the yard and using the switch on me?"

"I remember when I was responsible for you," she said. "Your parents were hard working people, and they didn't always have time to take care of you. They weren't always around the house, so I took care of you much of the time."

Jim was only four when Maria left the ranch to go back to Pine Ridge. He remembered seeing tears in her eyes as she climbed into their old truck before his mother drove her back to the reservation. Of course, he didn't understand why she was leaving. His father had just stood quietly by the barn as they drove away. He didn't even wave goodbye.

Jim also remembered the day Silas started working at the Williams ranch. He had a young son with him. Raymond was about four years younger than Jim, but they became good friends.

"Maria, please come and sit with me," Jim said, patting the table softly.

She sat next to Jim, and they talked for a long time, sharing both tears and laughter. Although Jim noticed a tenseness in Maria's demeanor, it was heartwarming to know that his mother always had a friend she could count on as she made her way in a white man's world.

He remembered some of the Bible stories his mother would tell him. She so wanted him to find God in his life, and she made it all sound so simple.

Jim's time with Maria turned out to be special. He learned that his mother was a devout person who *often* came into conflict with tribal elders and their links to the spirit world, but she wasn't one to upset the apple cart, so she generally kept her faith and devotion to herself.

After a while, Jim asked Maria to tell him more about Raymond. She hesitated at first, but she could see that Jim truly wanted to learn as much about him as possible.

"Silas wasn't his real father, you know."

"No, I didn't know that. Who was his father?"

She looked down and stared at the hands folded in her lap, much like Raymond did. Then she ignored his direct question and, in a broken voice, she said, "He was an orphan, and I brought him from the reservation to live with Silas when he was two. Of course, I helped Silas take care of him."

"Kind of like your own son?"

Maria immediately broke into tears, and Jim knew he'd struck a cord. Maybe Raymond was Maria's son? He decided not to press her, though, and changed the subject.

"Maria, can you think of a reason why Raymond would write the word *shaman* on a piece of paper when he knew he was going to die?"

She gasped, but then composed herself. "Raymond was caught between two worlds."

Seeing Jim's confused look, she continued. "He was bounced back and forth between white and red, and God and the spirit world as Lakota know it to be. He went on a vision quest as a young man and came back a changed person."

Jim wanted to ask about Raymond's fight with demons, but decided to let it go.

"Why did he go on a vision quest?"

"After you left for the academy, he became quite rebellious, and it got him into all kinds of trouble. An elder from the reservation invited him to seek a shaman, and Raymond told me that the trip his soul took led him to great understanding. He said he'd found truth. He also said that he felt the shaman was God's merchant, put here on earth to deliver him to the scared place, the place of his reversal."

As they continued talking, Jim found himself sharing his own story about crossing the prairie and encountering the Deer Woman. Maria just smiled through her tears. She understood. She also knew that Jim needed to seek the truth again, and she appeared anxious to help him solve Raymond's murder.

"Are you going on a vision quest?" she asked.

"I hadn't planned on it."

"I believe the note in Raymond's pocket was not only to help you solve his murder, but also to resolve the problems with law enforcement here in Houston County," she said.

Jim thought about Maria's words for a moment and then said, "You know, Maria, I think I will go on a vision quest."

She seemed pleased with his decision.

"If you go to the town of Blue Willow on the Pine Ridge Reservation, you'll find a solitary house at the edge of the village," she said. "There, you will find an elderly man. Don't go with his first offer, but seriously consider the journey he will set for you. Now, Mr. Grant, I'll get the guest room ready for you. Thank you for our talk and for trying to clear Raymond's name."

Maria then left the kitchen, leaving Jim to wonder about her connection to Raymond. It all fit, but if she was Raymond's mother, who was his real father? Was it Silas or someone else?

The next morning, Jim left the ranch and headed to the reservation. True to Maria's word, he found the house exactly as she'd described, sitting on the edge of town. It appeared to be a government issue house, probably built in the 1950s. It was gravely in need of repair, and, at first glance, he thought it might be abandoned, with boarded-up windows and a hole in the roof. Uncut weeds and buffalo grass grew in patches in the red dirt that defined the front yard.

His first inclination was that it had to be the wrong house. Surely a shaman would live in a nicer house. But then, most of the houses in Blue Willow looked rundown and could be mistaken for abandoned houses. In fact, with the exception of the occasional porch sitter and a couple of small children playing in the street, it appeared as if the whole town was abandoned.

Jim parked his Jeep on the side of the dirt road and walked toward the small house. He was hesitant about stepping onto the porch. Tilting about twenty-five degrees toward Seattle, it was riddled with broken and missing boards. He was curious to see who actually lived there. Stepping carefully so the heels of his boots wouldn't get wedged in the cracks, Jim reached toward the door, but before he could knock, it opened.

The man standing in front of him wasn't the person Jim had expected to see—no long white hair, no incredibly aged face, and no flowing gown. Instead, he saw a disheveled man with hair sticking out from a red bandana; he was dressed in blue jeans and a jean jacket. He was old enough, perhaps, but he just didn't look the part.

Could this man really be the shaman? Before Jim could absorb that surprise, he was greeted by another.

"Welcome, Jim. Please come in. I have been expecting you."

Jim hadn't announced his visit to anyone. Perhaps Maria had called the shaman, or maybe he was using his shamanic powers. Whatever the case, Jim stepped through the doorway and into the dimly lit front room. The smell of incense and sage permeated the room. It was so strong that Jim momentarily had to fight back a wave of nausea.

"Please sit," the man said.

As Jim sat down in an old large-cushioned chair, he noticed several plaques on the wall on the opposite side of the room. In the dusky light, he could barely make out what was written on them. Squinting, he read the old gothic letters arched across the top of one: "California School of Metaphysics." At the bottom was the name Harold Eagles.

Jim's mind began reeling when he recognized the name from Raymond's court records and saw that he was the old Indian in mourning dress who'd been standing by the fence at Raymond's funeral.

"I can lead you on a vision journey," the old man said. "Isn't that why you're here?"

The shaman's slow, penetrating voice sounded sincere, so Jim was interested in what he had to say.

"I can set you up on a journey for only $25 an hour," he said. "Next week, it goes up to $30."

Jim suddenly felt as if he was being hustled—as if he'd come to see a palm reader or fortuneteller. He was disappointed, not only in Harold Eagles, but also in himself for making such a foolish trip. He stood and began walking toward the door.

"Harold," he said, shaking his head, "I was only looking for information about Raymond. Thank you anyway."

As Jim stepped off the porch, he heard Harold say, "You're looking to solve Raymond's murder. You're at a dead end and not sure where to turn next. Raymond led you this far—I can lead you the rest of the way. I can help you find your answers. I can lead you to the truth."

Jim turned around and looked at Harold, who continued. "I sense that you have doubts. I can feel your unbelief, but you must purify before you can have trust in the spiritual realm. You must come with an open, accepting heart. Be here tomorrow at dawn and we'll begin the search together."

A short time later, Jim drove out of town, skeptical about Harold Eagles and his spiritual powers. Still, there was an air of curiosity about their meeting. How had Harold known about the information he was seeking? He'd heard that the Denver police sometimes used psychics to help solve particular cases when they reached a dead end. Why not see if Harold Eagles could help him? The shaman had been right about his having come to a blind alley in his search for answers.

Was the note in Raymond's pocket leading him in the right direction? Jim's law background told him he should use more scientific methods for gathering evidence against Sheriff Gillette. He felt as if he had a basic understanding of why Raymond had been killed, but to solve his murder, he'd need to align all the parts that made up the big picture.

His instincts told him that Raymond knew more about why he'd been killed and who was responsible than anyone else, and Jim's gut feeling was that if he could move on the single-word message Raymond had left behind, he could solve the murder and get Dean Gillette indicted. What did he have to lose? One thing was certain, however. If he decided to follow where Raymond's note might lead, he was going to need a good night's rest.

After some serious thinking while driving around the area, he arrived back at the rooming house after dark and prepared to hit the sack. He decided, unless the morning brought a change, he'd be leaving early for Blue Willow.

CHAPTER 16

Harold Eagles was waiting on his porch as Jim drove up to the house. The sun had just broken the horizon, and the long shadows it cast across the land heightened the dilapidated look of the small home. However, what the hard landscape couldn't provide in beauty, the sky did. In fact, the heavens were stunning dressed in robes of pale blue and reddish orange. The colors burst forth in explosive fashion like fireworks on the Fourth of July. It was another perfect Sand Hills morning.

Harold had on a full-length buckskin robe, tied at the waist with a multicolored, beaded, rawhide band. He must have put a wig on because today his hair was white and flowing down his back. A river birch staff he carried in his hand completed the look.

Jim remembered Harold's warning as he departed last night. He'd been troubled by Jim's doubts and questions and told him that he must believe if he hoped to be successful in his vision quest. As he had put it, Jim had to discover the divine sacredness of self. Harold's concerns were taken to heart and Jim was determined to have an open and receptive mind so that *Wakan Tanka*, the Great Spirit, could do its work.

Harold didn't have to remind him again, but he did. In fact, it was the first thing he told Jim when they began to talk that morning.

After a short sermon, Harold pointed west, and they started out. After fifteen minutes of brisk walking through tall prairie grass, they came to a lowland area that was dotted with several dozen large cottonwoods. As they entered the grove, Jim saw the frame of an old sweat lodge sitting off in the distance.

"This is a place for purification and spiritual cleanliness, surrounded by talking trees. It's sacred ground to the Lakota," Harold said. Jim didn't react. He just stared at the naked frame. It looked almost profane sitting there bare and unused.

Jim had heard about the *inipi*, which he knew meant *to live again*. Its frame was started from a dozen willow saplings arranged in a circle, their trunks placed in the ground. The saplings, three to four inches across the bottom, tapered to twig size at the top and were bent over. An old frayed rope finished the construction. It was wrapped around the twigs several times where they came together to create an oval-shaped dome. Most sweat lodges were shaped like that and were referred to by the Lakota as *Mother Earth's womb*.

"Jim, help me cover the sweat, would you?" Harold said, reaching behind a pile of cottonwood logs and picking up two heavy old wool blankets.

The blankets smelled damp and heavy with smoke as they tossed them over the willow frame. Harold was insistent that every square inch of the frame be covered. Then he picked up a couple of old brown tarps. Jim wouldn't have to worry about the old stale smoke smell of the blankets, since the odor of mold and mildew on the tarps was ten times worse. He fought back his gagging reflex as he helped Harold position the tarps over the blankets and peg them down.

There was a round hole in one of the tarps. Jim assumed it was a door opening.

"See those rocks?" Harold said. "Put the hole in front and face it toward them."

The door itself was made from another old blanket. Jim picked it up, shook out the crickets, and tossed it over the top of the hut as Harold instructed. Then, going around to the other side, he pegged the corners to the ground with rawhide straps that were tied to it. That allowed the blanket to act like a hinge. When flipped down in the front, it covered the opening, sealing the "sweat" and keeping the heat in.

In front of the door opening were countless burned-out, cracked stones, piled high in the shape of a U, to form a fire pit. Obviously, the lodge had been the scene of many sweats in the past. Alongside the burned stones were what appeared to be fresh ones.

Jim was curious about the discrepancy, so Harold summarized for him the ancient ritual.

"The stones are used only once. Not only do they split and crack in the intense heat, but the spirits possessed by the stones leave during a burn. Stones used in a sweat also represent Earth, as both Grandmother and Mother, an eternal kinship. This makes them alive, and they can absorb the power of fire."

Jim smiled. This was all new to him, even though he was half Lakota.

Harold continued. "The positioning of the logs and stones in the fire pit is important. They're placed in a particular design for spiritual benefits as well as for easy access. The heated stones are carried into the sweat lodge from the fire pit and placed in a circle. Water is then slowly poured over them to create a sweat bath. It represents one of two essential life-giving elements. The other is air."

Harold said that the sweat ritual had begun on the plains more that a thousand years earlier and was closely tied to Jim's Lakota heritage. The sweat is meant to purge and cleanse the body of both spiritual and physical impurities, signifying a rebirth. It prepared a person to walk into the heart of nature with a cleansed body and a clean heart and mind.

Harold suggested that Jim find a quiet spot in the cottonwood grove away from the hut while he started the fire and began heating the rocks. Then he asked Jim to strip down and put on a pair of leather shorts that were brought for him.

"People are usually naked during the sweat, like in the womb, but I've lost too much business by asking people to sit in the buff," he said matter-of-factly.

A statement like that didn't exactly inspire Jim to believe in the process, but it was too late to turn back. He put on the shorts, found a quiet spot away from the hut, and sat down to meditate and pray, although the mosquitoes made it difficult to concentrate.

Even with Harold's earlier warnings, Jim still felt uneasy with the ritual he was about to undertake. Most Lakotas went through their first sweat at a young age. Even if Jim believed wholeheartedly, doing a sweat at his age might prove unsuccessful. He knew he'd have to prepare more diligently, but prepare for what? What kind of vision did he hope to receive—or, perhaps more accurately, what kind of vision would he be led to?

After about an hour, Harold came over to where Jim was sitting. "It's ready," he said.

Jim didn't know if he was spiritually prepared, but he was certainly physically ready. His battle with the nasty bloodsuckers had been raging all that time, and he welcomed the relief. He followed as Harold explained how to use the heated stones and the water in the bucket sitting by the door. He also showed Jim how to switch cool stones for hot ones.

"I'll come for you when it's time," Harold said, and then he turned and walked away.

Jim picked up an old shovel from the ground and began carrying hot stones into the hut and placing them in the center of the fire pit. He flipped the blanket down over the opening and slowly absorbed the darkness that engulfed him.

He felt his way around, finally sitting on the flat cedar boughs that covered the floor. As he tossed some sage onto the hot, glowing rocks, Jim immediately smelled the strong, sweet odor rising out of the burn. Camouflaging the damp, musty smell of the tarps, it was welcomed. He was reminded of his visit to Harold's house. The smell produced by the sage and the dark ambiance were much the same.

He found the water bucket, lifted it, and began dripping water onto the glowing rocks. The more water he applied, the more steam came off the rocks, eventually engulfing the interior of the hut. The warm, dark, moist atmosphere began to produce the intended results. Jim felt as if he had returned to the womb—although he didn't remember the first time, he thought with a smile.

Inside the silent darkness, the sweat began. Jim closed his eyes and began to pray, lifting his prayers up to *Wakan Tanka* and asking for a clean heart and a clean mind to begin his vision quest. After about twenty minutes, he noticed that the stones were cooling off and the steam was evaporating. He stood up and went outside. Picking up the shovel, he began replacing the cool stones with hot ones from the fire pit. The warm weather outside actually felt cool by comparison.

After the second stone exchange, the newness of the situation was beginning to wear off, and the exhilaration he'd originally experienced was beginning to turn to discomfort. His sweating had created a parchedness in his throat, his temples were throbbing, and his mind was having a difficult time staying focused.

Harold had warned him of the uncomfortable conditions, since most city people weren't hardened to such an ordeal. In fact, he'd asked Jim before he started if he wanted to modify the ceremony for safety and comfort.

"No, I want to get the full effect and be completely cleansed," Jim responded. "I want the works."

Harold had also warned Jim about forgetting to drink, which Jim had done, so he picked up the bucket and gulped down about a quart as soon as he remembered.

Just when Jim thought he couldn't stand the heat another minute and was getting ready to burst out of the hut, a relaxing calm came over him. His overwhelming thirst lessened, his headache went away, and his thoughts returned to his need for purification and the answers he was seeking.

Just as the third stone exchange had started to cool, the flap on the door opened and Harold stuck his head in.

"It's time to move on to the scared spot, set aside for your vision quest. Let me take you to where you can see with the eyes of your heart."

Jim didn't know what that meant and he wasn't sure what to expect, but it couldn't be more tortuous then what he had just been through.

After a dusty thirty-minute minute ride in Harold's old pickup, they finally stopped at the edge of a rugged, barren plateau in southwestern South Dakota. The red-stained ground, with its rain-carved gullies running down to brush-filled ravines below, was as desolate a landscape as Jim had ever seen. There was a bleakness and austerity to the land. It was accounted for when Jim saw the eroded pinnacles and spires of the South Dakota Badlands rising up from the northwest horizon.

"Some call this place the devil's playground," Harold said, "but it's always been a sacred place to the Lakota people."

They walked to the edge of the plateau and Harold pointed to the spot where Jim's vision quest would take place. It was a circular area about ten feet in diameter, close to the edge of the plateau. Cleared of pinion, scrub cedars, and sagebrush, the circle had been dug out to form a slight depression in the ground. In the center was a tall pole stuck into the hard earth. Four smaller poles were evenly placed around the edge, representing the four directions. Surrounding the center pole was a thick bed of freshly cut cedar branches and sage.

On the drive over to the sacred spot, Harold had explained the vision quest ritual, so Jim knew that he was going to be there for three or four days, in his shorts, without food and with very little water. It wasn't a comforting thought for a pampered big city attorney.

While he was there, he was to pray continuously to the Great Spirit for guidance. He needed to let go of the cluttered, complicated life he'd left behind and pay close attention to the new world that surrounded him. It was that new world that would give him the vision of truth he was seeking.

Before he left, Harold gave Jim one more chance to back out. "Are you sure you want to go through with this?" he said.

Jim smiled at Harold's lack of enthusiasm when asking the question, since he knew it would cost Harold $25 an hour if he backed out now. He supposed that Harold's question amounted to a sort of a legal disclaimer. Even so, Jim did briefly think about backing out, but immediately changed his mind, since it might be his only chance to solve Raymond's murder.

"No," Jim said, "I need to do this!"

Harold's last words as he climbed into the pickup were meant to encourage Jim.

"*Wakan Tanka* will come," he said. "During the quest you must always be attentive and listen carefully. The message may come from anywhere, even in the form of an animal or bird, so be prepared. Deeper knowledge is only possible if the spirits, through other creatures, are able to share their knowledge with you. I'll be back in three days."

Then he waved and drove away, leaving Jim to wonder what he'd talked himself into. He was a novice, and the suffering and exposure would surely come down hard on him.

He sat on the cedar boughs, leaned his back against the center pole, and tried to relax, but he couldn't stop worrying about whether he could withstand the rigors of such a wild land for an extended period. Would he be able to let go and allow nature to give him a new vision, and if he did have a vision, would he know how to act upon it? It would be a test of his endurance, much more so than it had been for his ancestors. His life had become one of comfort and softness, and he worried he might not survive the ordeal he was about to undertake.

In spite of himself, Jim started to panic. He looked to the horizon for signs of Harold's old pickup, but there were none. He was stuck whether he liked it or not.

The afternoon was spent walking from one pole to another, offering up prayers to the Great Spirit, asking as sincerely as he knew how for a vision. All the while, he kept his eyes focused on the surrounding landscape. How would his vision come, and how would it help him solve Raymond's murder?

Daylight turned into dusk as the sun disappeared behind the far-off red rock spires of the Badlands. Jim's body was wracked with fatigue. The heat of the morning sweat and the unforgiving fervor of the afternoon sun had coalesced to sap his strength. He raised a sponge to his lips and squeezed out a few drops of water. It felt warm and cool at the same time. He had to conserve his water supply since he still had three days to go.

He again sat on the cedar boughs and leaned his back against the pole. In the remaining daylight, he could see nature playing out a roulette game in front of him as bright, colorful canyon wrens flitted among the piñon plants. Their playful darting antics were amusing as he watched them search for their supper among the pale yellow flowers.

High above, a chicken hawk was looking for his evening meal and noticed the wrens as well.

It circled, getting closer and closer, looking for an opportunity to strike—and when he saw it, in the blink of an eye he had carried out his deadly assault.

Then, amid the high squeaks of the captured wren clasped in its talons, it flew away. Jim knew about nature's life and death struggles, but he was still stunned to see it violently played out right in front of him.

While he was thinking about the natural order of things, Jim suddenly saw an enormous bull snake slowly crawl out from beneath the sagebrush a short distance away. With carefully measured, segmented movements, it wound its way toward him. Was this a message?

Darting its tongue in and out, the snake tested the scents floating in the air. Thanks to the inattentive canyon wren moments before, it had been spared a life and death struggle in the talons of an age-old enemy from the sky. Finding nothing of interest, the snake slowly disappeared back into the sagebrush from wince it came. No message from the serpent, Jim decided.

A short time later, nature continued its labyrinthal plan as Jim noticed two mule deer making their way up one of the gullies toward his outpost. The male, sporting a trophy rack, led the way, and walking behind him was a smaller female.

Jim's heart quickened. Could this be the message he was meant to receive from *Wakan Tanka*? Were those animals his messengers? Harold had told him that guardian spirits could appear from anywhere—but he'd just started his quest. Could an answer appear so soon?

Slowly, Jim rose and stood next to the center pole. The large stag stopped and sniffed the air. Then, quick as an arrow from a warrior's bow, he disappeared down the ravine. The doe hesitated, as if offering an apology for the intrusion, and then bolted down the gully after the buck, leaving Jim to ponder.

Harold had told him that when a messenger came, it would have a visible connection with a spirit. Since the signs hadn't been obvious and nothing physical had been left behind, Jim decided that his visit from the deer had just been a pleasant incident.

Darkness soon invaded the land. It was so intense it looked almost solid. Jim was determined to remain awake through the night, praying to all four directions so he wouldn't miss any message. He could sleep later, but tonight, he would do his best not to close his eyes.

From time to time, his mind would venture from praying and mediating, and he would begin thinking about how important a vision quest had traditionally been for the Lakota people. Nearly every man went on at least one. It was an essential step in life's journey. If he hadn't been drawn back to the land of his roots, he might never have had the chance to experience the spiritual rebirth that lay before him, and, for that, he was grateful.

He continued with his prayers, and after awhile, he found himself looking up into the clear summer sky. He'd forgotten how incredible the stars could be. City lights dampened their effect, but there in a darkness that covered every inch of the land, the stars shone full and eloquent, lighting up the sky in a complex pattern only the Great Spirit could orchestrate. The splendor of it was mesmerizing. Jim sat down with his head against the center pole and stared up at the sky for a long time.

Suddenly, he was startled from his trance by a low, guttural sound from behind him. Whatever it was, it was close enough that its breath was warm against his shoulder. His mind raced with thoughts, including a thought of turning around and coming face to face with a demon spirit that was lusting after his soul.

Jim gathered his courage and turned quickly. He was shaken by what he saw. There, nose to nose with him and staring straight into his eyes, was *sumanitu*. When Jim abruptly turned, the coyote was as startled as he'd been. Hesitating a second, perhaps in disbelief, the animal quickly disappeared into the darkness as Jim jumped to his feet.

Nothing physical had been left behind, as far as Jim could tell in the blackness, but it had been an incredible meeting between himself and a wild creature.

His heart was still pounding with a fervor reserved only for things that go bump in the night, and beads of sweat rolled down his neck.

"Some warrior I am," he said softly to himself.

Standing there, letting his heart recover, he began thinking about his empty stomach and lonesome heart, which reminded him of how uncomfortable he was. Putting those thoughts aside, he strained to see into the darkness, but the blackness seemed to be mocking him, teasing him. Was the Great Spirit off to the west? No, he was probably to the east. Instinctively, Jim walked from pole to pole, calling out in the dark. Then, after searching the black void for a long time, he suddenly remembered that the Great Spirit was an intelligent sphere whose center was everywhere and whose circumference was nowhere, and that thought brought with it an incredible sense of release.

The rest of the night was spent listening to the sounds around him and fighting a growing desire to close his eyes. He was also beginning to get cold, and, after several hours, sleep began to tug mercilessly at his eyelids. The pull of the earth against his body taunted him as he began to lose his battle to stay awake.

Then, like an upsurging wind of creative energy, the first rays of sunlight began to appear above the red earth. The sun would be up shortly, and the pull of the darkness would be gone. With the return of the light, Jim's desire to sleep was lifted.

The day awoke bright and clear. Jim turned to face the sun with closed eyes, taking in its radiant warmth as he continued to pray for the Great Spirit to reveal the truth he so eagerly wanted to find.

Soon the sun made its way up into the sky and the warmth he'd been craving began to beat down on his red, dry, sunburned skin. His hunger continued to increase, even though he tried hard to erase it from his mind. His mouth was dry, and his lips were starting to crack. He raised the sponge to his lips, savoring the cool moist feeling. Then, not wanting to give in to his discomfort, he placed the vile of water back on the ground, turned away, and resumed his prayers.

Several hours later, the sun was at its apex and its flaming, orange, radiant heat began to envelop him. It not only attacked from above, but its rays reflected off the silver-red alkali soil around him, making Jim feel as if he was sitting in a solar oven. Under those extreme conditions, he again found it difficult to concentrate on his prayers.

The sun continued blazing hotter and hotter as the afternoon wore on until, far off in the sky, Jim saw some hope of relief. Toward the northwest, he saw a wall cloud starting to build over the Badlands. Born eastward by a strong wind, it grew taller and taller as it moved toward him.

As Jim watched the approaching storm, he thought about Harry Bellows, his sixth grade geography teacher. An ex-meteorologist, Harry was always injecting weather tidbits into his teaching, and many times he'd forecast the weather. The class would laugh at Harry's predictions, but, thinking back, Jim realized that Harry was generally more accurate than the TV weathermen.

Jim remembered one of Harry's lessons in particular. Near the 100th meridian, where they lived, humid eastern and dry western air masses often collided, creating a unique mix of weather. Most of the time the rain fell sparsely, but during certain times in the spring and summer when conditions were right, torrential storms would hit with the full force of Thor himself. Jim wondered if he was about to witness such a storm firsthand.

Large cumulus clouds began filling the sky, bringing much-needed relief as they blocked out the blazing sun. Continuing to amass energy, thick, foreboding layers of moisture and wind-laden clouds started to roll in and the heavens grew darker and darker.

Then Jim saw a lighting bolt zap off to his right, followed by a much closer one. There was no sense applying Harry Bellows' 30-30 rule for lightning safety in a thunderstorm. The strikes were already closer than six miles. The second strike seemed to be a signal that the time was right for the rampage of weather to begin, and the rain started. At first it was misty, like a burst from a huge spray bottle, but then it started to come down harder. Soon it had turned into transparent sheets of liquid as the wind began to push it across the land with incredible force.

Jim lifted his head to feel the full force of pelting rain on his body. He opened his mouth wide and let the rainwater splash against his tongue. Although ferocious and stinging, the downpour was welcomed.

Suddenly, a bolt of lightning struck a nearby cedar. The flash blinded Jim for a second and its loud boom stung his ears. His thoughts immediately turned to mortality—his own. Was he about to die there on the prairie? Had his sins been so great that it was his time to go? Is that why he'd been led to that place?

His prayers turned from requesting a vision to asking *Wakan Tanka* to save his soul. He also prayed for the rain and lightning to stop, but the storm continued, and the rain began falling even harder. The assault was in full force as the landscape was savagely thrashed by the raging storm.

Water filled the depression around the pole to ankle depth, and it occurred to Jim that standing in water next to a tall pole with all that lightning was about as smart as tossing an electrical appliance into a bathtub full of water, so he stepped out of the depression and onto higher ground.

The storm continued for a least an hour, and then, as quickly as it had come, it blew over. The skies settled back to a steel gray color, heaven's gates closed, and the raindrops decreased to a trickle. It seemed as if Jim's prayers had finally been answered, even though evening was fast approaching, which meant he was about to spend another miserable night sitting in a wet, rain-drenched hollow.

He decided that he'd continue his prayers by walking from pole to pole, offering them up without sitting. But as darkness set in, so did a sense of deep depression. Even reaching out to the Great Spirit didn't lessen his mental state. He had begun to review his vision quest at that point, but it made him feel even more discouraged and beaten. Had *Wakan Tanka* deserted him?

The warrior in him now started to give in to nature. He didn't want to battle the sun, wind, and water anymore. Consequently, he no longer saw his quest as a necessity.

With the danger of lightning over, the aching in his legs and back made him decide to sit down in the mud. Just as he did, he heard the sound of a motor off in the distance. Looking that way he could see lights coming toward him from the direction of the sound.

A minute later, the motor wound down, the lights shut off, a door slammed, and he heard a voice say, "Jim, are you okay?"

"Harold? Is that you?"

"Yes, I didn't want to interrupt, but I was worried about the storm, so I thought I'd better check on you."

"I'm okay," Jim said.

"Do you want to finish the quest?"

Hesitant at first, but realizing the necessity, Jim paused and then said, "Yes, I need to."

"Well, then, here's something to chew on to help you through the night," Harold said as he handed Jim a dried out, jerky-looking herb. "This will relax you and help with your concentration."

Jim had heard that some vision quests are laced with hallucinogenic drugs to reach a desired affect. He wanted a pure experience but his now depressed frame of mind, after battling nature the past two and a half days, didn't care one way or another.

So, not knowing what it was, Jim took the herb, chewed on it tentatively, and then swallowed.

"I'll wait here for a few minutes in case you change your mind," Harold said.

After about five minutes, Jim told Harold he could leave.

The last thing he remembered after that was telling Harold that he was going to close his eyes for a few seconds.

CHAPTER 17

Jim was suddenly startled awake by a large shadow that blocked out the sun. He couldn't imagine what was causing it. Clearing the sleep from his eyes, he looked up. Standing in front of him was a large animal. It was the paint horse. Unusually tall—more than sixteen hands high—he stood proud and mysterious, his head tipped back, and his eyes lifted upward. What a magnificent animal—but how had he found Jim? He looked around to see if anyone else was around, but Jim saw no one. It was as if the horse had appeared out of nowhere.

Jim then followed the paint's gaze upward and saw a lone eagle circling high overhead. As he watched, the raptor suddenly swooped down and flew directly over the two of them. As it glided past, it let out a loud screech and one of its tail feathers came drifting to the ground at Jim's feet.

Jim knew that he need no longer worry about receiving a sign. He bent down, picked up the feather, and tied it to the paint's long mane. Then he swung up onto the horse's back, gave him his head, and they began galloping to the southeast, following the eagle. They raced down the bluffs and onto the flat land. The paint stretched out his legs and they sped to the banks of the Niobrara, across the river, and out onto the prairie. Above them, the giant bird, looking every bit the part of a mythical thunderbird, appeared to be flying directly toward the sun on wings untiring and strong. To Native Americans, the eagle was an extension of God, playing the role of soul-bearer and reaching up to the heights where the Great Spirit resided.

As the paint continued to follow the great bird, a verse from the book of Isaiah came into Jim's thoughts: "They shall mount up with wings as eagles; they shall run, and not be weary."

The verse played through Jim's mind as he felt the wind blowing in his hair, and he wondered if the Great Spirit of his ancestors and the God of the cross were one and the same. Was there a bridge where Indigenous people, who put faith in the Great Spirit, and Christians who put their faith in the God of the cross, could meet? Could that bridge be accessed from either direction? For a bridge to work, Jim thought, it had to be able to be stepped on from either end.

The paint galloped tirelessly, following the Great Thunderbird south. They ran for hours, seemingly transcending the paint's physical limits, until the large raptor dove out of the sky and landed on the top of a forty-foot sand dune. Finally slowing the pace, Jim guided the paint to the base of the dune and got off, but the magnificent horse continued up the face of the dune a few feet and began pawing at the grass-covered sand.

When the paint had finished, Jim walked up the dune and looked into the hole the horse had dug—then stepped back. He saw the sun reflecting off a portion of a shiny metal object in the middle of the hole. With his hands, Jim began to dig further, and, in less than five minutes, the opening was several feet long. Brushing away the last of the sand, he saw something that quickened his heartbeat. There, reflecting the sunlight, was a metal panel, and across the panel, in twelve-inch high, faded red letters, were the words "Denver Mint."

He'd found the lost government plane that had disappeared ten years before, with more than $3 million in gold coins aboard!

Had he been brought there by the eagle and the paint? Was that the message he'd been destined to receive? Although it solved one mystery, how could the discovery help solve Raymond's murder?

Then a thought came to Jim. Had he been led to the very place where Raymond's tortuous path had begun?

"One thing is for certain," he thought. "I'll need to find out more about the plane before I can make any association."

Jim knew it would take bigger equipment to unearth the plane, so he quit digging with his hands. He visually marked the area as best he could, focusing on the surrounding landscape so he could return later with the authorities to finish the dig. He needed to make sure of its location because the land in that area could be confusing, since much of it looks eerily similar.

He looked around for the paint so he could return to the ranch, but the horse was nowhere to be seen. Both the paint and the eagle had disappeared, leaving Jim alone again.

Jim guessed that Sandy's ranch was about ten miles away, so he started to walk. He'd call Harold Eagles later and tell him what had happened.

"Jim, wake up," he suddenly heard a voice say. "It's time to go back. Your vision quest is over."

Opening his eyes, Jim immediately became confused. It was daylight, and he was sitting in water-soaked sand, his head leaning against the center pole of the depression where he'd been before. Harold Eagles was standing above him, looking down.

"Where's the paint?" Jim asked.

"Sorry, Jim," said Harold. "There's no one here except you and me."

Then Jim realized that he must have fallen asleep and dreamed the entire thing.

Harold smiled knowingly and asked, "Were you led by *Wakan Tanka*? Did you experience a vision? Did you find the truth?"

Harold's questions were coming faster than Jim could respond. "A vision?" Jim said groggily. "I'm not sure. I think I had a dream."

The shaman smiled again as if to say his job was finished. Jim's quest had been successful. He handed Jim a towel, and Jim began to wipe off the caked mud and sand.

Then Jim reached into his pocket—and pulled out a single eagle feather.

That was all the evidence he needed. They jumped into Harold's pickup, and Jim urged the shaman to drive faster as they headed toward Blue Willow. Without knowing it, Jim was about to fulfill the third and final stage of his vision quest.

He'd gone through severance—the separating, detaching, and letting go of his inhibitions—from the sweat lodge to the center stake. He'd gone to the threshold, which had led him—with the aid of the paint and the eagle—to listening, seeing, and knowing, as the Lakota would say. Now he needed to follow through with the act of incorporation, bringing his vision back to the people to make the world a better place.

But first he had to pay his shaman the $25 per hour he owed him. Looking at Harold, Jim noticed the shaman was wearing a sly smile. Had the old man tricked him? Jim decided to pay him, but as for believing everything that had happened, he still wasn't quite sure. Perhaps it was a dream—but maybe it wasn't. Maybe he should believe in Harold Eagles' spiritual power.

Had Jim really found the remnants of a plane there in the sand, or had he imagined it? It had all seemed so real—more real than his encounter with the Deer Woman.

"Hurry, Harold," Jim said. "I'm anxious to get back to the ranch."

Jim knew that only a real-life trip to the crash site would quiet his inner turmoil.

CHAPTER 18

When they got back to Harold's house, Jim thought about driving to the ranch, borrowing Earl's pickup, and going directly to the crash site. But if it hadn't been a dream and the plane was there, he knew he'd need bigger equipment, so he decided to wait until the morning.

He plopped down on his bed at the rooming house, worried that he wouldn't wake up early enough. In fact, as tired as he was from his vision quest, there was a good chance that he'd sleep completely through the next day. However, he needn't have worried, because he didn't sleep much at all. He kept churning the vision quest experience over in his mind. Had it all really happened? Had he found the truth he'd been seeking? If it had been real, could he find the spot again, and, if he did, who could he get to help him excavate it? Should he call the federal authorities, or should he first make sure the plane was actually there?

His best bet, he decided, was to ask someone from the R Bar W for help, since the plane was buried on the western fringe of the ranch. It had to be someone he could trust, since whoever helped him unearth it would have to keep it a secret.

He decided to see the wreckage for himself before he contacted the authorities. He didn't know how it played into Raymond's murder, but he didn't want the news getting back to town.

He finally fell asleep just as his alarm went off. The sun was starting to peek over the horizon as he headed toward the ranch. He was in a hurry, knowing it would be important to examine the site for himself before any of the local officials could. He didn't want the site quarantined by the sheriff or county attorney.

With the exception of Sandy, Earl was the only person Jim trusted to help. He remembered seeing a tractor with a front end loader sitting next to the stables. It wouldn't be the best piece of equipment to do the dig with, but it was the only piece Jim knew of at the moment. He'd ask Earl to drive the tractor out to the spot where he believed the plane to be.

Jim hadn't seen Sandy since their rendezvous along the Niobrara four days before. It would be good to see her again.

The past several days, although somewhat of a blur, had been as close to hell as Jim ever cared to get. Baring his body and soul in searing heat, burning sun, and torrential rain, combined with the loneliness, had been tortuous. But it had moved him far beyond the raw experience. He had to admit that he felt good about it, though, and he felt he'd received what he'd set out to find—*if* his discovery of the plane had been real.

Before Jim drove up to the house, he stopped by the stallion barn, and there, grazing peacefully at the far edge of the corral, was the paint. The horse looked up at Jim momentarily and then lowered his head and continued eating. Just how special was that horse?

Parking the Jeep in front of the house, Jim knocked lightly on the large door and then walked in. Sandy met him just inside and, not wanting anybody to see them, she pulled Jim away from the open door and gave him a long hug.

They kissed and lingered in each other's arms as Sandy said, "I missed you, Jim. I'm glad you're back."

Jim smiled at her, realizing that the love they'd shared years ago was strong again. He also knew that because of her situation, they'd have to keep their love secret for a while. He realized that he wasn't going to challenge Christine's leaving. It was over between them.

Jim smiled and said, "I missed you, too."

As they sat at the kitchen table where the idea for Jim's vision quest had begun, he told Sandy all about it, from the sweat lodge all the way to how he'd been led to the crash site by an eagle and the paint horse.

Sandy didn't respond. She simply looked at Jim with a slightly unbelieving expression.

"I didn't examine it closely, but I suspect that the plane had been rifled," Jim said, "and all the gold had been removed. It will be interesting to find out what happened to the pilot and his security guard."

Jim was surprised at Sandy's nonchalant reaction. He sensed that she still felt uncomfortable about his persistence in solving Raymond's murder. Even so, she told him she wanted to come with him to the crash site, so Jim went out and found Earl while she changed into her work clothes.

"Are you crazy? You let a shyster like Harold Eagles talk you into sitting out on the prairie for three days without food?" Earl responded when Jim told him about his vision quest and his need for help.

"Can you keep it down a bit?" Jim asked. "I don't want the whole ranch to know."

"Unbelievable!" Earl said as he shook his head. "And now you think you've found the remnants of a long-lost airplane? It's crazy, but you bet I'll go with you! I'll go just to show you that a rich city lawyer isn't any smarter than the folks around here."

Jim was a little surprised that Earl would stray from his work, but he seemed eager to help. Jim and Sandy climbed into Earl's old Bronco as he fired up the tractor. As they backed the Bronco away from the barn, Jim saw something that he hadn't noticed before. In the back of the old Ford, among a lot of other junk, were two twelve-volt batteries. Everything else looked old and clunky, but the batteries looked brand new. Jim figured the ranch needed batteries from time to time, so he I didn't give it much thought.

In order for Earl to keep up with them with the tractor, Jim had to drive slower than he would have liked.

After about twenty minutes, Jim looked into the rear view mirror and saw Earl waving them toward the north. Jim was sure he was on the right course, but Earl kept waving northward. Jim stopped the Bronco and waited for Earl to catch up.

"Damn it, Earl, we need to go that way," Jim said.

"Well, from what you've told me, you're wrong. It's off that way," he said, pointing to the northwest. "Do you see that large group of dunes up ahead? That's where we need to go."

Jim still thought Earl was wrong, but who was he to question him? After all, Earl had lived on that prairie for the last forty years, so Jim steered the Bronco toward the dunes Earl had pointed to.

When they arrived, they found nothing but grass and sand. There were no signs of Jim's digging. Jim drove around a couple more dunes in the area, but they found nothing. Neither Earl nor Sandy said a word.

Jim's mind was reeling. The vision had seemed so real. He felt as if it had really happened.

Finally, he decided there was no need to detain Earl any longer. They decided to start back, in spite of the overwhelming disappointment Jim was feeling. But as he turned the Bronco around, Jim saw two large dunes to the southwest that were similar in height to the ones they'd just searched. They looked familiar.

"Earl, I'm going to check out the area down there," Jim said, pointing to the southwest.

"I'm out of time," said Earl. "Let's get back to the ranch."

"Tell you what," said Jim. "Let me take the tractor, and I'll look while you take Sandy back to the ranch house."

"I can't let you do a fool thing like that," said Earl. "I'll help you check out a couple more spots."

Again, Jim was surprised. Earl seemed to be hanging around on purpose. It wasn't like him to sacrifice his time this way. When Jim asked Sandy about it, she said she thought Earl was just being helpful.

The first of the large dunes was like the others—just grass and sand.

"I should have known the ones we originally looked at weren't the right ones. They weren't tall enough to have a plane buried in them," Jim said to Sandy.

Then he announced, "Okay, we'll look at one more before I give in to it all being a dream. This last one has to be it."

Earl suddenly turned the tractor toward the ranch house and threw it into gear. He appeared to be telling Jim that for him, the search was over. As Earl started back, Jim and Sandy began driving toward the last sand dune.

Then Jim thought he saw something, but dismissed it at first.

"When you want something to happen bad enough, you start to imagine it," he thought.

What he thought he saw was a hole in the side of the dune just ahead of them. For a few seconds, he couldn't distinguish whether it was real or not, but suddenly there it was—an eight-foot-long hole, just as he'd pictured.

They climbed out of the Bronco and walked toward the hole. Jim knelt down and saw the shiny panel with the words "Denver Mint" on it. He blinked back some tears. It was real. It had actually happened! He had ridden the paint, led by an eagle, across the prairie and had found one of the missing links to Raymond's murder.

Meanwhile, Earl had turned around and was driving the tractor back to the dune. His worried expression told Jim that somehow he wasn't really surprised that they had found the plane.

"Let's see what's under there," Jim said.

Hesitantly, Earl raised the scoop and slowly began pulling the grass-covered sand off the plane. In about ten minutes, the entire side of the fuselage had been uncovered. It was intact, which meant the plane had probably rough-landed and then barreled into the sand dune, knocking the ridge down over it. It had then either been covered up immediately or slowly covered during the night by a heavy rainstorm—but what had happened to the pilot and his security officer? Had they died in the crash or had they survived? And if they had survived, where were they? Why hadn't they come forward?

Then Jim had an idea. Maybe they had taken the gold with them.

He stepped up onto a broken-off piece of wing to get a better look into the fuselage. He brushed the sand off a cockpit window just enough to peer inside. The glass in the window had crystallized from years of burial, and it was hard to see through. Jim put his hand on the base of the glass and leaned closer. C-r-rack! A sharp, terrible sound echoed through the air as the window literally exploded under his hand.

Instantly, Jim yanked his arm out of the hole, and, as he did, he found himself gawking into the dark, sand-filled abyss of the cockpit. From atop a pile of sand, staring back at him were the eye sockets of a dead man. The skull tissue was like leather and half gone. The fleshy part of the eyes was completely gone.

No matter what Jim had been prepared for, the sight of a dead human with so much rot and decay was alarming. He stepped back quickly and took a deep breath.

"Jim, what do you see?" Sandy asked.

"Well, there's one body for sure, but I want to see inside the rest of the cockpit."

Climbing off the wing, Jim waded through the loose sand toward the door of the fuselage. He pulled on the latch, but the door was stuck shut.

"Earl, hook your chain to the door of the fuselage, and let's jerk it open with the tractor."

Earl hooked it up, gunned the motor, and the tractor began spinning its wheels as it lurched backward. Then, with a groan, the door gave way. In addition to the door, an entire section of the fuselage was torn away as well, allowing sand to pour out.

Looking in, Jim noticed a hole in the top of the fuselage. The collision with the dune must have punctured a large hole in the top, and as the sand came cascading down from the ridge, it not only covered the plane, it had filled it up as well. Or somebody found the plane, stole the gold, and knocked a hole in the top of the fuselage to cover up any traces of a crime.

Then Jim saw a second skull. It must have rolled out with some of the sand. He picked it up as Earl and Sandy backed away. Turning it over, he noticed something unusual. Just above the foramen magnus, where the spinal cord entered the skull, was a smaller hole. It appeared to be a bullet hole.

From the position of it, Jim suspected that the man had been executed. He set the skull back inside the fuselage, his curiosity deepening. What about the skull he'd seen through the broken window? He stepped onto the wing again and took a closer look at the skull in the cockpit. It also had a large hole in its temple.

Earl shouted up, "What is it? What do you see?"

"I think this is a crime scene," Jim said. "Let's go back to the ranch and phone the authorities before we inspect it any further."

Jim carefully replaced the skull.

"I need to get back to the ranch quickly," Earl said. "I've wasted enough time here already. I'll take the Bronco and you and Sandy come back on the tractor, okay?"

Jim thought that was a dumb idea, but before he could object, Earl jumped into the old Ford and took off. Sandy and Jim bounced along in fourth gear, up one dune and down another, with Jim cussing out Earl all the way back to the ranch. Why couldn't he have taken them back with him in the Bronco and picked up the tractor later?

As soon as they got back to the house, Jim placed a call to the United States attorney's office in Denver. It would normally be out of their jurisdiction, but since the plane had been the property of the United States government, Jim knew they'd be interested. He also decided to place a call to Abigail Finnigan.

CHAPTER 19

The federal authorities in Denver had been searching for the site of the plane crash for years, so Jim's call created quite a buzz, and the wheels of recovery were quickly set in motion.

"United States marshals will arrive as soon as possible to secure the site," said a voice on the other end of the line, "and crime scene investigators and personnel from the NTSB will be there soon afterward."

Jim's call to the state attorney general's office also created a stir. When Abigail answered the phone, she told Jim she was about to call him with some important information. In fact, she said that Jim could expect someone from her office first thing the next morning to discuss the new information and to view the crash site. She seemed anxious to get involved.

After Jim hung up the phone, Sandy picked it up and made a call to her press secretary in Lincoln. It seemed as if everyone wanted to get in on the action.

After Sandy hung up, Jim confronted her. "I don't think that was such a good idea. There are going to be people crawling all over the area, and bringing in the press might add to the confusion."

"Relax, Jim," she said. "We'll have a press conference here at the ranch tomorrow. After the federal authorities take care of their business, we can take anybody who wishes out to the site."

Jim smiled. He shouldn't have underestimated her desire as a politician to claim a share of the spotlight.

"Sandy, I want to get out to the plane crash and be there when the federal authorities arrive. Can I use your pickup?"

"Sure, I'll have Earl drive me out later."

Jim knew it would be several hours before authorities would arrive, so he wasn't in a hurry. Sandy asked Maria to prepare a late lunch for them, and, while it was being prepared, Jim walked down to the stallion barn to check on his old friend, the paint. As Jim stood by the corral fence, the horse trotted over. Jim watched curiously. The paint's magical appearance at the sacred site during Jim vision quest was unexplainable—almost godlike.

As he stood thinking about the incident, Jim heard Sandy call from the front porch. "Lunch is ready."

With all that had transpired over the past three days, he'd almost forgotten to eat. In fact, the last solid food he'd had was on the morning of the sweat. Small snacks since then did the job.

"A vision quest is one way to go on a crash diet," he thought with a smile.

They sat in the screened porch and ate a delicious lunch of lean beef, fruit salad, and sweet rolls. It was refreshing and gave Jim time to relax and think before heading to the crash site. It also gave Sandy time to restate her position on appealing Raymond's murder conviction—she seemed more adamant than ever that Jim let it go.

"I have to pursue it, Sandy," Jim said. "It's something I *need* to do."

"Please, Jim, just let it go," Sandy pleaded.

Her voice was troubled as she tried to convince Jim to drop the case, but Jim was just as adamant about continuing. When he'd finished eating, he stepped off the front porch and walked toward Sandy's pickup. He wanted to be at the site when the authorities arrived.

Then, looking toward the barn, he saw a cloud of dust coming up the dirt road toward the ranch. Soon he heard the sirens and saw the red flashing lights. He hadn't expected the federal marshals that soon—and he was right. Two Houston County police cars came to a dusty stop in front of the ranch house. Dean Gillette and Ed Hardin climbed out of the first car while two deputies waited in the second one.

"Jim Grant," Gillette shouted, "I have a search warrant to inspect the crash site you found, and I'm ordering you to take us there right now!"

Jim hesitated, not because he was hiding anything, but because he was surprised and curious at the same time. How had they learned about the discovery so soon? Obviously, someone had called them, and the only ones who knew were Earl, Sandy, and himself—but the only one he suspected was Earl, because he'd acted rather suspicious during their search for the wreckage and had insisted on taking the pickup, leaving he and Sandy to drive the tractor back to the ranch. Even so, Jim wasn't ready to finger Earl at that point; Sandy seemed to trust Earl implicitly.

"Mr. Grant, you'll either take us to the site now, or I'll arrest you for obstruction of justice," Gillette said menacingly.

"Just as you say, Sheriff." Then Jim turned back toward the porch and asked Sandy to follow them out in the pickup.

Jim climbed into the backseat of the squad car as Gillette slid behind the steering wheel. As Gillette quickly backed up, spinning the tires, he noticed that Ed Hardin was still standing outside. Realizing his mistake, Gillette slammed on the brakes, reached across the seat, and opened the front door.

"Damn it, Ed, get in! I'm in a hurry."

The ride across the prairie reminded Jim of a *Dukes of Hazzard* car chase, but he kept wondering why the other police car had stayed back at the ranch. Not seeing Sandy's pickup, he figured they had instructions to detain Sandy and keep her from leaving. Gillette wanted control of everything.

As they sped along, the sheriff kept asking for directions. Jim thought he'd mislead him to buy some time, so he pointed to his left. "It's over that way," he said.

Gillette frowned and said with a scowl, "Yeah, right. I think it's this way."

Jim wasn't totally stunned because he had the sense that Gillette and Hardin already knew where the site was! What Sandy had been saying about them was true. Jim began to worry that they would tamper with the evidence before the feds arrived—and he'd be powerless to stop them.

Even though it felt like they were going 100 miles an hour, the hills and loose sand kept the patrol car down to a much slower pace. Even so, Jim knew that it would only take about twenty minutes to get to the crash site. That meant they'd be there nearly two hours before the marshals could get there from Denver. By then, it might be too late.

As they drove between two sand dunes and down into a low area, Jim saw the spot they had excavated. Gillette saw it, too. He pulled up to the site, turned the car around, and he and Hardin got out slamming their doors. Jim reached to open his door, but it was locked.

Jim pounded on the window and pointed to the latch, but Hardin shouted, "We want you to stay in the car."

Jim felt like a fool. How had he allowed himself to get into this mess? After all his effort to locate the plane, he was now going to have to sit in the car and watch as Gillette and Hardin destroyed any evidence that would point to them. There'd be nothing left that might incriminate them in the deaths of the pilot and the security officer.

While Gillette and Hardin were making their way toward the plane, Jim began to run different scenarios through his mind. The last one, he concluded, seemed to fit. Raymond had found the wreck and had gone into town to tell the sheriff. Gillette saw an opportunity to cash in on some unexpected wealth. Seeing the enormous cargo of coins, he killed the men in the plane and took the gold. Later, since some of the gold had shown up in the southwest, Jim figured the sheriff had used it to pay for drug deliveries.

There was no doubt about it. The evidence from the wrecked plane had to be preserved, or he'd never be able to prove that Gillette had framed Raymond for murder and then had him killed in prison. Both he and Hardin would go scot-free. But what could he do? He was locked in the squad car!

Suddenly, Jim heard a chopping sound that grew louder and louder. It was a sound he recognized but was surprised to hear so soon. He turned around and looked out the back window of the squad car just in time to see a blue-and-white helicopter fly over top of the dune. With its blades churning up dust, the chopper nosed around and started to set down about fifty yards from the wreckage. Gillette and Hardin watched in shock, not sure what was happening. As the helicopter's props slowed down, the doors on each side opened, and two men jumped out. Ducking their heads, they hurried toward the sheriff and county attorney.

"Gentlemen," one of the officers said, flashing his badge, "I'm United States Marshall Clint Buzzard and this is Marshall William Thoms."

"I'm Sheriff Dean Gillette and this is County Attorney Ed Hardin," said Gillette. "We're investigating the crash scene for the county. Why are you here?"

"We've been authorized to secure this site by order of the U.S. Attorney's office in Denver," Buzzard said. "So please, the two of you return to your squad car."

"This is my county, I'm in charge here!" shouted Gillette. "Attorney Hardin and I have already secured the site, and I can tell you that you're wasting your time here!"

"Sheriff," Buzzard said firmly, "this is a *federal* crash scene, and therefore it's out of your jurisdiction. Now, please return to your car."

Jim had suspected that Dean Gillette was a bit stupid, but what he did next confirmed his suspicions. It also proved that Gillette must have thought he had a lot to lose if those investigators found evidence of tampering—and maybe even of murder—at the crash scene.

Pulling a revolver from his holster, Gillette started toward Buzzard. Instantly, Thoms lunged at the sheriff, tackling him and wrestling him to the ground. Within seconds, Gillette was face down in the sand, his hands cuffed behind him. Buzzard reached into his jacket, pulled out a revolver, and ordered Ed Hardin to the ground as well. Soon both men were cuffed and being led toward the squad car.

From his cage, Jim happily watched the scene unfold. It did his heart good to see Gillette and Harden in handcuffs, even though they'd probably be released as soon as they got back to Cottonwood Springs.

Thoms opened the back door of the squad car and was surprised to see Jim.

"And who are you?" he asked.

"I'm the one who found the wreck and called the authorities," Jim said.

Thoms motioned for Jim to get out of the car, and then he forced Gillette and Hardin into the backseat, still handcuffed.

"How did you guys get here so quickly?" Jim asked. "Doesn't it take more than three hours by helicopter from Denver?"

"We're not from Denver," said Thoms. "We're from Rapid City. We were alerted earlier this morning about the plane being found. Somebody called our office from the Pine Ridge Indian Reservation. He didn't leave his name, but he did tell us where it could be found. We were already in the air when federal authorities called us from Denver. We might have been here even sooner, but it was difficult to find the exact spot."

Jim was confused. If the call had come from Harold Eagles, he must have known about the crash sight all along. This made Jim question whether or not the vision had actually happened, or if he had hallucinated about it. Whichever, he made a mental note to pay the shaman a little extra for his help.

Since there was nowhere else to go and no way to get there at the moment, Jim stood by and watched as the marshals began securing the crash site. He would have stayed all day, but Thoms asked if he'd help drive Gillette and Hardin back to Cottonwood Springs.

"I'll wait at the scene until investigators from the NTSB arrive," said Marshall Buzzard. Then Jim told Thoms about the deputies back at the ranch, so he was told to stop there first.

Jim drove the sheriff's car up to the ranch house. Needless to say, the deputies were shocked when they saw Gillette and Hardin handcuffed in the backseat.

Thoms got out of the car, flashed his badge at the deputies, and said, "I want you to take these prisoners into town." Seeing their shocked expressions, he added, "I don't want you to put your jobs in jeopardy, so you can release them once you get to town." Obviously, Marshall Thoms wasn't concerned about the sheriff returning.

"Meanwhile, I'm going to commandeer your squad car, so both of you will need to take the sheriff's car into town."

The deputies climbed into the sheriff's car and took off, but the car rolled to a stop just past the stallion barn. Then one of the deputies got out and uncuffed the prisoners, who were undoubtedly yelling at them from the backseat. Then they took off again.

"I'm going to take the squad car back to the crash scene," Thoms said.

"I'm going with you," said Jim.

"No, I can find the spot."

"But I'd like to help with the investigation."

"No, please, remain here," said Thoms. "I promise we'll keep you informed."

Watching Thoms drive away, Jim knew there was nothing to do at that point but wait. He went into the house and sat in one of the club chairs as Sandy brought him a cold beer. He leaned back and took a swig, and though light beer wasn't his favorite, it was cold and tasted good.

"You know, aside from being troublesome, this whole episode has been confusing," Jim said.

"What do you mean?" Sandy asked.

"Lots of things don't add up," said Jim. "First, there's you. Why did you change your mind about appealing Raymond's conviction? Then there's the matter of Harold Eagles' knowing about the crash site and Earl's apparent call to the sheriff. It feels like I've been set up by everyone involved. Have I?"

"I think it's all just coincidence," she said. "I think it's admirable that you took it upon yourself to find the plane."

"Then why do I feel like I was the last person to know about it?"

Sandy said nothing, but her silence told Jim a great deal. He'd come back to Cottonwood Springs to find a path, not a maze, yet he seemed to be caught in a complex one, full of dead ends and trick turns.

Even though the sense of being used by Sandy was heavy on his mind, Jim still wanted her. In fact, his feelings for her were stronger than ever, but as she walked over to him, he instinctively backed off and told her he needed to be alone to do some thinking.

He felt a horrible emptiness on the drive back to town, and twice he almost stopped and turned around. He didn't know if it was weakness or strength that made him change his mind, but he eventually arrived back at the rooming house.

He threw a frozen pizza into the oven and settled down in the only soft chair in the room. He stared at the empty wall across from him and wondered why he'd ever managed to get himself involved in such a mess. A couple of beers and a cardboard-tasting pizza later, he closed his eyes and drifted off, but he was awakened by a soft rapping at the door.

He staggered sleepily across the room and opened the door to find Sandy on the landing, looking squarely into his eyes. Instantly, he reached for her and wrapped his arms around her, lifting her off the floor. He kissed her long and hard, feeling her warm body against his.

Very few words were spoken. They just enjoyed each other until long after midnight.

Afterward, while Sandy slept, Jim again went into the living room and sat in the overstuffed chair. His life had certainly changed, but he had to admit that he was excited about the possibilities of having Sandy back in his life.

He sat in the dark for a long time, and when he returned to the bedroom, Sandy awoke, somewhat startled for a moment. Realizing where she was, she gave Jim a loving smile.

"I have to leave," she said sleepily. "I want to get back to the ranch before the morning activities get underway."

"Can I drive you back?" Jim asked.

"No, that's okay. I'll drive back. The less commotion, the better," she said. Then, to Jim's surprise, she added, "I love you, Jim."

To his even greater surprise, Jim heard himself respond, "I love you, too."

He walked her out to her pickup and watched as she drove off into the night.

CHAPTER 20

Jim didn't go back to sleep after Sandy left. He just lay there thinking about their future together. At six o'clock, he decided to get up and go for breakfast. He was eager to find out what evidence the crime scene investigators had come up with, but he knew nothing would be available until later that morning, if it was ever made available, which was entirely possible. He imagined they'd hold a news conference sometime after Sandy's press conference.

Walking out to his Cherokee in front of the rooming house, Jim saw that the sky was heavy with dark clouds. He didn't know if it was the weather or the circumstances, but he began to feel uneasy. He couldn't nail it down, but the morning had an eerie feel to it. It was as if the whole town was waiting for something to happen. There was absolute silence—no barking dogs, no traffic, nothing. After a few seconds, however, Jim relaxed, realizing that such lack of noise was normal in a small town that early in the morning. He'd forgotten how quiet some places away from the city could be.

He opened the door of the Cherokee, but before he climbed in, something told him to turn around and look down the street— and what he saw froze him. Sitting about a block away was an old pickup. Jim strained to get a better look. The truck looked familiar.

Then he saw a man standing in the bed of the pickup, leaning on the top of the cab . . . he was pointing a rifle his way. Jim dove headfirst into his Jeep.

He heard the lever cock, and then a loud crack as the rifle went off, followed by the sound of shattering glass as the bullet ripped through the rear window and tore into the seat beside him with a thud. Those sounds were quickly followed by another shot and then another. Jim felt like a possum, trapped in the middle of the highway looking on as an eighteen-wheeler bore down on him. The only chance he had of staying alive was to get the Cherokee started and get the hell out of there. He reached up, put the key in the ignition, and turned it. As he did, he looked in the rearview mirror and saw that the pickup was moving slowly toward him.

Another shot rang out, hitting the Cherokee's tailgate with a loud crack. The engine roared to life, and Jim jammed the vehicle into gear while shoving down hard on the gas pedal. Immediately the Cherokee lurched forward, causing Jim to lose control momentarily, but after a couple swerves back and forth across the centerline, he regained control and headed hell-bent for leather out of town.

He reached the blacktop just as two more bullets tore into the back of the Cherokee. Jim was now in a desperate run for his life, and his choice was clear: he needed to work harder at staying alive than the other guy did at wanting him dead. His Jeep had never exceeded ninety miles an hour before, but it did that morning, racing along the blacktop out of Cottonwood Springs. As the speedometer teetered between 100 and 110, Jim again glanced at the rearview mirror. No pickup. The driver must have given up, knowing the old truck could never keep up with him.

Jim eased off of the gas petal a bit and continued looking behind him from time to time. At the first sign of trouble, he was ready to floor it again.

He brought the Cherokee's speed back down to seventy, and after several more glances in the mirror, he was convinced he'd lost them. He slowed even further and continued driving toward the R Bar W.

"What had all that been about?" he wondered.

He couldn't decide if they'd really been trying to kill him or whether the shots had only been meant as a warning. Either way, those bullets *had* come awfully close. After thinking about it for a few moments, Jim decided the shots had been a warning. After all, he'd learned that folks around that part of the world were usually excellent shots, and rarely missed something they really wanted to hit.

Then it struck him why the old pickup had looked familiar. It was the same truck that had tried to run him down a couple of weeks ago. That attempt had failed, too, which made Jim even more convinced that both incidents were meant as warnings—but it only made Jim more determined to carry out what he had gone to Cottonwood Springs to do. The environment in northwest Nebraska was more threatening than ever, and somebody needed to do something about it. He had to take Gillette and Hardin down to stop this harassment and murder.

The ranch was bustling as Jim drove up to the house. Sandy's pickup was sitting in front of the ranch house, so he knew she had made it home safely. Stepping onto the porch, he rapped the door knocker, but when no one answered, he let himself in. As he stepped into the foyer, Jim heard loud voices coming from Sandy's office.

"Damn it, Sandy, why did you let him find the plane? That's all we need."

"I didn't let him find it, Mick. He was led to it by Harold Eagles. Do you think I wanted him to find out about what happened?"

"Then why the hell did you bring him out here in the first place?"

"Look, we agreed that it would be best if we tried to get Raymond released."

"Hey, I didn't agree to that. That was your idea. If you hadn't caused Silas' death and then felt guilty about having Raymond sent to prison, we wouldn't be in this mess."

Hearing Mick's statement made blood rush to Jim's head. Could he really have heard what he thought he had?

"How are we ever going to get out from under Dean Gillette—or should I say, how are *you* going to?" Mick continued. "As long as Gillette has you under his thumb, he's going to continue bleeding you to death."

"Mick, I know your only concern is what you're going to get out of this ranch, and frankly, that was my only concern at the time—but things are different now."

"You mean because you're sleeping with that half-breed attorney?"

"You son of a bitch. Maybe I should shoot *you!*"

Then there was silence.

Jim slowly and quietly stepped back outside and closed the door. He wasn't about to get into the weeds of the moment—not quite yet.

He again opened the door, but before entering, he called out, "Anybody home?"

Sandy came rushing out of her office. "Jim, did you just get here?"

"Yeah. Nobody answered when I knocked, and the door was unlocked, so I let myself in."

No longer worried about being seen, she walked over and gave Jim a big hug.

"Either she's glad to see me or relieved to think I didn't hear their conversation," Jim thought.

A moment later, Mick came out of the office, saw Sandy and Jim embracing, then jammed his hat down on his head and walked by without saying a word, slamming the door hard behind him.

"Did I interrupt something?" Jim asked.

"No, we were just discussing some ranch business."

"I could use some breakfast, especially a cup of strong black coffee," Jim said, trying to break the ice.

A short time later, Maria brought them breakfast as they sat out on the porch. While they ate, Jim agonized over the conservation he'd overheard. He desperately wanted to ask Sandy what Mick had meant about her being responsible for Silas' death. Had she ordered it done or had she actually shot him herself? Or was it an accident? Either way, Jim simply couldn't believe that she was involved with Silas' death and then had let Raymond take the blame. There had to be some other explanation.

He also wondered about Mick's statement referring to Gillette bleeding her. Was he blackmailing her? Did he have something on her? The murder, perhaps?

Jim decided to let it all go for the moment, but the pictures being conjured up in his mind were disturbing—especially now that he and Sandy had once again become intimate. He decided to focus on the plane wreck, but in spite of himself, his thoughts kept returning to Mick's statements.

While enjoying a breakfast he was earlier denied, Jim saw a limousine come around the barn road toward the house.

They certainly generate interest way out here. After it reached the parking area, the driver got out and opened the back door. His passenger stepped out and removed her sunglasses. It was Abigail Finnigan. Jim certainly hadn't expected to see her.

He stood up to greet her, but as she entered the porch, she brushed right past him and walked over to Sandy. "It's nice to see you again, Senator Gibbons."

"Ms. Finnigan, welcome to the R Bar W."

It was obvious that they knew each other, but Jim could tell by the somewhat icy inflection in their voices that it wasn't a friendly reunion.

"What brings you here, all the way from Lincoln?" Sandy asked.

"I have a surprise for Sheriff Gillette," Abigail said, "and I don't think it will make him very happy.

"What do you mean, a surprise?" asked Sandy.

"I'll let you know when the time comes," Abigail replied.

Only then did she turn and acknowledge Jim's presence.

"Good morning, Mr. Grant. Thanks for the phone call. I'd like to enlist your assistance, but first I want to see the report from the United States District Attorney's office on the plane crash."

"The report isn't in yet," said Jim

Sandy had a worried look on her face, as if things around her were starting to unravel. It was the first time Jim had seen her let her guard down. In fact, it was the first time he'd ever seen Sandy lose her composure.

"Please excuse me," said Sandy. "I have to check on some things before the press conference."

Then she hurried into the house.

With all the events that were swirling around him, Jim was beginning to get a sick feeling in the pit of his stomach.

"Have you been out to the crash site this morning?" Abigail asked.

"No, I was waiting for the investigators to finish," Jim replied.

"Would you like to go out there with me?" she asked.

"I don't think your nice car could navigate the sand dunes," Jim said with a smile.

"Don't worry about that," replied Abigail. "I just borrowed it for the day. I have a helicopter waiting at the edge of Cottonwood Springs. Once we get back to town and airborne, we'll be there in less than five minutes."

"I should have known a person in Abigail's position wouldn't have driven all night to get here," thought Jim. Then he said, "Sure. I'm curious to see what's been going on out there. I'm also worried that they won't find any significant evidence. I know it could take weeks, but I'm anxious to get this case resolved. I'm concerned about gathering enough evidence to nail Gillette and Ed Hardin for Raymond's murder."

"Well then," said Abigail with a smile, "I think you're going to like the surprise I have in store for Sheriff Gillette. Come on, I'll tell you about it in the helicopter."

Abigail's pilot was waiting as they drove down Main Street toward the landing strip. When he saw them, he started the helicopter's engine and the blades began to rotate. By the time they had parked and gotten out, the propellers were whirling at full speed. Running through a swirl of wind and dust, they finally reached the door and climbed aboard.

Once inside, Jim could tell Abigail wasn't used to such conditions as she tried to rescue her physical appearance from its unkempt circumstance. As she worked to tidy her hair and clothing, Jim asked how she knew Sandy. He figured she knew her as a state senator, but their meeting at the ranch had suggested a more personal relationship.

"Oh, Senator Gibbons and I ran against each other in the last election. Her campaign got extremely negative, and she struck out at me personally. An unmarried woman in her forties can leave certain impressions, and Sandy took full advantage of that, whether it was true or not. She ran a very bitchy campaign."

Abigail continued as the helicopter lifted off. "In my position, I can be cordial, but that doesn't mean I have to like the woman, even though I have to work closely with the legislature."

That explained the cold greeting at the ranch, but it also opened the door to more pain for Jim. It was one more thing that he had a hard time believing about Sandy.

The brown-and-green prairie was a blur beneath them as Abigail shouted to Jim over the noise. "Now let me tell you about the real reason I'm here. I called the warden at the Nebraska state penitentiary. At first he was vague about the investigation into the murder of Raymond Two Bears, but after some pressure, he agreed to focus on the guard you told me about. We issued a search warrant and found a large number of gold eagles in the guard's home. Because they appeared to be part of the shipment from the Denver Mint plane and could be considered stolen contraband, he loosened up immediately. In fact, we have a sworn statement from the guard that Gillette ordered him to have Raymond Two Bears murdered."

The surprise look on Jim's face was evident as Abigail continued. "The bombshell I have for Sheriff Gillette is a warrant for his arrest. He wasn't around earlier this morning. One of his deputies said he was out of town, but I think he caught wind of the warrant, and he's in hiding. As soon as we get to the crash site, I am going to enlist one of the U.S. marshals to help us find Gillette and place him under arrest. I also have a warrant to search the jail as well as his home. I want to connect him with the missing gold, and, Jim, I want you there when we do the search."

Jim was filled with excitement and relief. Abigail's words were exactly what he'd been hoping to hear.

"That's the best news I've heard in a long time!" he said. "The only problem is that I don't think Gillette is dumb enough to have kept any of the gold coins in the evidence room or in his house."

"Don't worry, I'm prepared for that," Abigail assured him. "If no physical evidence shows up, I'll bring in the state auditor, and we'll examine every record, every payout, and every money trail leaving from his office for the last ten years. Want to bet that we dig up some damage?"

Seeing the crash scene ahead, the pilot swung around and nosed down for a landing. Marshal Buzzard met them as they got out of the chopper.

"Good morning, Abigail. It's good to see you," the marshal said, giving her a hug.

Jim was surprised by their informal greeting. Evidently, they knew each other well.

Buzzard said, "From first indications, it appears that the two occupants in the plane were murdered, thought there's still no evidence as to when and by whom. Apparently, they were shot execution-style. None of the gold coins have been found, either."

"Clint, I need your assistance to serve a warrant on Sheriff Dean Gillette for murder. Can you help me?" Abigail asked.

Buzzard seemed excited about the idea, though Jim wasn't sure it was because of his law enforcement background or whether he had a thing for Abigail, but it didn't matter. The tide appeared to be turning his way, and it was entirely possible that he was going to be able to help his old community reclaim its former power.

CHAPTER 21

The courthouse was quiet as they drove up and parked in front of the sheriff's office. Jim was curious as to how the sheriff would react to the warrant that was being issued for his arrest. Would he react violently or stay calm, thinking he was still in control of things? Whichever, revenge was going to be sweet for Jim. He was glad that Abigail had invited him along.

As they walked toward the office, one of the sheriff's deputies came out to meet them.

"Sheriff Gillette isn't here. Can I help you?" the deputy said.

He must have known something was up the way he phrased his greeting. He seemed to have been waiting for them.

"Where can we find him?" Clint asked.

"I don't rightly know. He didn't leave a—"

"Young man," Clint interrupted. "We have a warrant here for his arrest, and unless you tell us where we can find him, I'm going to place you under arrest for obstructing justice."

Jim supposed that Clint knew he didn't have the power to do that, but his threat worked.

"He went hunting," the deputy said.

"Where?"

"I don't know for sure—," the deputy stammered.

"Where?" Clint demanded.

"He has a hunting lodge—two counties over—where he stays sometimes," the deputy said.

"Take us there," Clint said forcefully.

Jim wanted to go along, but the helicopter wasn't big enough to carry five, so he volunteered to stay. He'd have to relish the look on Gillette's face and exact his revenge when they got back. Maybe he could even convince Clint to lock Gillette up overnight. He'd love to see that.

As Abigail, Clint, and the deputy departed, Jim realized he was going to have to bum a ride back to the ranch. It would be at least a couple of hours or more before they got back, so he had time to go to Sandy's press conference. Maybe a quick stop at Malarkey's might scrounge up a ride with one of the reporters heading out to the ranch.

His hunch was right, but Jim was in for a surprise when he walked into the tavern. Coming toward him were Christine and Darren Hinkle, a bureau chief out of New York.

"Christine, what are you doing here?" Jim said.

"Darren and I heard over the wire about the plane wreck being found and the news conference at the R Bar W Ranch. He was in Denver on business, so we flew out early this morning. As important as this story is, we couldn't trust it to just any reporter."

"How you doing, ole boy?" Darren said as he reached for Jim's hand. "How are things going out here in cow country?"

They'd met before. In fact, Darren actually spent quite a bit of time in Denver. Jim had never liked him, though, and Darren's snide comment really irked him.

"He's nothing but a pompous ass posing as a real life person," Jim thought as the sight of Darren with Christine began to raise his blood pressure.

"Darren," Jim said firmly, "welcome to the real world. Watch out where you walk so you don't get any of that cow country dew on your patent leathers."

"Would you like a ride out to the ranch?" Christine asked, stepping between them. "I've arranged for a young reporter from North Platte to take us to the ranch. I think we can squeeze one more in the news van."

"She always was a good peacekeeper," Jim thought with a smile, but he wasn't sure he wanted to squeeze into a news van with his soon-to-be ex-wife and her new boyfriend.

Even so, it was a way to get to the ranch, so Jim accepted Christine's offer.

The ride was made more unpleasant by Darren's constant complaining about the dust and heat. Luckily, it wasn't far to the ranch, and, even as unpleasant as it was, the ride was definitely more relaxing than Jim's first trip earlier that morning.

He longed to ask Christine about Molly, but didn't think it was the right time and place. The last time he'd talked to his daughter on the phone, she'd seemed a bit down. He knew that their separation was going to be hard on her and determined that he'd need to spend some special time with her as soon as possible.

A large number of newspaper and TV reporters were gathered in front of Sandy's house. The news had spread fast after a few well-placed phone calls. Vans with Nebraska, South Dakota, Wyoming, Colorado, and Montana license plates were parked all the way from the cow barn to the ranch house. Jim directed the reporter from North Platte to park his van at the side of the house.

"Are you going in?" Christine asked as Jim started to climb out of the van.

He thought it was an odd question, but when she asked if she and Darren could go in with him, he understood. They just wanted to scoop the rest of the news organizations and were using him to get it.

Jim looked at Darren, who was waiting like a child expecting a box of candy. Jim smiled and said, "I don't think so."

Then he jumped from the van and ran through the mob of reporters to the front door, sorry that he'd had to miss the expression on Darren's face.

Earl and a couple of his cowboys were standing guard at the entrance, so they let Jim in. Sandy met him at the entrance to the great room. They kissed, and Jim gave her a long hug. She was dressed in her best state senator look.

"Jim, what did you find out this morning at the crash site? The U.S. marshals aren't letting anyone past the ranch buildings, so I haven't been able to get out there."

When Jim told her about the arrest warrant and search for Gillette, she looked stunned. Once they were through with the commotion, he intended to sit down with Sandy to find out what was going on. He wasn't sure he really wanted to hear her answer, but they needed to get it all out in the open.

A moment later, Sandy's professional nature took over and she gathered herself. Then, stately and composed, she stepped toward the door.

"Jim, would you stand by my side during the press briefing, in case I need some assistance?"

"Look, Sandy," Jim said, "this is your show. They want to hear from a state senator, not an attorney from Denver. You can do it. I'll wait for you here."

He was surprised to hear Sandy ask for help. Usually she took control of a situation, and he had no doubt that she'd do the same thing in a few moments. He was right. The press conference went well and Sandy controlled every second of it. The reporters didn't get the answers they'd come for, but that would be resolved when the investigation of the crash scene was completed. Sandy was at her best and got out of the briefing exactly what she'd intended— her name and position were in the national news.

As she finished taking questions, Sandy extended an invitation for all the reporters to go out to the crash scene. It was something the marshals weren't excited about, but there was little they could do, especially after the invitation had been made. The crowd was just too big.

Sandy's invitation was like a gun going off at the start of a stock car race. Reporters and cameramen ran to their vehicles and tore off across the prairie. Jim suspected that many didn't even know where they were going. They just followed the dust cloud toward the horizon. The marshals would restrict them once they get there, but with telephoto lenses, every newspaper in the country would have a close-up of the wreckage on their front page.

Jim wondered briefly if Harold Eagles had anticipated that.

"Sandy," he said, "I'm going to drive into town so I can be at the courthouse when they bring Dean Gillette in. I'll stop back later this evening."

As Jim started his Cherokee, the passenger door opened, and Christine poked her head in.

"Jim, I need to talk to you."

"I'm in a hurry to get to town," he said. "Can't it wait?"

Before Jim could say another word, she climbed in and shut the door. "Darren's off with the other reporters. Can we talk while I ride into town with you?"

Jim knew he had no choice.

As they drove down the lane toward the blacktop, Jim could tell she was troubled.

There were several long moments of silence before she finally said, "Jim, I filed divorce papers yesterday. I want as speedy a process as we can get. I'm not contesting many property rights—I just want it over. You can have the mountain home, but I want to sell the house in Littleton."

"Sell our home? Why? Where are you and Molly going to live? I assume you've thought about that!"

"Jim, Darren and I are going to get married!"

Although Jim didn't swerve into the ditch or anything like that, it certainly was a surprise moment!

"That didn't take long," Jim said.

At that moment, it occurred to Jim that Christine and Darren had known each other much better than he had thought, and apparently it had heated up considerably after their separation.

Maybe she hadn't been as upset as she had let on when he had announced his decision to go back to Cottonwood Springs and continue working on Raymond's case.

A jumble of thoughts was swirling through Jim's mind when Christine dropped another bombshell. "Darren has taken a job in Paris as the new overseas bureau chief, and I'm going to go with him."

Suddenly, Jim grew defensive.

"And what about Molly?" he said firmly. "Christine, you may want a quick resolution, but I'm not going to let you take my daughter to Paris. I'm telling you now—I'll fight you long and hard about that."

"Now take it easy," said Christine. "That's something else I want to talk to you about. I've decided to let Molly live with you."

Jim slammed on the brakes and pulled the Cherokee to the side of the blacktop.

"You've decided to let her live with me!" he shouted. "Don't you think our daughter should make that decision? Christine, this whole thing is bunk. You're acting irrational. It's just not like you."

"What's the matter?" Christine said. "Don't you want Molly to live with you?"

"Of course I do," said Jim. "I'm just worried for her sake. Does she *want* to live with me? Did you ask her?"

"We talked about it, and she wants to stay in Denver, but that's not an option," Christine said calmly. "I can see Darren and myself living in Paris for a couple of years, three at best, and then she can move in with us, if she wants to, when we return to the States."

Jim looked at Christine, amazed by her cold resolve. She seemed to be tossing their daughter around like a rubber ball for her own self-gratification.

"She'll definitely be better off living with me," Jim thought.

Then he remembered that he didn't have a place to live at the moment. He didn't even have a job. He shook his head, started the Cherokee, and pulled back onto the blacktop.

Christine kept talking as they made their way into town, but Jim had little to say in return. She seemed to have everything all planned out, and it was obvious that she and Darren had been talking about it a lot.

"I want to talk to Molly first. I'll be back in Denver this week," Jim said as he let Christine out next to her company plane.

He offered to wait with her at the courthouse until Darren got back, but she declined.

"I'll just wait in the plane," she said.

Jim's mind was reeling as he drove toward the courthouse. In one way, it was as if a huge weight had been lifted from his shoulders, but on the other hand, it also meant that he would soon be caring for his daughter by himself, and it would be up to him to see that her life was organized and happy. Even so, it was a challenge he would gladly accept.

Sheriff Gillette still hadn't arrived back at the courthouse, so Jim got out of his Jeep and walked down to Malarkey's to have a longneck and to think things out. If Molly agreed to live with him in Cottonwood Springs, he'd need to start looking for a house, but where would he find one?

Then a wild idea hit him. It was a long shot, but it was worth looking into. What about his parents' old ranch house? He'd have to convince Sandy to sell him the land and buildings, and they'd need a lot of fixing, but it was definitely worth a look.

He smiled, thinking about the old saying, "Life comes around full circle!"

Suddenly, the sound of Abigail's helicopter could be heard in the distance, and Jim knew that revenge was about to be his, providing they had found Dean Gillette. As the noise grew louder, Jim downed the last of the longneck's contents and stepped outside.

Apparently, Jim wasn't the only curious one. Many other townsfolk had come out of their stores and houses and were lining the sidewalks of Main Street. It was as if they were expecting a parade. Word had gotten out, and Jim sensed that he wasn't the only one who was hoping to catch a glimpse of Sheriff Gillette handcuffed and riding in the back of a squad car.

Abigail didn't disappoint them.

Shortly after the helicopter had landed, a patrol car that had been parked at Vauder's slowly started down Main Street, its lights flashing and siren blaring. When the large crowd of people saw who was in the backseat, they began to yell and clap.

Ethically, Jim thought, Abigail's stunt could be put at the bottom rung of law enforcement, but she knew what she was doing. She wanted any local within earshot to hear the commotion and to see that Sheriff Dean Gillette was now under *her* control.

Jim quickly walked to the courthouse, just in time to see a U.S. marshal pull Ed Hardin from his car in front of the courthouse. On the courthouse steps, the crowd began to cheer, and a number of people shouted profanities at the sheriff as he was escorted past them and into the building.

Abigail waved for Jim to join her, and he pushed his way through the crowd and walked in the front door right behind the sheriff. It was all he could do not to add his own insult to those of the crowd, but Jim refrained, trying to hold on to his professional dignity.

Gillette was put into a cell next to Ed Hardin, with a U.S. marshal stationed outside the cell door, in case one of the deputies got any ideas about releasing the sheriff.

It seemed as if everything had been wrapped up into a nice tight bundle. Jim had to hand it to Abigail. The woman definitely knew what she was doing.

"He started blabbing as soon as we found a cache of gold coins hidden under the sink in his cabin," Abigail told Jim. "I don't know how much of what he said we can use, but he certainly gave us lots of information to work with while he was trying to incriminate others and take the blame off himself. We now know a lot more about the mysterious plane landings, the wreckage, and even about some of the other lawlessness that has been going on around here for years."

"I still want to clear Raymond's name," Jim began to say, but Abigail interrupted him.

"Jim, I think I can help you with that, too, but right now, I need to file some paperwork, and since the county attorney seems to be indisposed, I need to appoint someone to have jurisdiction over the case," Abigail said with a smile.

Then she pulled Jim aside and said softly, "Look, Jim, I'm optimistic about nailing Hardin and Gillette, but it's going to take time. The first step is to convene a grand jury. Then, if we get an indictment, we'll need an arraignment, and, finally, we'll go to trial—and that could take months. Both Gillette and Hardin will be released following their booking. Jim, I think you'd better keep your eyes open. If Gillette thinks the odds are against him, he may come after you and try to take you down."

Jim was well aware of the process, and he knew the potential danger that Gillette represented. The sheriff had killed before, and, with his own life at stake, he probably wouldn't hesitate to kill again.

For the next few months, Jim would constantly have to be on guard for trouble.

CHAPTER 22

Jim felt good about the progress that had been made in solving Raymond's murder, but he still had a number of questions on his mind as he drove up the blacktop toward the ranch. With the news that Molly would be living with him, a whole new set of problems had arisen.

The first thing he needed to do was get with Sandy and discuss their future. Even though he was uncomfortable with some of her lifestyle patterns, Jim knew he wanted to spend the rest of his life with her.

Then there would be the negotiations with Mick and Sandy to purchase his parents' old homestead so he and Molly would have a place to live. He was looking forward to living there and having his daughter learn about her Native American heritage and the Sand Hills culture.

Of course, living in the area would mean having to deal with Mick. It was something he didn't relish, but if he was going to live in the Sand Hills, he would have to learn to tolerate him.

The issue of who Raymond's mother and father were also made him curious. Jim wanted to find the truth because he felt it would bring some closure to his relationship with Raymond.

Before turning onto the ranch road, Jim decided to take another look at his parents' old homestead. He failed to notice the old pickup truck that was following him, because his mind was thrashing around his decision to purchase the property.

Maybe it had been too rash of an impulse to want to fix it up and start a new life there, but if it appeared doable, he was determined. It was important to him that Molly have a nice place to live.

As he pulled up to the abandoned house, his doubts mounted. The house seemed to be in too much disrepair. He'd have to hire an architect and a contractor—if he could even get a bank loan. However, as he got out of the Cherokee and started walking around the house, the project began to feel less daunting, and the longer he stared, the more doable it seemed. Finally, he made up his mind to make it happen.

"Yes!" he yelled loudly, as if making a verbal contract with the house and surrounding landscape. "Yes, I can do this—and I will!"

His plan was to begin making arrangements the next day. It needed to be made livable before Molly arrived.

As Jim prepared to leave, the pickup that had been following him drove into the driveway. Turning around, he caught sight of it and recognized the old truck as the one that had nearly hit him along Main Street several weeks ago. It was also the vehicle that transported the shooter when his Jeep was filled with bullet holes.

His first thought was to go into flight mode, but, realizing his situation and knowing there was no place to run, he decided to stand his ground as the pickup came to a stop in front of him.

He could see two men through the windshield but wasn't able to make out their faces in the darkened cab.

They just sat there in front of Jim. Then the passenger door opened, and a man with a nylon cover over his face stepped out. He had a ball bat in his hand, and Jim knew it meant only one thing.

Switching from defense to offense, Jim immediately rushed the man standing there with his legs astride, the bat in ready position. His shoulder made contact in the man's gut and knocked him off balance. They both hit the ground and the bat went flying. Jim immediately pounced on the assailant and started pelting the man's nylon-covered face with his fists.

Meanwhile, the driver had exited the pickup and came around behind Jim. With a full arc swing, *his* bat made contact in the small of Jim's back. A sickening thud echoed across the farmyard as it buried into Jim's flesh, only to be stopped by his rib cage.

Jim struggled to get up, but as he did he was struck again by a second blow from the assailant. This time the bat hit his shoulders so hard that part of it cracked off and went flying into the side of the pickup. The blow knocked Jim to the ground. Again, he struggled to get to his knees. The first man whom Jim had been pummeling now saw his chance. As Jim kneeled in the dirt collecting himself, the man placed a hard, quick kick that landed right beneath his chin. The blow not only made contact with his jaw, it glanced off his throat, causing Jim to gasp for air.

Falling face down in the dirt, Jim struggled again to raise his beaten body. He couldn't move. It was then he knew his life was about to be over. As he lay there waiting for a deadly blow to his head, he heard the cracking sound of a rifle. And another. Then he heard the doors of the pickup slam shut. Painfully, he turned his head to the side just in time to see the old pickup tear out of the farmyard and race down the blacktop.

He collapsed into the dirt.

The next thing he remembered was waking up in a bed at the Springs Medical Clinic. Sandy was standing by his side.

"You have some cracked ribs and a number of deep body bruises, but you're going to be all right," Jim heard her say as he opened his eyes.

"Who were those men?" Sandy continued. "It looked like they were ready to kill you. I think I put a bullet in one of them, but they got away."

Most of Sandy's conversation was coming at Jim like it was filtered through a funnel. Although awake, his senses were still doped up. As the seconds went by, he began to realize where he was. He struggled to sit up, but a sharp pain in his side forced him back down to the bed.

"You fired the shots I heard?" Jim asked. "How did you know I was in danger?"

"The paint horse," she said. "Most of the "news people" were out at the crash site or had left altogether. I was talking with Mick out by the stallion barn when, suddenly, with brute force, that horse barreled through the corral fence and raced down the lane. I jumped in my pickup and tried to run him down. Then near the blacktop he leaped clear over the cattle grate and galloped up the road toward your old house. I saw the commotion and yelled at the men, but they ignored me, so I took out my rifle and shot over their heads. One of the shots must have hit the driver as he held the bat above his head.

"But, Jim, you still haven't answered my question. Who were they, and why were they trying to kill you?"

I don't know who they were, but it was the same pair who has been threatening me the past few weeks. I recognized the pickup. Every time I get to close to the sheriff with something that makes him uncomfortable, they show up. Unlike the last couple of times, whereby they were only scaring me, this time I think they had instructions to kill me."

"Sandy, you definitely saved my life."

"Well, you better thank your paint friend. He was the one who led me out there. Now come on, before the painkillers wear off. Let me get you to the ranch," Sandy said.

Jim had a lot of questions but wasn't feeling that well as they drove back to the ranch.

The pain was starting to come back.

As they drove by the stallion barn, Jim saw the paint come trotting over to the corral fence. Suddenly, he was stricken by a need to go to his old friend even though his pain was now coming in sharp twinges. He agonizingly stepped out of the pickup and walked over to the poised animal. Stroking the paint's forehead, Jim began to feel an upsurging of strength in his own body. His breathing was now more even, and the sharp pain in his side was diminished somewhat. He wondered why.

Then a thought hit him. This animal is more than just an ordinary horse. "What kind of powers does he possess?" he asked himself. If the paint could stimulate recovery from a simple petting, what would be the results of an all out gallop across the prairie?

Suddenly, Jim needed to ride the paint. He told Sandy that he was okay and that he would be gone only a short time. The important reason for a talk would have to wait: asking Sandy to marry him.

With Jim now on his back, the paint raced out of the corral onto the prairie toward the Niobrara.

At first, the pain in Jim's side was horrendous, but as he rode further away from the ranch buildings, the pain began to ease more and more. Soon it was almost gone.

Reaching a sand dune that overlooked the winding river below, Jim climbed off the paint and walked over to a cottonwood log lying in the grass. He slowly sat down to clear his mind. This spot had a sacred feeling to him.

Sandy tried to ignore Jim's sudden departure, but after a while she became worried when he didn't come back. The commotion at the ranch had died down, and Sandy was free of further responsibilities for the rest of the day, so she decided to ride out and look for him. She knew where he would be.

After about 30 minutes, she saw the paint. Dismounting, she walked up the grass-covered dune to where Jim was. At first he didn't look up.

"Jim, are you okay? I got worried when you didn't return."

"Ya! I'm fine. I just needed to air out my head."

They sat and watched the meandering river for a long time in silence.

Across the way, Jim could see the same river bluffs that were so vividly portrayed in Cormish's "Niobrara Crossing." He smiled at the irony that this could be one of the happiest moments of his life, with Sandy there, as opposed to the horror depicted in that painting.

"Sandy, I want you to know how I feel about you," Jim said. "I want our relationship to grow, and I want you with me for the rest of my life. I want to live here in Cottonwood Springs, marry you, set up shop, and continue to work at clearing Raymond's name. Sandy, will you marry me?"

Sandy's response hit him like a thunderbolt.

"Jim, I'm sorry. I can't."

He was stunned. How could he have misread her intentions? She had actually told him that she still loved him!

"Sandy, I don't understand," Jim stammered. "What do you mean, you can't? I thought you wanted me!"

"I do, Jim! I want you more than anything in the world, but don't you see? I can't marry you. There's too much hanging over our heads." Then she looked down and covered her face with her hands. She started to cry.

"We can overcome any obstacle," Jim said. "Please don't cry."

"No, it's too complicated," she said.

Then, lifting her head with tears streaming down her cheeks, she looked at Jim. "Don't you understand? I killed Silas Two Bears!"

At first, Jim acted unsurprised.

"I know you feel bad about it," he said, "but don't blame yourself. Once we find out who *really* killed him, I know you're going to feel better."

Jim tried to put his arm around Sandy, but she recoiled from his embrace, sobbing. "Jim, you don't understand. I shot Silas! I stood by the corral and shot him through the window. I killed him! Nobody else! I killed him!"

Again, Sandy put her face in her hands. Then she began sobbing uncontrollably.

For several long moments, the only sound that could be heard, besides the gentle murmuring of the Niobrara below, was Sandy's sobs. Jim said nothing. He just sat in stunned silence, his arm around her shoulder as he waited for her to collect herself.

With her head in her hands, she continued. "Silas came by the ranch house that night and he'd been drinking. I asked him to leave, but he wouldn't. He grabbed me. I tried to fight him off, but he was too strong."

Then she screamed, "Silas Two Bears raped me—right there in my own home!"

Jim was in shock, and though he tried to reply, the words simply wouldn't come. He didn't know what to say, but the whole scenario was finally beginning to become clear. At last he knew why Sandy had wanted him to lay off the appeal—but he still couldn't understand why she'd let Raymond take the blame. How could she have been that cold-hearted?

After a few moments, Sandy's sobbing subsided, and, with tear-filled eyes, she turned to look at Jim. Speaking softly, she said, "I couldn't tell anybody. There was no one I could trust, so I decided to take matters into my own hands. I got my rifle and went to find him. When I walked by the corral, I saw him in his easy chair sitting by the window as if nothing had happened. I pointed the rifle toward the window, lined it up at his head, and pulled the trigger. Then I killed him—that son of a bitch."

Jim couldn't believe what he was hearing. The woman he loved more than life itself was telling him she had committed murder.

Sandy continued, "Raymond came out and saw what had happened. Without saying a word, he went into the house and brought out his rifle and laid it on the ground by the corral. Then he told me to go into the ranch house and call the sheriff. I was afraid for Raymond, but he insisted.

Mick met me at the door and I told him what happened. He told me to hide my rifle and said he'd handle it. I heard him tell Gilbert on the phone that Raymond had just shot his father and that he had better come out right away. Meanwhile, Raymond disappeared. Before I knew it, I got caught up in all the lies and Raymond was being hunted down. After two days they found him on the Reservation and, with the help of federal agents, arrested him, extradited him from Pine Ridge, and put him on trial."

Sandy paused and looked into Jim's eyes, tears again rolling down her face. "Jim, you may think that I'm cold-hearted and don't care, but the last eight years have been hell for me. I know Raymond took the blame because he wanted to protect me. He never said so, but I know he was in love with me.

Finally, I just couldn't live with myself anymore, so I decided to try to get Raymond released. I thought I could rescue him somehow without being implicated in the murder, but Gillette wasn't happy about that, because it meant destroying his safety net—and Hardin's. The sheriff knew what had really happened, and he tried to blackmail me, but without indicting themselves, they couldn't expose my crime to the world, so I felt safe—until they threatened my life. By then, though, I wanted to make things right more than I wanted to protect myself."

"Sandy, who else knows about this?"

Unless the sheriff told, only Hardin. Jim, I want you to know how sorry I am for what's happened, and I'm sorry for dragging you into this. I wouldn't blame you if you never wanted to see me again."

For a long moment, Jim sat in silence, staring out at the bluffs. His heart was heavy. His mind flashed back to those who had died at Wounded Knee. He could now see the soldiers racing across the Niobrara toward the doomed village, and he felt at least some of the pain his ancestors must have felt.

He was standing at a crossroads as his mind raced with questions. Could he live with the injustice? Would Sandy's confession haunt their relationship? After all, she had a good reason for shooting Silas. Rape is a horrible, lawless thing, and sometimes backs people into a corner. But was he just making excuses to ease his mind? It didn't take long to decide what he needed to do.

He took Sandy's hands, looked into her eyes, and said, "Sandy, I love you. Nothing will change that. I still want our relationship to grow, and now that Gillette has been accused of ordering Raymond's murder, I believe we need to let it go. We shouldn't let ourselves be held captive by the past. It's over and done with. I couldn't bear to lose you again."

Sandy didn't say anything. She just reached out and hugged Jim tightly. In his heart, he knew that everything would someday be right again, but it would take time for Sandy's pain to heal.

The sun was disappearing in the west as they started their ride back to the ranch. Along the way, Sandy not only agreed with Jim's plan to restore his old homestead, she insisted on deeding it to him without any payment.

"Mick will have to sign off on it, which could be a problem," she said, "but I think he'll do it, since it would get you out of our house!"

At least that much was settled, Jim thought, but there was still a great deal to do. He'd have to begin remodeling the house right away, bring Molly from Denver, and then start building a new life with Sandy—in his beloved Sand Hills.

CHAPTER 23

If Jim wanted to bring the old house up to a level he was comfortable with, he knew he'd have to do most of the work himself; he still didn't have much of an income, and he didn't want to sell his mountain home. After being away from the city for several months, he'd grown accustomed to hard work, so a little sweat equity didn't scare him. Molly would be joining him in a few weeks, and the house needed to be ready.

Meanwhile, a grand jury was set to begin deliberations on Dean Gillette's case. Ed Hardin would go before the grand jury later. In Jim's estimation, Abigail didn't seem as intense as she should have been in preparing her case. For one thing, she'd let the case slip out of the county to North Platte. He thought the case needed to be more aggressively pursued and should have been tried close to the local jurisdiction, but for whatever reason, Abigail was dragging her feet. She seemed to be preoccupied with other things.

As for Jim and Sandy, they were enjoying their time together, and if a concern about what had taken place eight years ago came up, they either discussed it calmly or pushed it aside as their love continued to grow stronger.

One day, as they were blowing insulation into the walls of Jim's house, Earl came driving up in his old Bronco. He jumped out and ran into the house.

Above the roar of the machine, they heard him shout, "Have you heard?"

Jim shut off the machine and took off his mask. "Heard what?"

"Dean Gillette wasn't indicted for murder!"

"What?" Jim said, stunned by the news. "What do you mean, he didn't get indicted? That's impossible!"

Earl shook his head. "He was indicted on fraud and conspiracy, but not for murder. They're only going to try him for stealing the gold from the wrecked plane. No indictment on drug charges, no indictment for money laundering, and no murder indictment."

The news hit Jim and Sandy like a thunderbolt, because they knew that a slick lawyer stood a good chance of getting Gillette off, and, if that happened, Hardin's lawyer could duck it all as well. Jim knew that if Gillette and Hardin got off, the money laundering, drug running, and abuse of power would never stop—and Raymond's murder would never be resolved.

"What should we do?" Earl asked.

"What do you mean?" Jim said.

For a long moment, Earl was silent, and then added, "Oh, nothing. I guess I was just thinking out loud."

Earl's question was puzzling. Had he been involved with Gillette's underhanded activities and was now fearful for his life? Jim had thought for quite a while that some of Earl's actions were suspicious—especially at the crash site—but Sandy seemed to trust him more than anyone else on the ranch.

Jim and Sandy stopped work and headed back to the ranch. As they walked into the house, they heard cries of anguish from the kitchen. Jim stepped into the kitchen just as Earl was walking out the back door. Maria was sitting at the table crying, so Jim assumed that Earl had just told her about Gillette and Hardin.

As Jim walked toward her, Maria whispered between sobs, "My boy, my poor baby boy. Why have they treated you this way?"

Now there was no doubt in Jim's mind that Raymond was Maria's son. He had suspected it, but now he was sure.

Jim put his hand on Maria's shoulder. "Maria, I'm sorry. I want to help. Please talk to me about Raymond."

Maria looked up at Jim and said, "All his life, Raymond was treated like an outcast. I tried my best to give him a good life, but the Sand Hills were against him. I never should have brought him here from the reservation."

As Maria continued to talk, the picture became clearer. Maria had gotten pregnant with Raymond while working for Jim's mother and father. She wasn't married and, according to tribal custom, she went back to the reservation to give birth to her son. After nurturing Raymond for a year, she turned him over to the elders, then came back to Nebraska and started working for the Williams family. When Raymond was about four, Maria brought him back to the ranch; to soften matters, she had him live with Silas.

Sandy told Maria to take the rest of the afternoon off. As Maria stood, she stared straight at Sandy. The look was more than amicable. Jim noticed the stare and wondered how much Maria knew about Silas' murder.

Sandy saw it as well and soon answered Jim's thoughts as they sat down in the great room.

"Jim, I can't live like this," she blurted out. "Everyone around here looks at me in a secretive way like they know what happened. I can't go on this way. It was a mistake to think I could. I'm going to admit my part in Silas' death."

"No, Sandy, I won't let you," Jim said firmly. "Just give it time. You and everyone else around here will forget—and besides, nobody knows. You're just reacting because of guilt. Think of it as a good deed. Silas deserved to be shot after what he did to you."

Jim couldn't believe what he'd just said. He was a servant of the law. How could he be rationalizing murder that way? Finally, taking Sandy in his arms, he talked her into not saying anything.

When Sandy had regained her composure, Jim said, "I need to get back to Denver to clear up some business things, though I know this might not be the best time to do it. I worry about you now that Gillette is free awaiting trial. I love you, but I think we need a few days apart to get our heads straight. I'll be back in a week. Meanwhile, don't do anything rash, okay?"

Sandy agreed that a few days apart might be a good thing. She'd been spending so much time with Jim that she'd been neglecting her duties on the ranch.

She promised not to talk to anyone about Silas' murder, but added a disclaimer, saying, "We need to seriously consider the direction our lives are going when you get back."

Jim agreed and left for Denver the next day.

———

Jim was happy spending time with Molly and looked forward to having her live with him. During the day, while Molly was in school, Jim worked on getting his affairs in order. He put their home up for sale, made contact with friends in the law business—just in case he ever needed to lean on them—and, when school was out, he and Molly explored the Denver area. They even took a drive into the mountains and took a late summer ride on a ski lift. As they enjoyed their explorations, Jim realized how much he'd missed his daughter and vowed that when she came to Cottonwood Springs, they'd spend much more time together.

On the other hand, Jim stayed as far away as he could from Darren Hinkle and Christine. Every time he thought about their taking Molly to Paris with them, he shuddered. He wouldn't be able to stand being away from her that long, and he was glad that Christine had decided to leave Molly with him. He'd worry about the rest of it later.

By the end of the week, Jim had completed his business in Denver and was ready to return to Cottonwood Springs.

"I wish you could come with me now," he said to Molly as he left, "but it's the middle of the semester, and our house isn't livable yet. I'll be back for you in twenty days, I promise."

Jim then went to the airport to make arrangements to lease a small plane so he could fly back to Nebraska. He had been put on to Esse's Flying Service but when he got there, they were short on planes. The only one available was an over-the-top Cessna 210. It wouldn't have been his first choice, but it would work. It would just mean being in the air longer, since its cruising speed was considerably slower than that of the turbo prop he was used to flying. It did have one advantage, though: it was cheap, which was a good thing for Jim at the time.

He called Sandy to let her know he was coming. She sounded glad to hear his voice.

"Jim, it's been lonely around here without you," she said. "What time are you coming home?"

It was a simple question, but it had tremendous implications for Jim. It had been a long time since he'd heard the Sand Hills referred to as his home. Still, he liked the sound of it.

"Yes," he thought, "I'm finally going home."

As Jim and Sandy talked, it wasn't long before Gillette's name was brought up.

"Jim, I'm concerned," she said. "Gillette has been making up for lost time. He came out to the ranch a couple days ago, and I saw him talking with Earl before he came to the house. He hinted to me that I needed to consider a donation to his retirement. I'm sure he's going to try to hold Silas' murder over my head."

"Sandy, don't do or say anything until I get there. I'll be there about six tomorrow morning. Can you have Earl leave his Bronco at Vauder's so I'll have a ride out to the ranch?"

"I'll tell him to do it tonight, because they're going to be busy in the morning."

As he hung up the phone, Jim again thought about how nice it was to be going home. He was going to need some quality sleep if he was going to take off at two the next morning, so he immediately went back to his motel.

The next morning, the lights of Denver lit up the still-dark sky as Jim sped down the runway and lifted off into the darkness. Without visual representation, he'd have to rely on the instrument panel to get him on the right course. Then he could settle back for a long flight through the blackness.

After about three hours, rays of sunlight on the eastern horizon told Jim that he was getting close to Cottonwood Springs. Scanning toward the north, looking for the familiar water tower, he saw what appeared to be a dark cloud in the sky far ahead of him. As he got closer, he saw that it was a cloud of heavy black smoke, coming from the vicinity of the Springs. There must be a large fire somewhere in town, he thought. Then a bright orange flash lit up the night sky as intense black smoke blasted out in all directions.

Soon he was close enough to see flames lifting high into the sky—and suddenly, he knew where the smoke was coming from. The Houston County courthouse was on fire.

He veered off course so he could circle the town before landing. From his high vantage point he could see the flashing red lights of emergency vehicles as they raced toward the burning building. The sun was just popping up as he broke out of the circle and guided the small plane down toward the narrow runway.

As he got out of the plane, he could hear sirens blaring in the distance. It was if the commotion in the small town had reached a fever pitch. He looked for Earl's Bronco but didn't see it, so he began to run down Main Street toward the courthouse.

A large crowd of people had gathered as firefighters fought to get the fire under control. Flames were leaping hundreds of feet into the early morning sky and had already engulfed the central tower of the building.

Then someone yelled, "Look out! Get back!"

As the crowd on the courthouse lawn quickly moved into the street, the central tower of the courthouse started to collapse. To Jim, it was like watching a slow-motion movie. Finally, with a twisting motion, the tower plunged inward and down onto the main floor of the building before crashing into the basement—and, in that one moment, the courthouse was gone.

All that was left standing was a charred brick shell with the stone window frames left naked from the blown out glass. Thick black smoke curled up from the hollow pit in the center and surrounded the occasional licks of flames that were devouring the buildings remains.

There was nothing firefighters could do amid the smoldering ruins except keep the flames under control.

After the inferno had destroyed the tower, ashes, pushed out by the wind from the building's collapse, covered the courthouse square.

The crowd, sensing most of the excitement was over, slowly dispersed. That's when Jim saw Earl's Bronco parked on a side street. No wonder he couldn't find it. He began to wonder why Earl had left it there instead of at Vauder's. As he walked over to it, Jim caught the heavy smell of gas. Examining it further, he noticed a liquid dripping out from under the Bronco. It appeared to be coming from a tipped over gas can in the back.

As he bent down to get a closer look, he saw one of Gillette's deputies run up to a group of firemen and shout, "Have any of you seen the sheriff?"

No one had seen him, but they were sure that there had been no one in the courthouse when it had caught fire. After all, it had started at three in the morning. There had been some brief concern about the night custodian, but he showed up in the crowd later, so they were certain that the building had been empty.

Jim was curious. There was just something strange about it all. Gillette was missing, and Earl's Bronco was sitting on a side street with a half empty gas can in the back, but he'd have to wait until the state fire marshal was called in before he'd get some answers. He decided to leave the Bronco sit there.

Jim walked to Marlarkey's to use the pay phone. When Sandy answered, she said that she'd heard about the fire but didn't know why Earl's Bronco wasn't at Vauders.

"Actually, it's kind of funny," she added. "Earl wasn't here this morning to give out the work assignments, and it's not like him not to show up for work."

Now Jim was even more curious about the Bronco and its cargo.

"I'm going to snoop around a bit," he told Sandy. "Can you come in later and pick me up? I don't think Earl's Bronco will be available to drive out."

When Sandy agreed, Jim hung up the phone and went inside for some breakfast.

The tavern was full of people talking about the fire, how it started, and, of course, how much it was going to cost to replace the courthouse. Only time would tell, Jim thought. After all, they still hadn't found the cause of the Denver Mint plane crash, and that investigation had started over a month ago.

Noticeably absent from the crowd, both in front of the courthouse and in Malarkey's, were Gillette and Hardin. Where were they? After all, their offices had been destroyed. Why hadn't they shown up to witness the destruction?

Suddenly, the front door flew open, and Joe Hermes from Harris Feed Mill ran in, shouting.

"They found Gillette and Hardin!"

Amid the commotion, Joe, still excited, continued. "They were both in the building—and they both burned to death."

Jim was surprised by the news, but he was stunned by what happened next. The entire crowd in Malarkey's erupted into loud applause. He had suspected that Gillette and Hardin weren't popular, but he was still taken aback by the crowd's reaction.

As a lawyer, it wasn't the kind of news that could be taken at face value. For one thing, how could they have identified the bodies so quickly? Leaving his coffee half finished, Jim headed back to the courthouse to see if what Joe had said was true.

When he got there, yellow crime scene tape surrounded the burned-out building.

The state fire marshal's office had begun taking charge of the investigation, so Jim slipped under the tape and walked over to the man who appeared to be in charge.

"I'm attorney Jim Grant," he said. "Can you tell me yet what happened?"

At first the marshal just looked at him. Then he turned away, but Jim insisted on more information, saying, "I just heard they found the sheriff and the county attorney inside. Is that true?"

The fire marshal turned back toward Jim. "It's too soon to identify the bodies. In fact, we found three bodies in there. Two of them were—and please keep this to yourself—handcuffed to one of the jail cells. Somebody wanted them to die and, I might say, in a very horrible, tortuous way. It appears as though they were crushed to death when the tower fell in, which spared them from being burned alive. One of the local firemen recognized them, so I can tentatively say that is was Dean Gillette and Ed Hardin. The third body was found by the west exit. It was burned beyond recognition. It appears that whoever it was got burned up trying to escape when the tower fell in."

Then the fired marshal lowered his voice and said, "This is off the record, but we found a burned-out gas can in the basement of the ruins, so it looks like the fire was intentionally set. That means there's an arsonist loose in town."

Although Jim didn't say it, he had a hunch that the fire marshal was wrong. In fact, he had a strong suspicion that he knew the identity of the third body. Pointing toward Earl's Bronco, he told the fire marshal what he'd discovered.

Jim thanked the marshal for his time and then walked over to a bench by the sidewalk. Brushing the ashes off, he sat down to wait for Sandy. Finally a clear picture was starting to emerge. As he suspected, Earl had been working for Gillette. It was probably Earl who had hooked up the batteries to the lights out on the prairie, to help guide in the planes suspected of delivering drugs. Earl was no doubt responsible for distributing the gold eagles around the country—and he *had* been trying to divert Jim away from the plane wreck that first day.

When the sheriff beat the murder wrap, Earl became concerned for his life. He knew Gillette would want to clean up all loose ends, so he acted first, but he hadn't managed to get out before the tower collapsed on top of him.

Things were starting to make sense. Jim didn't think he would have to deal with the mystery pickup and its occupants again. With Sheriff Gillette dead, they were officially off his case. And as for Mick, it appeared as though he was just an angry, disgruntled man fighting for his share of the ranch.

As Jim sat thinking, he looked up to see an elderly man walking toward him.

Jim recognized the man from years past. He was one of the town's old-timers.

"Mr. Grant, I have something here I think you should hear," the man said.

He pulled a small tape recorder from his shirt pocket. As he turned it on, he told Jim that he'd been standing near the courthouse and had it running when the fire started.

Jim put the recorder up to his ear to hear better. He could hear men shouting in the background, and he could hear sirens approaching in the distance. Nothing unusual about that—but then he heard something else. Starting quietly and then growing louder were two men's voices in the background. As the tape continued to run, Jim heard the voices begin to yell louder and louder. They were voices now terror-stricken and screaming for help.

Suddenly, a loud explosion could be heard on the tape. Then the silent humming of the recorder. Jim had never heard anything like it before and was very disturbed.

He asked the old man if he could have the tape. The elderly gentlemen agreed and handed it to Jim. As the man walked away, Jim knew there was only one thing to do.

A few minutes later, Sandy pulled up to the curb, and, as Jim rose from the bench, he tossed the tape into a nearby trash can. As far as he was concerned, justice had been carried out, and there was no need to have all the gruesome details laid out for the town to hear.

"Sandy, I don't think Earl will be coming back to work," Jim said as she turned the pickup around and drove back toward the ranch. "And I think most of our troubles are over."

CHAPTER 24

Two weeks had passed since the fire, and Cottonwood Springs was starting to get back to normal—if something so horrific could ever bring back normalcy. The courthouse had been totally destroyed, along with all its records. Some of the courthouses built in that era had concrete or steel vaults where copies of all official records were kept, but the Houston County center of government didn't, so most of the official records were lost. Depending upon where you stood, that was either a good thing or a bad thing.

After a brief investigation, it was determined that arson was the cause of the fire and Earl Sweet was eventually identified through dental records. Everyone in town had known him, but officials had to wait for proof, since Earl's body had been burned beyond recognition. He was blamed for setting the fire that killed him, but nothing official was ever said about the murders of Dean Gillette and Ed Hardin, though it was assumed that Earl had cuffed them to the jail cell.

Many people found it hard to believe that Earl could have been that cold-hearted, but no one understood how cruel Gillette could be while running his totalitarian regime. Sandy would probably have been the next on his shit list and was only saved by his death.

Until official word came through, the case remained open, and Jim knew from experience that the faster a court rendered a verdict, the sooner a community could get back to healing. However, most of the loose ends had been tied up. No one would ever know for sure about the various disappearances and lawlessness that had taken place over the last several years, but residents would finally be able to live without fear, which would make Cottonwood Springs a good place to live again.

As for Jim and Sandy's struggle, only time would tell. The burden they carried would either bring them closer together or tear them apart. One of Sandy's battles was still to be fought, though—dividing the R Bar W. She had been so adamant about keeping it all in the family—her family, not Mick's—that she had lost her direction, but reality was setting in, and she knew that she was going to lose as much as half of the ranch.

"Jim, I think you should stop the remodeling of your old house and live here at the ranch," Sandy said one morning as they sat at the breakfast table.

"I don't know, Sandy. I think for my daughter's sake I need to finish the house and have it ready when she comes here next month. I'd love to live here at the ranch with you, but not right now."

Suddenly, a loud crashing sound came from the kitchen. They both jumped up and ran to the door. As Jim pushed it open, he saw broken glass from a meat platter strewn all around. Maria must have dropped it, but where was she?

"My god!" Sandy screamed. "It's Maria—over there behind the table."

Jim rushed to her lifeless body on the floor.

"Quick! Call 911!" Jim said. "I think she's had a heart attack."

Jim tried mouth-to-mouth resuscitation, but after a few minutes he stopped and turned to Sandy, who was watching in horror.

"I think she's dead," Jim said as he rose to his feet.

As the ambulance left with Maria's body, Jim and Sandy stood in the doorway watching with tears in their eyes.

"A wonderful lady has left this earth," Jim said. "A beautiful woman with such tragedy and heartbreak in her life. I want to make sure she's buried properly—next to Raymond."

To gather information about Maria for her obituary, Sandy took Jim into Maria's room.

"She kept her things in that chest over there," Sandy said.

Jim raised the lid of the cedar box and carefully began going through the chest. He soon learned that Maria had been born on the Pine Ridge Reservation more than sixty-five years ago. There were two birth certificates. One read *Maria Red Cloud, born September 23, 1920,* and the other read *Raymond Two Bears, born January 24, 1948.* There it was finally—the truth about who Raymond's mother really was.

As they continued to search for information among the keepsakes, Jim noticed an envelope in the corner of the chest. It was postmarked February 1948. Inside was a note, folded in half. At first he hesitated about reading it, but then he decided that it might shed more light on Maria's life. He took the note out of the envelope and began reading.

Maria,
   I'm so sorry about what happened. Please, if I can do anything, let me help. I don't want you to carry the burden of this child all by yourself.
                              Jim

Stunned, Jim just sat, staring straight ahead, holding the letter in his lap.

Sandy sensed something was wrong. "What is it?"

"Nothing," Jim said as he put the note back in the envelope. "Just a note someone wrote to Maria. Nothing we can use for her obituary."

He laid the envelope on the floor beside him. When they were nearly finished, Jim asked Sandy if she'd get him a cold drink. As she'd left the room, Jim picked up the envelope and put it in his pocket. He didn't want anyone to find out what he'd just learned. Later, he would tear up the note and throw it away.

————

The mourners, all friends of Maria, stood on the same barren hillside next to Raymond's grave as her body was lowered into the ground. Harold Eagles now stood with them.

"Another warrior has gone on to be with the Great Spirit," Jim thought. "A real warrior—not of battle, but of sacrifice and perseverance. Maria chose to follow the way, painfully keeping her secret for a lifetime while watching over her son."

It saddened Jim's earthly heart, but the tears streaming down his face were really tears of joy.

As the mourners began to leave, Jim paused and stepped over to Raymond's grave, where he knelt and offered a silent prayer. When he'd finished, he stood and quietly said, "Raymond, my brother, your mother's secret is safe with me. Now you and she can rest in peace."

Then he turned and walked toward Sandy. He reached for her hand, and they slowly left the cemetery.

————

Sandy was in Lincoln for the start of the legislative session when Jim received word that Abigail Finnigan had gotten Raymond's conviction overturned. He hadn't even known she was working on it. When a posthumous request comes to the court, they are usually dealt with it in a quiet way, which had been the case with Raymond's appeal. Abigail had convinced an appellant court to waive normal procedure since all the parties involved were dead.

Jim wasn't sure why Abigail had proceeded with the appeal—probably because it would look good on her record if she ever ran for public office again. But it wasn't long until Jim knew the real reason.

The Nebraska Senate had just gone through a procedural vote and the senators were either sitting at their desks or milling around the senate floor. Sandy was packing up some of her paperwork when she heard a commotion near the entry door. Suddenly, in opposition to a screaming sergeant at arms, the door swung open and Abigail Finnigan, flanked by two Nebraska BCI agents, came storming down the center aisle.

"Sandy Williams-Gibbons, I have a warrant for your arrest," Abigail said. "You are charged with the murder of Silas Two Bears. Please be reminded that you have the right to—"

She continued reading Sandy her Miranda rights. When she finished, Sandy was tussled around and handcuffed in front of the entire senate. Then, while leading her out of the chamber, Abigail stopped just long enough to allow a reporter, no doubt one she had summoned, to take a picture of the event. The story was front page news, not only in Nebraska papers, but across the nation.

Abigail had accomplished her mission. Like parading Dean Gillette after his arrest, her actions smacked of unethical procedures, but she didn't care. That was just her style.

Jim received word of Sandy's arrest from her secretary and flew to Lincoln immediately. He learned that the charges against Sandy were involuntary manslaughter. He also knew that if Abigail had had a leg to stand on, she would have pushed for a more severe charge, but she took what was available to her. He also knew why Abigail had gone through with Raymond's appeal. It kept the case open and made Sandy's arrest possible. Revenge would be hers, he thought.

As Jim and Sandy flew back to Cottonwood Springs, the small plane was filled with emotion. Jim talked about bringing in the DMMK team from Denver, but Sandy refused.

"I don't want you involved in the least bit," she said. "Even though you're no longer associated with your former firm, I don't think that would be a good idea. Besides, are you sure they'd even want to take up my cause? Maybe I should just plead guilty to get it all over with."

"No!" said Jim emphatically. "We're going to fight this together, and we're going to win!"

As the weeks went by, Jim, Sandy, and Molly went on with their lives in Cottonwood Springs, but thoughts of the upcoming trial were always on their minds. The first bad news after Sandy's arrest was that Abigail had obtained a change of venue, moving the trial from Houston County to North Platte. That was bad news, in light of the political constituency. Sandy had garnered the fewest votes from that district during her bid for the senate. Abigail definitely knew what she was doing.

Finally, the trial day was here. Sandy's defense team was composed of well-known lawyers from Rapid City, and by the end of the third day, the jury had been selected. It was time to get to work and for her defense team to show their stuff. Jim wasn't part of the team, but he maintained close contact with them. He was at the courthouse every day.

On the fourth day, after the procedural process was over and the jury had been seated, the judge entered and gaveled the court to order. Then something strange happened. Sandy's defense counsel immediately asked for a side bar. Since that was unusual, it brought an objection from Abigail, but the judge ruled for the defense, so the attorneys for both sides stepped up to the bench.

"Your honor, my client would like to change her plea," Sandy's attorney said.

"Come again, counselor?" the judge asked.

"Your honor, against my wishes, my client would like to change her plea to guilty."

"She can't do that!" Abigail shouted. "The trial has already begun."

"Please restrain yourself, counselor," the judge said, slamming his gavel down loudly.

It was an unusual set of circumstances, and the judge was somewhat flustered, so he did the only thing he could at the moment.

"This court will be in recess for thirty minutes," he said. "I want to meet with the defendant and all the counselors in my chamber immediately."

Jim and the rest of the courtroom sat quietly, not sure what had just happened. He wanted to be in the judge's chamber, but he wasn't allowed.

Abigail began complaining the minute she walked into the chamber, and only stopped when the judge threatened her with contempt of court.

"Now, counselor," the judge said as he turned to the defense, "tell me what this is all about."

"Your honor, my client is very adamant about pleading guilty. She wants to cop a plea and get on with her punishment."

"Ms. Williams-Gibbons, is that correct? Do you really wish to change your plea?"

"Yes, your honor."

"You understand, don't you, that the court could sentence you to the maximum penalty under the law, even if you plead guilty?" the judge said.

"Yes, your honor, I do."

"I won't let her!" Abigail shouted. "She knows she can't beat me and is trying to soften the blow. I won't accept her guilty plea."

"Ms. Finnigan, sit down and shut up!" the judge said loudly, pointing to a chair.

"You can't talk to me like that!" Abigail shouted back. "I won't stand for it."

"You're right," the judge said. "Bailiff, if this woman doesn't sit down right now and shut up, I want you to place her under arrest."

Abigail realized that she'd met her match. She followed the judge's order and sat down, but she clearly wasn't happy. Sandy's move had diminished her possibility of exacting revenge, and, in Abigail's mind, it meant that Sandy had won again.

After the attorneys had filed all the proper paperwork, the judge stepped back into the courtroom. Without explaining, he dismissed the jury. Jim was surprised at the turn of events.

Even though he was not sure what was going on, seeing the jury dismissed gave him a good idea. Sandy had copped a plea on her own, without involving him.

Sandy was led into the courtroom by the bailiff and stood in front of the judge, tears streaming down her face. The judge spoke as her attorney stood next to her.

"Ms. Williams-Gibbons, in light of the change in your plea from not guilty to guilty, I hereby order the court to hold you overnight in the county jail to await sentencing. After I listen to the impact statements of anyone who knew the victim, I'll pronounce sentence tomorrow afternoon at 2:00."

The bailiff then removed Sandy from the courtroom and escorted her to a cell in the county jail. Jim just sat in the courtroom, stunned by what had just taken place. He knew he needed to visit with her before the sentencing tomorrow, even though it was too late to get Sandy to change her mind. He needed to find out why she'd given up a 50-50 chance of being set free.

A short time later, they were sitting together in the visitors' room, not knowing what to say. They both realized that Sandy had put an end to her career as a Nebraska senator. Sandy's half of the ranch could be put into a trust until she was released, but how was it all going to affect their relationship? They'd just have to wait until Sandy completed her sentence before they could try to continue on together—at least, that's what Jim thought.

But Sandy put an end to that line of thinking when she abruptly said, "Jim, it's over between us."

"No!" Jim blurted out. "We can survive this. Our love is strong. We'll make it."

Sandy looked into his eyes, and Jim saw a look of fear that was similar to the one he'd failed to notice in Raymond's eyes, but Sandy's look wasn't a fear of death like Raymond's—it was a fear of losing *at* life.

Sandy spoke softly. "I didn't plead guilty to hurt you or to create distance between us, Jim. I did it to own up to my responsibility. I realized that whichever way the trial went, I was going to lose. It didn't matter if I was found guilty or acquitted. The consequences would have been the same. I knew that I wouldn't be able to live without pain or guilt."

She took Jim's face in her hands and looked deep into his eyes.

"We thought our relationship could withstand this, but it would never survive. Don't you see, Jim? I'm doing this for you. I want you and Molly to have a life—free of the pain and heartbreak we'd have together. I know you love me, but a lost love can be healed faster than a false, auspicious one. You'd eventually grow to hate me.

Maybe when my sentence is over, we can—no, you have to forget about me."

Jim struggled for words, but they wouldn't come. Placing his head in Sandy's lap, he sank to the floor and cried as Sandy put her arms around his shoulders to comfort him.

"I can't give up on you," he finally said, raising his head and looking into her eyes. "I will *not* give up on you."

Jim got up and sat on the bed, where they held each other for a long time in tearful silence.

Then Sandy said softly, "Jim, please don't come to the courtroom tomorrow. Let's say our goodbyes now."

She kissed him firmly on the lips, lingering as long as possible. Then she turned and walked down the corridor.

A headline in the local newspaper two days later said it all: "Senator Williams-Gibbons Sentenced to Five Years for 1974 Killing."

Sandy was sent to the Nebraska women's penitentiary, located just outside of Lincoln, where she'd remain confined until she'd served her time.

As Sandy had requested, Jim wasn't there to hear the sentencing. The next day, he and Molly packed up their belongings and were preparing to leave Cottonwood Springs for good. But for Jim, it was important to say a proper good-bye to his brother. He soon found himself at the cemetery, kneeling by Raymond's grave.

"Yes, I'm leaving, my brother. I want to thank you for bringing me back to my Lakota ways. When trouble confronts me down the road it's your face I'll see, the face of a brave Lakota warrior. I'll never forget you. I'll always carry your spirit with me."

After saying good-bye, Jim crossed the Niobrara one last time. Stopping at the ranch, he picked up his daughter, loaded the paint horse into a trailer, and together they headed off down the road to begin their new lives . . . in Lincoln, Nebraska.

EPILOGUE

I would caution the reader, not to think this is a chronicle about love and hate, secular versus spiritual, or good versus evil. It is an account built on much more.

It is a story about the human spirit, a story about each of us as we journey through life and the choices we make.

So, as *you* transcend through this life, take the lessons of the Niobrara Crossing with you. And, may your *crossing* be admiral, may your hopes precede you and May God go with you.

P.
S.

About the author

Meet the Author

Reading group guide

Questions for Discussion

Other

Dear Reader

Up Coming Book

Order Form for Niobrara Crossing

MEET THE AUTHOR

To me it was special growing up east of the Nebraska Sand Hills. North Bend, during the time of my youth was a small bustling community, not on the Niobrara, but on the Platte River.

Borne into a Scotch-Irish, German family my roots were barely set before I pulled them up to venture across the Muddy Mo and take up my life's career in education.

A product of the one-room school (not unusual in the rural expanse of Nebraska), much of my time as a boy was spent on our home-made baseball diamond or trekking the narrow expanse of the Rawhide Creek. Lessons learned in all these areas were invaluable to me as I journeyed through life to make my lot.

My fathers father, laid the foundation for my transition into writing and I still sit and read for hours his notes and historical writings about the state of Nebraska.

Schooled in the sciences and physical activity, I have always had a yearning to tell the story. Retirement has given me both time and inspiration to do the research necessary in putting a novel together. My first, the *Niobrara Crossing* has been a work of love tethered with a need to get the story out.

QUESTIONS FOR DISCUSSION

1. Life is rarely neat and tidy and like Jim Grant many of us come to terms with our wounds we suffer and the love we fail to acknowledge. What do you find most striking about how Jim comes to terms with Raymond's death? Does it remind you about anything in your own life?

2. How did G. Gray McVicker use a paint horse in the novel to convey messages of anguish and redemption? What images particularly stick in your mind?

3. How does the point-of-view perspective that remains the same throughout influence, for you, the significance of the story?

4. When Jim receives a phone call from Sandy he quickly finds himself moving in a direction he never anticipated. Or did he? Discuss the emotional challenges he is confronted with.

5. Spirituality plays a big part in Jim's character. Recount the scenes that show various revealing moments in the story that eventually lead him to question his spirituality.

6. How does the novel's structure; chapter one jumps ahead, strengthen the story for you?

7. Growing up in the Sand Hills did affect Jim physically, mentally and emotionally. What affects were evident and what links can you make between his behavior in the present to incidents in his past?

8. What do you think of Sandy? How does her influence on Jim affect the story? What does she represent to the community? To the novel.

9. In Chapter 6, the great room scene is an important eye-opening experience for Jim. Discuss the revelation he has after staring at the portrait hanging on the mantel.

10. The author uses the land as a metaphor for the story. Discuss how he does so in the story.

11. Dean Gillette and Ed Hardin's behavior is harmful to many people yet they seem to have control of the community. What does this say about the community, laws, and society in general?

12. Despite their seeming distance from each other, Jim and Sandy keep ending up together. Why is that? Do you think they need each other in some way?

13. Harold Eagles led Jim on a vision quest. Discuss your feelings as they relate to the process and to the outcome.

14. Sandy suddenly changes her plans at the end of the novel. Why does she plead guilty? Do you think she has forgiven herself?

15. How do you feel about Jim's decision as the story ends.

DEAR READER,

I hope you've enjoyed the adventures of Jim, Sandy, Raymond and others involved in the Niobrara Crossing. I'd love to know which characters or scenes you liked best, or just that you enjoyed the book. Please drop me a line, via e-mail at geomcv@msn.com or at G. Gray McVicker, P.O. Box 25113 West Des Moines, Iowa 50265. I really look forward to hearing from you.

Also please visit the publishing web site at PaintHorseBooks. com. There are a number of free items (short stories, book markers, writer's information, etc.) as well as information about my upcoming book scheduled for fall 2008.

Rapiemur. (Sub title; To Be Snatched Away) It is a compelling story about a cardiologist who learns he is suffering from early onset Alzheimer's. The journey he embarks on, to return to his home town, before he sinks into a mist where there is no escape, and where no one else can follow, will make you laugh and cry at the same time.

G. Gray McVicker

Niobrara Crossing Order Form

Yes, I want to purchase the novel, below book store price

Each Book Personally Autographed by G. Gray McVicker

Quantity

_____ (Each Book-Niobrara Crossing $12.95 + Shipping)

_____ (Five–Nine Books @ $10.95 each + Shipping)

_____ (Ten or More Books @ $9.95 each, free shipping)

Larger Quantities Please Contact PaintHorseBooks.com

(Shipping comes to $1.95/book)

Name: _____

Address: _____

City, State, Zip: _____

Payment (check or money order only to: Paint Horse Books)

(ForCredit Card purchases please go to PaintHorseBooks.com)

Number of books ( )	Total	
Sales Tax 6% (Iowa Residents Only)	Total	
Shipping	Total	
	Grand Total	

Send to: Paint Horse Books, P.O. Box 25113
West Des Moines, Iowa, 50265
Please allow two weeks for shipping

Niobrara Crossing Order Form

Yes, I want to purchase the novel, below book store price
Each Book Personally Autographed by G. Gray McVicker

Quantity

_____ (Each Book-Niobrara Crossing $12.95 + Shipping)

_____ (Five–Nine Books @ $10.95 each + Shipping)

_____ (Ten or More Books @ $9.95 each, free shipping)

Larger Quantities Please Contact PaintHorseBooks.com

(Shipping comes to $1.95/book)

Name: _____

Address: _____

City, State, Zip: _____

Payment (check or money order only to: Paint Horse Books)
(ForCredit Card purchases please go to PaintHorseBooks.com)

Number of books ( )	Total	
Sales Tax 6% (Iowa Residents Only)	Total	
Shipping	Total	
	Grand Total	

Send to: Paint Horse Books, P.O. Box 25113
West Des Moines, Iowa, 50265
Please allow two weeks for shipping